*That's My Baby!*

## He could see her sitting on her bed with little Anna in her arms.

She was looking down at the child, her finger slowly stroking a rounded little cheek, the alabaster slope of her breast visible between the sides of her pink shirt. One tiny fist rested against that fullness and the baby's eyes were closed.

Emily's expression looked utterly peaceful.

Justin wasn't sure what caused the odd tug in his chest just then. He wasn't a man easily impressed, much less easily moved. Yet, he couldn't seem to look away. Had he been standing before a painting, he supposed the eroticism was what would have caught his attention, the pure sensuality of soft light on skin, the gentle part of Emily's mouth, the suckling of the baby's. But there was an element far beyond that, a Madonna-like quality that made him feel as if he were witnessing something infinitely… precious.

The thought had his conscience kicking hard as it told him to look away. He was intruding here. But it was already too late.

Dear Reader,

Welcome to a spectacular month of great romances as we continue to celebrate Silhouette's 20th Anniversary all year long!

Beloved bestselling author Nora Roberts returns with *Irish Rebel,* a passionate sequel to her very first book, *Irish Thoroughbred.* Revisit the spirited Grant family as tempers flare, sparks fly and love ignites between the newest generation of Irish rebels!

Also featured this month is Christine Flynn's poignant THAT'S MY BABY! story, *The Baby Quilt,* in which a disillusioned, high-powered attorney finds love and meaning in the arms of an innocent young mother.

Silhouette reader favorite Joan Elliott Pickart delights us with her secret baby story, *To a MacAllister Born,* adding to her heartwarming cross-line miniseries, THE BABY BET. And acclaimed author Ginna Gray delivers the first compelling story in her series, A FAMILY BOND, with *A Man Apart,* in which a wounded loner lawman is healed heart, body and soul by the nurturing touch of a beautiful, compassionate woman.

Rounding off the month are two more exciting ongoing miniseries. From longtime author Susan Mallery, we have a sizzling marriage-of-convenience story, *The Sheik's Secret Bride,* the third book in her DESERT ROGUES series. And Janis Reams Hudson once again shows her flair for Western themes and Native American heroes with *The Price of Honor,* a part of her miniseries, WILDERS OF WYATT COUNTY.

It's a terrific month of page-turning reading from Special Edition. Enjoy!

All the best,

Karen Taylor Richman
Senior Editor

Please address questions and book requests to:
Silhouette Reader Service
U.S.: 3010 Walden Ave., P.O. Box 1325, Buffalo, NY 14269
Canadian: P.O. Box 609, Fort Erie, Ont. L2A 5X3

# CHRISTINE FLYNN

# THE BABY QUILT

Published by Silhouette Books
**America's Publisher of Contemporary Romance**

To Karen Euritt,
with thanks for your help.
We really miss you guys!

**SILHOUETTE BOOKS**

ISBN 0-373-24327-8

THE BABY QUILT

Copyright © 2000 by Christine Flynn

This edition published by arrangement with Harlequin Books S.A.

Visit Silhouette at www.eHarlequin.com

**Printed in U.S.A.**

**Books by Christine Flynn**

## CHRISTINE FLYNN

admits to being interested in just about everything, which is why she considers herself fortunate to have turned her interest in writing into a career. She feels that a writer gets to explore it all and, to her, exploring relationships—especially the intense, bittersweet or even lighthearted relationships between men and women—is fascinating.

Dear Reader,

One of my sisters called while I was cleaning a closet the other night. While we were talking, and I kept sorting, I came across the worn-out old quilts I keep there, all neatly tucked in tissue and plastic cases. One had been made by an aunt, the other had been the patient work of my husband's grandmother. My sister mentioned the old quilts she, too, treasures, and remarked that their only value was the time and love that had gone into creating them for their families.

That would be how Emily, the heroine in my story, feels about her baby's quilt. Knowing how much love her mom put into each stitch would make her cherish it. It's nothing fancy. And it's not the sort of thing the worldly, sophisticated Justin Sloan would value. At least not until she shows him how. After all, as we know from every THAT'S MY BABY! title, it's the *little* things that count.

Best wishes,

Christine Flynn

# Chapter One

Justin Sloan's mood was as black as the storm clouds churning in the Western Illinois sky. His car had a dead battery. In a fit of rebellion, which he was rapidly coming to regret, he'd left his cell phone recharging in his fifty-second-floor condo in Chicago. And since he hadn't had the foresight to throw rain gear into his trunk along with his fishing pole and a spare T-shirt, he was about to get soaked to the skin. Those clouds were too leaden to hold back their moisture for long.

The wind shifted and danced, fanning the tall grasses and wildflowers as he continued his trek along the narrow country road. According to his map, the town of Hancock was ten miles from the little bridge he'd just crossed, a good thirty miles closer than the freeway exit he'd taken to reach the fishing spot a client had told him about. Spending a Saturday making long looping casts into a secluded stream had sounded like a fine idea when he'd been staring at the ceiling above his bed at 6:00 a.m. Five hours later, he almost wished he'd fought his insomnia with a run along the shore of Lake Michigan instead.

Almost.

The same edginess that had prompted his escape from the city still stirred in his gut. He'd had to get out. Get away. The need had felt too urgent to question. He wasn't even questioning it now. It had been there ever since he'd left last night's celebration dinner—a dinner given in his honor—and still hadn't quite eased.

The road ahead took a gradual rise over the gently rolling land and made a dogleg turn to the right. His glance narrowed on a house to the left.

The modest old farmhouse sat back from the road, a relic from the turn of last century and painfully austere. It stood ghostly white against the charcoal-gray sky, its stark appearance unrelieved by any hint of decoration except a single window box overflowing with blooms of bright-red. The porch was a utilitarian square, the railings utterly plain. But the land surrounding it burst with every imaginable shade of green. Nearest the road, row upon row of brilliant emerald plants glowed jewellike against dark, loamy earth. Farther back, miles of corn merged on a large square of land planted with what looked to be a vegetable garden. A windmill, its blades spinning madly, guarded a tidy utility shed and a chicken coop.

Relieved to know he wouldn't have to walk ten miles in the rain to get to a phone, he set his sights on a woman disappearing into a greenhouse and jogged across the road and up the property's long graveled driveway. Thirty feet from the building, he slowed his pace. The young woman had appeared again. With her calf-length blue dress tangling around her legs, she headed for a long rack of plants.

Slender as a willow branch and just as supple, she bent to hurriedly tuck a flat of plants under each arm and headed for the greenhouse once more. Wisps of flaxen hair had escaped the braid that dangled nearly to her waist. The wind whipped those gleaming strands into a halo around her head, but it was the way the gusts of air plastered the shapeless garment to her body that had most of his attention as he moved toward her.

The thought that she was probably half his age immediately jerked his attention from her intriguing curves. Mentally disrobing the farmer's seventeen-year-old daughter wasn't likely to make the farmer eager to lend him a hand. Considering the bolt of lightning streaking against the wall of black in the distance, he wasn't interested in jeopardizing his welcome.

"Is your dad around anywhere?" he called, an instant before a crack of thunder shook the windows in the house behind him.

It was hard to tell which caused her footsteps to falter when her head jerked up—finding a large, male stranger in her yard, or the jarring boom that sent a covey of wrens screaming from the sweeping arms of the walnut tree shading the house. She'd been so focused on her task that she hadn't even noticed his approach.

That task obviously took precedence. Ignoring him, she dropped her hand from where it had flattened at her throat and, with her hair streaming across her face, disappeared into the greenhouse.

"Great," he muttered, looking around for signs of someone who might be a little more cooperative.

There wasn't anyone outside that he could see. There weren't any lights on in the house to indicate anyone was inside, either. Wondering if someone might be in the greenhouse, he looked through the plastic-covered windows that had already fluttered loose in places. The milky material rustled in the wind, echoing the snap of the blinding white sheets billowing on the clothesline. There were no shadows to indicate a human inside. The only other form of life seemed to be the chickens who were abandoning their wire enclosure for the white clapboard coop.

A flash of pale blue streaked from the greenhouse.

In no mood to wait until she decided to acknowledge him, he moved with her.

"Look, I'm sorry to bother you, but my car won't start. It's not far from here," he explained when she'd kept going without giving him so much as a glance. "Is your dad around?" he called. "All I need is a jump."

She hurriedly lifted two more flats of tiny green plants from the rack near the vegetable garden. "My father doesn't live here."

She finally looked up. Justin didn't know which caught him more off guard, the velvet soft quality of her voice, her faint accent, or the angelic quality of her delicate features. Her eyes were the clear blue of a summer sky and her skin looked so soft it fairly begged to be touched.

His glance dropped to the lush fullness of her mouth. Soft and ripe, that sensuality was as unexpected as the innocence.

So was the jolt of heat low in his gut.

Her lips had parted with an indrawn breath when their eyes met the first time. When they met again, her glance faltered and she grabbed another flat.

"What about your husband?" he asked, forcing his focus to her hands. She appeared older than he'd first thought. Her left hand was hidden, but she could easily be married. "Can he help me?"

She was trying to balance a third tray between the two she held when he saw her hesitate. Harried, distracted, she darted a furtive glance from his dark hair to the logo on his polo shirt and murmured, "No. He can't."

An instant later, seeing she couldn't carry more than two

trays without smashing what she was trying to save, she hoisted a flat to each hip and took off again.

"Then, how about a telephone?"

Grabbing the plants she hadn't been able to carry and another flat for good measure, he hurried to catch up with her.

"There is no telephone here," she said, still moving. "The nearest one is at the Clancy farm. It's up the road by the bend. I'd imagine Mr. Clancy is bringing in his cows. For a telephone, you'll have to go to Hancock."

"Isn't there any place closer? A gas station?"

"Only in Hancock."

"How about another neighbor?" He could jog to the little town if he had to. He ran four times a week as it was. But a ten-mile run in the rain wasn't exactly what he'd had in mind when he'd decided to play hooky. "I'd really like to avoid getting drenched," he admitted, tossing her a rueful smile. "That sky looks like it could open up any minute.

"I drove out from Chicago to do a little fishing," he explained, wanting her to know he wasn't some lunatic out stalking farmers' wives. "I'm taking the day off, you know?" he asked, wondering what the rush was with getting the plants inside. He'd have thought rain would be good for them. "I noticed the weather changing and decided to head back, but my car battery's dead."

She didn't reply. Nor did she slow by so much as a step as they reached the plant-filled building. Not sure if he should follow her in—or if she was even listening—he stopped by the doorway while she shoved her load onto the nearest table and spun back toward the door.

Spotting the flats he'd carried, she pulled them from his hands, slid them next to the others and hurried back out.

He arrowed a frown at her back, practically biting his tongue to keep that scowl from his voice when he fell into step beside her. "Look, I can seen you're busy here, but all I need is a jump. If there's a vehicle—"

"What is this 'jump?'"

"Jump-start," he explained, never guessing that a farm girl would be as mechanically challenged as most of the women he knew. "You know. Hook up a car with a good battery to a car with a dead one to get the dead one going again?"

Puzzlement merged with the lines of concern deepening in her brow. But all she said was, "There is no car here."

"Then how about a tractor?" he called to the back of her retreating head.

There was no tractor, either. She told him that as the first fat drops of rain soaked into his shirt and ticked against the tin roof of the utility shed. Another bolt of lightning ripped across the black horizon. In the three seconds before the thunder rolled in to crack overhead, the rain turned to pea-size hail and the woman had tucked herself over the plants she picked up to keep them from being shredded by the little pellets of ice.

"This Clancy place," he said, hauling another load himself. "How far is it?"

"A mile by the road." Looking torn between encouraging and declining his unexpected help, she headed into a gust of wind. "It's shorter if you cut through the soy field."

"Which one's that?

"Hey," he muttered when she shot him a puzzled glance. "I recognize the corn over there, but I'm from the city. Is soy tall or short?"

"Everything is short at one time," she replied ever so reasonably. "I'll show you the route, but you'll want to stay until this passes. You'll need shelter."

She was right. The sky grew darker by the minute and the air had taken on a faint glow of pink. The clouds overhead looked as if they'd been flipped upside down, their boiling bellies suddenly a little too close, a little too ominous. Between the shades of slate, misty tails of pearl gray undulated and teased, dangling downward, pulling up.

They were nearly to the greenhouse when everything went dead still. The hail stopped. Not a single leaf on the trees moved. The air itself turned too heavy to breathe, the pressure of it feeling as if it were crushing him in an invisible vise. The woman felt it, too. He could tell by the fear that washed her expression an instant before the wind hit like backwash from a jet and the trays they carried were ripped from their hands.

Everything was leaning. Trees. Cornstalks. Them. A sheet from the clothesline sailed past. The blades of the windmill clattered wildly, fighting for a direction to go. Another sound rumbled beneath the tinny cacophony. Not thunder. The deep-throated hum sounded more like a million swarming bees.

The house sat a hundred yards behind them. It looked more like a mile as he grabbed for the woman's wrist to stop her from running for the greenhouse.

"It's not safe there! Get in your house!"

The wind snatched his words, muffling them in the growing roar. He could barely hear the "No!" she screamed back at him. But he saw the word form, and the sheer terror in her eyes as she tried to struggle free of his grip.

Panic had robbed her of reason. He was sure of it. She had to know there was no way the unfinished building would offer any protection. It was nothing but two-by-fours and tearing plastic that, in another minute, could well be nothing but matchsticks.

He swore. In the distance, a funnel of ghostly gray twisted against the black wall. At its base, a swirling cloud of dust began to form. "That thing could be on us any minute," he growled, finally comprehending why she'd been in such a rush. "I don't know what your problem is, lady, but I have no intention of playing Dorothy and Toto. Come on!''

He couldn't hear what she said. He was more concerned with the way she gripped his wrist to pull his hand from hers while he practically dragged her toward the house. Thinking he'd do better carrying her, he swung around to get a better grip when his shift in momentum allowed her the leverage she needed.

She broke free with a sharp twist of her hand. An instant later, a Volkswagen-size chunk of tree ripped past, the tips of its branches barely missing his face as it flew through the space she'd occupied seconds ago. He thought for sure that the heavy branches had grazed her, but frantic as she was, nothing slowed her down. Through the cloud of straw and dust now billowing around them, he saw her bolt through the greenhouse door.

Swearing violently, he raced after her.

The plastic covering the window holes rippled and snapped as wind shredded the flimsy covering. Through the doorway, he saw her duck beneath the long, plant-filled table just inside. He was thinking she had to be crazy not to see that the place was disintegrating around her when she jerked upright and ran back toward him with a hooded white carrier.

He'd barely noted the thick mauve liner and a pair of tiny legs when he realized there was actually an infant inside it.

*Dear God,* he thought, realization slamming into him. *She had a baby out here.*

"The cellar!" she hollered, fear stark in her eyes. "By the back door!"

He didn't ask if she minded him carrying the kid. He just grabbed the carrier from her and pushed her out ahead of him, bent on getting them moving as fast as he could. The wind tore at them like the claws of an invisible dragon, grabbing her hair, her dress, stinging his eyes with the dust that turned day into night. A wheelbarrow blew across the yard ahead of them, flipping end over end. Eyes shielded by their forearms, they raced across the grass while behind them the funnel bore down on the land with the speed and sound of a freight train.

She reached the angled, in-ground door to the cellar two steps before he did. Using both hands, she pulled back hard on the handle. The thing wouldn't budge.

Without a word, he shoved the carrier into her arms and jerked on the door himself. The pressure of the wind crushed down on it, making the long panel feel as if it were weighted with bricks. He could feel the muscles in his arms and back bunch as he battled, but he edged the solid wood up enough to wedge his foot between it and the frame before giving a powerful pull.

The wind shifted, catching the door, ripping it from its hinges, spinning it upward, slamming it into his shoulder.

Pain, barbed and jarring, shot down his arm. Gritting his teeth, he snatched the carrier again and practically shoved the woman down the steep and narrow stairs. He was halfway down himself when she reached up and pulled the baby from the hard plastic shell. The moment he saw that she had the tiny blond bundle of pink in her arms, he dropped the carrier and pushed her to the corner of the deep, shelf-lined space. With his back to the suction created by the raging vortex, he watched her clutch the baby to her chest and wrapped his arms around them both.

Thunder boomed. The wind shrieked. He had no idea how safe they were, but he figured that even with the door gone, they were better off tucked back in the confined space beneath the house than they would be anywhere else. At least, they were as long as the wind didn't make missiles of the hundred or so jars of fruits and vegetables gleaming on the shelves surrounding them.

"We need to get away from this glass."

"By the potato crates. On the other side of the stairs. There's none over there."

He glanced behind him. Wooden boxes were stacked a dozen feet away. Neatly folded burlap bags filled a galvanized tub, apparently waiting to be filled with onions like the lone bag leaning next to it. Even with the boxes of empty canning jars lining the shelves next to where they huddled, it seemed better to stay where they were. If the shelves fell, they'd land right on those boxes and bags.

"Do you think we should move?" she asked, her voice trembling.

"I don't see any place safer. We'll have to ride it out here."

He didn't have to see her to know she was terrified. She had the baby's tiny head tucked beneath her chin, her hand covering its downy blond hair. With his arms curved around her shoulders, her slender body angled against his left side, he could feel her trembling from neck to thigh.

A blinding flash of lightning turned the space pure white. Thunder cracked. He felt her whole body go taut as a spring an instant before she buried her head against his chest.

"It's okay," he murmured, hoping to heaven it would be. He cupped the back of her head the way she did her child's, protecting it, tightening his hold. "Just hang on. These things don't last that long, do they?"

"I don't know, Mr.... I don't know, " she repeated, apparently realizing she didn't know his name. "One's never come this close before."

She shifted a little, her thigh slipping along his. Given the intimacy of their positions, he found her formality a tad incongruous. "It's Sloan. Justin," he added, thinking she might appreciate a first name, too.

"Justin Sloan. Thank you."

He wasn't sure what she was thanking him for. It didn't

seem important anyway. The breath he drew brought her scent with it, something clean and fresh and far too innocent to seem so erotic.

He cleared his throat, training his focus on the wide planks above them while dust swirled and the apocalypse raged overhead. Wondering if those boards would stay put seemed wiser than wondering if that scent was in the silken hair braided and draped over his arm or if it was clinging to her skin.

He glanced back down. "And you're...?"

"Emily Miller. My daughter is Anna," she added, then jumped again at the crash of ripping timber.

A huge tree limb arrowed through the open doorway above them. The projectile crashed into the crates of potatoes and onions, splintering itself and the shelves and sending vegetables rolling over the packed dirt floor. Another crash reverberated above them, this one echoing with the sound of shattering glass.

With his back to the melee, his head ducked and his neck exposed, Justin held his breath. He was pretty sure the woman in his arms held hers, too. Only the baby moved. He could feel it wriggling in protest to her mother's tight hold, but he doubted there was any power on earth, including the fury being unleashed overhead, that could make the woman ease her grasp.

"Justin Sloan?" The sound of his name was faint, muffled by their positions and the cacophony overhead. "May I ask you something?"

He thought for sure she wanted reassurance. It sounded like the end of the world up there. At the very least, it was the end of her house. But if she wanted to know if he thought they'd be all right, her guess would be as good as his.

"Sure," he said, thinking he'd do the decent thing and lie if it would make her feel better.

"Who are Dorothy and Toto?"

"What?"

"Who are Dorothy and Toto?" she repeated. "And what did you mean when you said you had no intention of playing them?"

He had to sound as puzzled as she did. "You know. From *The Wizard of Oz.* The movie?" he prompted, thinking she must be trying to distract herself. "The tornado hits Kansas and the girl and her dog get sucked up?"

"Did they survive?"

He would have thought she was joking, except her concern when she looked up at him was too real, the fear in her eyes too tangible.

"Yeah. They did."

"That's good. I don't know of this Oz," she admitted, the fullness of her bottom lip drawing his glance as she spoke. Her mouth looked soft, inviting. Provocative. With her clear blue eyes locked on his, it also looked enormously tempting. "I've heard of Kansas, though. I've read that it's very flat."

The woman wasn't making a lick of sense to him, but she was definitely taunting his nervous system. The fact that she was reminding him of just how long he'd gone without the comfort of a woman's body wasn't something he cared to consider at the moment. Given their proximity, it seemed best to concentrate on something—anything—else.

Ruthlessly reining in his libido, he focused on the sound of her voice, her accent. She didn't have much of one, just enough to broaden the sound of her vowels. It was more the pattern of her speech that told him she wasn't a native—which could easily explain why she hadn't heard of the movie nearly every kid in America had seen by the time he was six years old.

"I take it you're not from here."

"No," she admitted, putting his very logical mind at ease. "I'm from Ohio."

Emily had no idea why her response made the big stranger frown. With the swiftness of the lightning arcing above them, the dark slashes of his eyebrows bolted over his pewter-gray eyes. His lean, chiseled features sharpened. The dark expression intensified the sense of command surrounding him, an aura she imagined to be possessed by men like kings and warriors in the library books she devoured. Or like the powerful men who stole women's hearts on Mrs. Clancy's soap operas. But she really didn't care that she confused him. All she cared about was that Anna was safe—and that his deep voice held the power to distract her from thoughts of what would have happened had he not come along.

Shaking deep inside, she glanced from the little red polo player embroidered above the pocket of his navy-blue shirt to her baby, soothing Anna's fussing by rubbing her back. If not for this Justin Sloan, she never would have been able to get inside the cellar with the wind blowing so hard. While she'd struggled with the door, the wind would surely have blown her little girl away, sucked Anna up as he said the wind had done with Dorothy and her dog. It might have blown her away, too, or caused her to be injured so she couldn't help her child.

The thoughts drew a shudder to the surface. They were too close to the nightmares she battled every day. Only this time her fears had nearly become reality.

But nothing had happened, she reminded herself. They were safe. For now. Safe and protected by this man who had come out of nowhere and was using his own, very solid body to shield them both.

He must have felt her trembling. His big broad hand slipped along her shoulder, drawing her closer. She sought that contact willingly, too overwhelmed by what she felt at that moment to do anything else. She knew there would be damage to face. She knew that very soon she would have to start rebuilding with whatever nature had left her. But for now, for these precious seconds, she wasn't having to cope all alone.

The need to absorb that feeling was so acute that it bordered on physical pain. She didn't know if it was right or wrong to want something so badly. She just knew that she was desperate for what she felt just then. He made her feel secure—and security was something she hadn't felt in a very long time. The desire to stay in the safe haven of his arms was the strongest yearning she'd experienced since long before her husband had died.

The thought of leaving that shelter was unbearable. But she wasn't given a choice. She was keenly aware of how solid his body felt, how strong. She was also aware of the tension tightening his muscles and a tingling warmth where her breast and hip crushed his side.

In the pale light, she looked up to find his glance fixed on her mouth.

Her heart gave an odd little lurch an instant before he jerked his attention to the baby nuzzling the fabric covering her breast. The tension she'd felt in his body seemed to settle in hers when he looked up and met her eyes.

Suddenly looking as if he could use more space, he eased back far enough to break contact without leaving her vulnerable and nodded toward Anna.

"Is she okay?"

The question had Emily easing her hold as she tucked her head to see her daughter's sweet little face. In the pale-gray light, she saw Anna give a great, toothless yawn and scrunch her nose to show her displeasure with the position. She much preferred her head on her mom's shoulder to having it tucked under her chin.

"She's fine," Emily assured him, compromising by shifting her little girl up a bit.

"You're lucky she is."

"I know," she whispered. "If it hadn't been for you—"

"I'm not talking about me. I'm talking about what you were doing."

At a loss, she blinked at the hard line of his jaw. "What do you mean?"

"I mean, you obviously knew this was coming, but you were out there trying to save plants instead of getting her inside where it was safe." His intent gray eyes glittered like quicksilver as they swept her face, reproach melding with disbelief. "Why'd you have her out there, anyway? What would you have done if you'd been hurt yourself?"

His low voice rumbled through her, stiffening her shoulders at his demands, pulling up her chin at the accusation behind them. Not a single day went by that she wasn't conscious of the fact that she alone was responsible for the welfare of her precious daughter. Everything she did, the backbreaking hours of digging in the fields while Anna slept protected in the shade or cuddled against her in a tummy sling, the planting, the weeding, the canning, the housecleaning for the Clancys—all of it was done with her child in mind.

Moments ago, he'd made her feel protected. Now, he'd jerked away the shield of numbness that had kept her from looking too closely at the enormity of her situation—and left her feeling even more exposed.

"I had her out there because I always keep her with me. She's safer than she would be alone in the house. And those plants are my livelihood," she informed him, totally unfamiliar with the sense of challenge he evoked. "I already lost one planting this year to frost. I was trying to save this one because I can't afford to lose another."

She swallowed hard. She'd probably lost the planting,

anyway. Profoundly aware of the sudden quiet, torn between gratitude for what he'd done and resentment at his implications, she figured she'd best get started saving what she could.

She glanced up, avoiding Justin's suddenly guarded expression. "The wind has died."

He didn't acknowledge her deliberately diverting observation. He didn't push to know what she'd have done had she been hurt, either. He simply watched the resignation wash through her pale features as she shifted the infant to her shoulder and smoothed the little white T-shirt over her back.

Turning to the foliage and smashed boxes, he jammed his hands on his hips and heaved a sigh. He was out of his element here. He knew nothing of relying on the land for a living. He knew even less about kids—except it seemed to him that something so tiny should be inside in a crib-thing in a nursery or something. What he had known, though, was that he'd been far too conscious of the surprising fullness of her breast, the gentle curve of her hip. Since he'd already been wondering what she'd been using for brains, he'd figured it wiser to focus on that.

He just hadn't intended to sound so abrupt about it.

Feeling his conscience kicked hard, he frowned at the large limb blocking the steeply pitched stairs.

She slipped from behind him. "At least the steps aren't broken."

"Spoken like a true optimist."

"I'm trying to be," she murmured, glancing uneasily toward the light filtering through the leaves.

She had no idea what she'd find out there. Seeing her uncertainty, not caring for the twinge of empathy he felt, he shoved aside the limb blocking the first few stairs and held it aside with his back. Pushing through the splintered limbs and leaves wouldn't be a problem at all. They'd just have to edge up the side. "I'll go up first and help you out."

"It might be easier if I go first. You can reach farther than I can. Here," she said, stepping close to hold out her baby. "When I get to the top, you can hand her up to me."

Justin froze. Despite the twinge of pain in his shoulder, his hands shot out in pure reflex. He would have done the same thing if someone had thrown him a ball. Only he would have known what to do with a ball. He hadn't a clue what to do with the little bundle of big blue eyes blinking up at him.

The impossibly light little body was barely longer than his forearm. The tiny fist waving around before finding its way to that wet little rosebud mouth was smaller than the top half of his thumb. He'd never seen fingers so small.

With her hands tucked beneath his, her mom suddenly looked as if she weren't sure she should let go. "Do you have her?"

His nod was more tentative than he'd have liked. With one palm cupping the back of the baby's head, he gripped what little there was of a backside with the other. "Yeah. Go on."

*Just don't fall,* he thought as Emily slowly withdrew her support and retrieved the carrier that had rolled under the stairs. The last thing he wanted was to have to figure out what to do with her child if the woman should need help. He'd gone toe-to-toe with three-hundred-pound linebackers playing college football. He'd bested the toughest negotiators in world-class business deals, but he freely admitted that this infant had him feeling completely helpless. Accustomed to being capable, he didn't like the sensation at all.

"Okay," he heard Emily call when the rustle of leaves quieted. "I'll take her now."

He hadn't moved. He hadn't taken his eyes off the perfect little face, either. Glancing up, he saw Emily framed against the lightening sky. She'd set the carrier on the ground above her and crouched two steps from the top, her arms stretched toward him.

Watching the baby as if he were afraid it might do something to upset his balance, he edged up the bottom steps and carefully lifted the blissfully oblivious bundle past the leaves quivering along the wind-splintered barrier. The sharp scent of fresh pitch swirled in the slight breeze, reminding him to watch for the jagged spikes of wood where the branch had snapped in the middle so they wouldn't catch the tail of the blanket.

He actually felt sweat bead near his temples when the baby jerked her arm and popped herself in the eye. Her face screwed up at the self-inflicted assault, but she didn't make a sound. He did, though. When Emily's fingers slipped beneath his and he felt the baby's weight shift to her hands, his sigh of relief was definitely audible.

## Chapter Two

Justin's first thought when he stepped onto the wet lawn was that the rain had apparently stopped as abruptly as it started.

His second thought was of his car.

With a sinking sensation, he moved beyond where Emily stood clutching her baby and glanced toward the road. Beneath the heavy clouds, he could barely see the tops of the trees near the little bridge and the curve of the road leading down to it. But the trees were still there, as thick and tall as when he'd parked his car beneath them. Closer in, under a sky that was opening with streaks of brilliant blue, the verdant land remained untouched.

The frustration he'd prepared himself to feel over hassles with transportation and insurance adjusters never materialized. His biggest problem—at the moment, anyway—was still his dead battery. Emily Miller, he was sure, hadn't fared as well.

When he looked from the coop where the chickens were pecking the ground, he found her staring at the walnut tree. What was left of it, anyway. All that remained was a short, jagged spike that had been blasted clean of its bark. The bulk of the sizable trunk was nowhere to be seen—though Justin figured it a safe bet that the branch poking out of the cellar had once been attached to it. So had the even larger branch that had been stuffed through the back porch. That massive limb had taken out the porch's center support, but the house itself was still standing. By some miracle, so was the greenhouse. Even the windmill, its blades now turning with laconic ease, appeared unscathed.

He'd expected to see nothing but rubble.

"Are you all right?" he asked, since she'd yet to move. He pulled a white sheet from where it had tangled around an upright water pipe. Tossing it over the T of the clothesline pole, he cautiously scanned her profile. "It's too bad about your tree. And your porch," he added, since that was actually the bigger problem. "But it doesn't look like you lost anything else."

"No. No," Emily repeated, responding to the encouraging note in his deep voice. "I don't think I did." Her own voice lost the strength she'd just forced into it. "It could have been much worse."

Brushing her lips over the top of Anna's soft, sweet-smelling head, she stared at the mass of leaves and branches obliterating her back door. She'd immediately noticed that the greenhouse and chickens and the fields had survived, but she hadn't let herself breathe until she'd turned to her house.

It really *could* have been worse. And losing a tree and a cellar door and having to patch her porch was nothing compared to what could have been. There was always some good and some bad. The sweet balanced the sour, her mother and her aunts had always said. That was life. It didn't matter that her own life had swung wildly out of balance. She was to take with relief and thanks all that had been spared. And take in stride and with grace that which hadn't.

That was how she'd been raised. It was all she knew to do, though she was the first to admit that she'd never mastered the easy acceptance part. As she stood hugging her child, the thought of the extra work it would take to cut up the tree was enough to bring her to tears. There weren't enough hours in the day as it was. But she didn't dare let herself cry. She was afraid that if she did, she'd never stop. And she had to be strong for Anna.

At the moment, she also needed to check on her neighbors.

The rows of corn nearest her little plot of land swayed in the diminishing breeze. Where the land gently rose a couple of acres away, she saw nothing but churned-up earth and a chunk of red-and-white siding that looked suspiciously like part of a barn.

"I need to see if the Clancys are all right," she said, uncomfortably aware of her rescuer's eyes on her. "Mrs. Clancy just had a hip replaced and their son and his family are away for a few days. There's no one there to know if they need help."

Justin stood with his hands on his lean hips, his broad shoulders looking as wide as the horizon. He stared right at her, his wide brow furrowed. He was very direct with his stares, she'd noticed. Not at all subtle the way the few men she knew were when they looked at her. But then, he seemed very direct about his needs and opinions, too. "You wanted to use their phone. Come with me and I'll show you the way."

"Thanks, but I think I'll head on in to town. From the looks of things over there," he said, nodding toward the cornfields, "the lines are probably down."

She lifted one shoulder in a shrug, the motion not nearly as casual as she wanted it to be. "I understand tornados are strange. The way they pick and choose what they destroy, I mean. I've heard of walls being ripped off, but nothing in the room being disturbed. I think that's part of Mr. Clancy's barn," she said, pointing ahead of her, "but their phone could still be working."

She was telling him he might be able to save himself some time by coming with her. Whether she knew it or not, she was also making it as clear as the raindrops clinging to the grass that he disturbed her. Her wary glance would barely meet his before shying away, as if she were embarrassed at having been up close and personal with a perfect stranger. He was pretty certain, too, from the strain that had settled into her delicate features that she was more upset than she was letting on about the damage. Yet, even as unsettled as she had to be, she sounded unbelievably calm.

As he watched her kneel to tug a piece of denim from beneath the baby carrier's thickly padded mauve liner, he couldn't believe her attitude, either.

He didn't know a single soul who would walk away from their own crisis to help out someone else with theirs. The fact that she remembered he still had a problem caught him a little off guard, too. After the way he'd jumped on her about leaving her kid outside, he wouldn't have been surprised if she'd left him to fend for himself.

She carefully tucked the baby's little legs through two holes in what looked like a denim tube and slipped her own arms through its two long straps. As she did, his glance strayed down the thick braid lying against her back to the fabric covering the sweet curve of her slender hips.

"Even if the phone's out," he said, wondering how all that hair would look unbound and spilling over her body, "maybe he can give me a jump."

Annoyed with the direction of his thoughts, he pointedly

pulled his attention from her. "It looks like you've been through this before. The greenhouse," he said, eyeing the skeletal structure to keep his glance from wandering over her again. "You only have a few windows back there. Did another storm take out the others?"

A long strand of loosened hair swayed over her shoulder. Snagging it back, she rose and tucked a soft-looking square of white fabric under the chin of the sleepy-eyed child in her tummy-carrier. "Those are the only windows that were put in. My husband built the greenhouse for me last year, but winter came before he could finish.

"I hired a man," she continued, absently rubbing the baby's back through the denim as she motioned for him to accompany her across the lawn. "He put in the windows Daniel framed and I gave him money to buy the rest, but he hasn't come back yet. I'm sure I don't have enough plastic to replace what was torn," she added, more to herself than to him. "I hope he returns soon."

"How long has he been gone?"

"Two weeks and two days. He wanted to find the best price, so he said it might take him a while."

They angled toward a dirt road lined with rows of corn. The wind had calmed to a warm breeze that rattled the leaves on the stalks and fanned the ankle-high grass growing on either side of the ruts. "Is this someone you know?" he asked, leaving her to walk on the near side of the road while he headed for the grass on the other side to avoid the mud in the middle.

"I didn't before he came looking for work. He said he'd worked for a lot of people in the county, though." A pensive frown touched her brow. "I wonder if he would repair my porch when he returns."

He should let it go, he told himself. He should concentrate on how quiet it was compared to the cacophony of only minutes ago. It was so peaceful here. Almost...serene.

There was no traffic. No horns, sirens, squealing brakes. He should just think about the stillness. He should not question her about something that undoubtedly had as reasonable an explanation as she'd provided for why she'd had her kid out in a tornado.

"He'd *said* he'd worked for people around here?" he asked, too curious to know what that explanation was to let the matter drop. "You didn't check out his references yourself?"

"Even if I'd heard of the names he mentioned, I had no way to speak with them. Besides, there was no need. If he couldn't do the work, it would be obvious, wouldn't it?"

There was a certain literal quality to her logic, a simplicity Justin would have found quite eloquent had she not entirely missed his point. He'd bet his corner office that the guy was an itinerant.

"I don't suppose this man is from around here, is he?"

"He didn't say."

Fighting incredulity, he cast her a sideways glance.

"Do you know his name?" he asked, all but biting his tongue to keep his tone even.

The look she gave him was amazingly patient. "Of course I do. It's Johnny Smith."

John Smith. How original.

"So you gave this man you really don't know money to buy something for you and you haven't seen or heard from him in two weeks."

"He said he wanted to shop for the best price for me," she reminded him, looking at him a little uncertainly. "And he did put the other windows in. He did a good job, too."

"Do you mind if I ask how much you paid him?"

"Twenty dollars."

"What did you give him for the windows?"

"I only had a hundred."

There was such innocence in her lovely eyes. And caution. And concern. The myriad impressions registered with Justin moments before she glanced away to watch where she was stepping.

Johnny Smith had done a good job, all right, he thought. A snow job. "You might want to report Johnny to the authorities, Mrs. Miller. He stole your money."

"I don't believe that," Emily said, incredulous. "Not for a moment." She blinked hard at the distance, her hand still protectively on the little bump resting against her stomach. "He was far too nice to want to do any harm."

The air of innocence he'd noticed about her before now struck him simply as naiveté. She obviously wanted to believe the best about the man. About people in general, he suspected, though he found the aspiration more dangerous than admirable.

"There are a lot of 'nice' crooks out there," he countered, wondering if the woman had ever set foot off the farm. "I take it you've never been conned before?"

"Conned?"

"Swindled, cheated, deceived? No one's ever taken advantage of you or your husband?"

Her glance darted from his, something like guilt shadowing the delicate lines of her face. "He took nothing that I didn't give him from my own hand."

The flatness of her quiet voice could have been recrimination for her own actions. It could just as easily have been defense for those of the man who'd quite probably absconded with her funds. Justin was far more interested in the part of his question she'd chosen to ignore. The part about her husband.

She tended to speak in the singular. And she'd made no reference at all to her husband having anything to do with the handyman. But what struck him as truly odd, now that he thought about it, was that she'd exhibited no concern at all for a husband during or after the storm. The only person she'd expressed concern about needing shelter was him.

All things considered, he strongly suspected that Mr. Miller wasn't even around anymore.

That she felt it necessary to keep up the pretense tugged hard at his conscience.

"Look," he murmured, disturbed to know he made her that uncomfortable. He was accustomed to people with better defenses. Harder edges. Even when she was trying to protect herself, she was totally without artifice. "We all make bad judgments sometimes. Don't let that stop you from turning the guy in. He's just going to rip off someone else."

"Even if what you say were true…which I don't believe it is," she hurriedly clarified, "I wouldn't know what to do. I know nothing about your…about the law."

"I do. I'm a lawyer. This isn't my area of expertise," he admitted, more concerned with her tolerance than her correction. "Criminal law, I mean. I handle corporate matters. But I'd be glad to tell the local sheriff what you've told me and ask him to come talk to you."

She gave him a smile as soft as the sunshine breaking through the clouds. "I thank you for your offer. It's very kind. But it's possible that he could come back. If he does—*when* he does," she corrected, turning her glance back to the horizon, "then I would have unjustly accused him. He will come back." Her quiet voice grew quieter still. "I need to believe that."

For a moment Justin said nothing. There was an odd anxiety in the way she spoke, a quiet sort of desperation. It was almost as if she didn't want him to challenge her nebulous hope because hope was about all she had.

He had no idea why the thought struck him as it did. But he rarely questioned his instincts, and now those instincts were telling him he was right on the mark about this woman's circumstances. He couldn't fault her argument, though. He didn't even want to. He could explain how brilliantly her handyman had duped her. He could point out how the guy had set her up to believe that if he was gone awhile it was because he was trying to help her save money—which would give him plenty of time to disappear. But the chances of recovering her cash at this point were somewhere between zip and nil—and there wasn't any point in badgering her about something it was too late to do anything about.

"How long has your husband been gone?" he finally asked, gingerly rotating his aching arm.

Emily glanced at the man openly watching her, then promptly looked at the ground. "I didn't say that he was."

She didn't like the suspicions Justin raised, even though she, too, had been wondering what was taking the handyman so long. She didn't like the feeling either, that he sensed how ignorant she was of the ways she was trying to assimilate. There was so much she didn't know. So much she didn't understand. And she had no idea at all how he'd known Daniel was no longer there.

"No, you didn't," he agreed, his tone surprisingly mild. "And I can understand why you wouldn't want a stranger to know you're out here alone. But with this storm, if you had a husband around, you'd be wondering if he was all right. The only people you've mentioned are your neighbors."

He'd moved closer when the road had become cluttered with the torn vegetation. She just hadn't realized how close until she caught his clean, faintly spicy scent. The instant she breathed it in, she was hit with the memory of standing in his arms with her head buried against his rock-hard chest.

He wasn't anything like the handyman who'd shown up looking for work a couple of weeks ago. The man who'd called himself Johnny Smith had seemed too shy to even make eye contact, much less make personal observations. And there was no way on God's green earth he would have caused the odd heat that had just pooled in her stomach.

She ducked her head, disconcerted by that heat, determined to ignore it. "Are you always so good at drawing conclusions?"

"My record's pretty decent."

His lack of modesty came as no surprise.

"I suppose all lawyers must be good at such things. I've never met one before, but I've seen one. On Mrs. Clancy's soap opera," she explained, thinking of the commanding, demanding and powerful man who, according to Mrs. Clancy, had stolen the heart of every female character in the cast. "You have much of the same manner about you."

"Is that good or bad?"

"It's neither. It just is. But you're right about Daniel," she continued, assuming he was frowning because she'd yet to answer his question. "He is no longer here."

His expression relaxed as it shifted from her to her child. "Has he been gone long?"

"Since last spring. He worked for Mr. Clancy," she told him, her voice growing hushed. "Daniel was raised on a farm, but he didn't know anything about the big machinery they use here. He was killed trying to repair a piece of equipment while Mr. Clancy wasn't around."

The movement of her hand over Anna's little back was automatic, a soothing motion that gave her as much comfort as it did the baby snuggled against her. "I didn't understand the talk of gears and tilling blades. But he had forgotten to set some sort of brake."

There were times when it felt as if it had been only yesterday that she'd received that awful, numbing news. There were other times when she could hardly picture her husband's boyish face. When she thought of Daniel, she tried to recall how happy they'd once been. But that had been almost too long ago to remember.

"I'm sorry," she heard Justin say, his voice subdued.

"Me, too. Daniel was a good man."

"How old is your baby?"

A small smile relieved the strain around her mouth. "Eight weeks yesterday."

It was now mid-July, Justin thought. That meant she'd been alone when the baby had been born.

He didn't like the way that bothered him. He didn't much care for the way she confused him, either. He'd still been trying to figure out the soap-opera reference when she'd hit him with the reason her husband wasn't around.

He'd figured the guy had simply taken a hike. He hadn't expected her to be widowed. But that little jolt had just been replaced with a decidedly skeptical curiosity over how someone who'd farmed all of his life would know so little about farm equipment.

It wasn't like him not to seek an answer when one was readily available. But he had no desire to chip any deeper at the brave front she wore. With her slender frame, her translucent skin, and that pale-as-cornsilk hair, she looked as delicate as spun glass. When he thought about how desperately she'd been trying to save her plants, and the work she had waiting for her when she returned to her house, he was quietly amazed that the front hadn't already shattered.

Ignoring his curiosity had another advantage. He hated tears. Granted, the only women he'd ever seen cry had used them either to get something from him, or out of fury when they didn't. And he suspected Emily to be far stronger than she looked. But he didn't want to push any buttons that would crack her composure. He'd never been around a woman who honestly needed comfort before. He wasn't sure he'd even know what to do.

"You can see the Clancy place up there," she said, relieving him enormously when she shielded her eyes against the sun and looked up the road. "Oh, good." She sighed, smiling at him. "It didn't hit their house."

It had hit something, though. Just ahead of them, an untouched section of cornfield opened up to a wide stretch of gravel and an overgrown sweep of lawn. From that same general direction came the deep-throated and distant bawl of something that sounded large and undoubtedly four-legged.

What the Clancy place lacked in architectural interest, it made up for in simple appeal. Approaching from the side, Justin scanned the boxy gray house with its lacy curtains and window planters overflowing with pink petunias. The deep green grass was dappled with the first rays of sunlight filtering through the cottonwoods. Standing sentinel over the home's steeply pitched roof, a huge aluminum grain silo gleamed like a giant silver torpedo against the clearing sky.

The bawling grew louder as they headed toward the brick red barn. Damage was more evident here. So was the path of the storm. From atop the gentle rise, it looked as if a giant scythe had taken a swipe across the earth.

The tornado had sliced across a pasture, leaving a path of debris and flattening most of the windbreak on its way. It had wiped out a section of the big barn, uprooted a few more trees, taken out a huge section of fence, then veered right toward the bottom land, missing Emily's place by little more than a couple of city blocks.

"There he is." Emily headed for a gnomelike little man pulling at a pile of boards and scattered straw by the barn. "And there's his wife," she muttered, spotting a flash of movement by the hay bales to her left. "What is she doing out here?

"Mrs. Clancy?" she called, disapproval etched firmly in

her brow. "You shouldn't be outside. You're going to hurt yourself."

"That's what I've been telling her," the barrel-chested farmer shouted across the distance, tossing aside a board with a muffled clatter. "Get her back to the house for me, will you, Emily? I got me some animals trapped back here."

The woman with a head full of pink-foam curlers in her salt-and-pepper hair balanced herself on a chrome cane and lifted a hand to shield her eyes from the sun. Her rose-print house dress flapped around the knees of her white pressure stockings, her expression bouncing between Emily and Justin in open curiosity.

"Are you all right, child?"

"We're fine. I only lost a tree and door. And a porch post. No one got hurt."

"Then let me sit down and take that baby so you can help Sam." Her sharp hazel eyes cut to the man who slowed his stride, letting Emily hurry ahead of him. When Emily stopped beside her, the older woman's voice dropped like a rock. "Who's he?"

"A lawyer. He was fishing and needed a…jump. His car isn't working. I said maybe he could use your telephone."

The late-fifty-something Connie Clancy ran a considered glance from Justin's meticulously cut dark hair to the tips of his expensive hiking boots. "You'd be welcome to use the phone," she called out over the frantic bawling coming from the damaged building, "but the storm took it out."

"I figured as much," Justin replied, dubiously eyeing the pink things protruding from the woman's head. He'd already noticed the phone and power lines dangling from the utility pole near the downed fence. Considering the damage, he wasn't about to ask for help with his car.

He glanced toward the barn. At the near end, the siding had been peeled off as neatly as the skin from an apple.

The far end looked rather like a bomb had gone off in it. Wires and roofing dangled over a gaping hole. Beams and posts slanted every which way. The man in coveralls wrestled one of those beams, his bulky body straining as he tugged and jerked on the unyielding timber. All the while a chorus of low-pitched and pitiful bawling pierced the air.

The cacophony was joined by a piercing squeal.

Even from forty feet away, the farmer's sense of urgency was obvious. On either side of his back coverall straps, sweat stains darkened the man's worn white T-shirt from the strain of lifting the heavy boards. His face was the color of the barn. With the extra thirty pounds the farmer was packing around the middle of his banty-legged frame, he looked like a heart attack waiting to happen.

Justin swore, softly and to himself, but the terse word pretty much summed up how he felt about the course the day had taken. He'd gone looking for escape and landed smack in the middle of Oz. If he'd wanted to deal with dilemmas, he could have stayed in Chicago and gone to the office.

"You stay here and take care of the lady," he said to Emily. One crisis a day was enough. There was nothing to do but step in and make sure he wasn't faced with another. "I'll go help him."

"There's a cow and calf trapped inside," Mrs. Clancy explained as Emily's baby began to make little squeaking sounds. "The weaner's in there, too."

"The dog?" he asked, thinking 'dachshund.'

Mrs. Clancy hesitated. "The pig," she replied, looking as if she were speaking to the daft. "Dogs don't sound like that."

"I know what a dog sounds like. You call a pig a weaner?"

"You do one that's recently been weaned from its sow."

The baby squeaked again. Because she'd started getting

fretful, her mom held her closer, moving with a gentle rock-ing motion. The movement wasn't what she seemed to want. With her little head turning from side to side against her mother's swollen breast, her face screwed up, trans-forming her features from cherubic to prunelike and her fussing into an impatient, hiccuping squall.

The older woman leaned more heavily on her cane. "I'd say she wants to nurse."

"She does."

"Well, I can't help you there, dear."

Emily's voice was soft, her soothing tone lacking any trace of exasperation as she ducked her head toward her child's. "She just wants her mom. But this isn't the best time, you know, Anna? I need to help Mr. Clancy."

"I said I'll help your neighbor." Justin took a step back, not entirely comfortable with the course of the conversa-tion, trying not to look it. "You can take care of her now."

"It sounds like the animals might be injured. You might need—"

"I'll deal with it," he insisted. "Stay here."

Puzzlement entered Emily's eyes with his terse order, but he turned before she could say another word and headed for the barn. Even if her baby hadn't needed her just then, he didn't like the idea of Emily climbing around the broken planks and timbers that blocked the end of the towering building. He was even less enthralled with the idea of her dealing with the animals he could hear battering the boards and bawling over the racket Mr. Clancy made when he pulled out a plank and the piece of wall it supported col-lapsed. He wasn't crazy about the idea of dealing with them himself. What he knew about farm animals was pretty much limited to the meat counter at his local supermarket. But he was pretty sure a terrified animal was as unpredict-able as it was dangerous. It was hard to tell how much damage one could do. Rather like a rejected woman.

The comparison balled a leaden knot in his gut. The last thing he needed to be thinking about right now was how to deal with his senior partner's daughter. He hadn't rejected Cameron Beck, anyway. Not yet. He was too busy avoiding the involvement her father was pushing on him to let her know he wasn't in the market for marriage. Never had been. Never would be.

Given a choice, he'd rather take on the cow.

"That looks pretty heavy there. Let me help you with it."

The old farmer glanced over his shoulder, his ham-hock fists grasping the end of a beam. Beneath the shadowing brim of a green cap embroidered with the word *Pioneer,* his spiky gray eyebrows knitted in a worried slash.

"Thanks. Need to get a path cleared," the man said, his need for haste battling curiosity over who was offering the unexpected assistance. "Brought my animals in to get 'em out of the storm. Now they're trapped in their pens. They're going to collapse that wall the way they keep knocking into it."

He hauled on the beam, dust billowing.

Judiciously avoiding a protruding nail, Justin reached for a door on top of the pile. The tines of a pitchfork were imbedded in its frame. Incredibly, so were stick-straight pieces of straw.

Not Oz, he thought. It was more like a rabbit hole.

Vaguely aware of two pairs of female eyes on his back, not pleased at all to find himself comparing his life to children's stories, he pulled the door upright. Wincing at the pain in his shoulder, he tossed the door aside and added to the cloud of dust himself.

"You say he was fishing?"

"That's what he said."

"Bet he's staying at that fancy bed-and-breakfast in Hancock that young couple from Des Moines opened last year. He looks like one of those yuppie-types, or whatever it is they call themselves nowadays. Can't imagine who else would wear one of those designer shirts to go fishing. I'll bet you can get three shirts from the JCPenney catalogue for what he paid for the one he's wearing.''

''I suppose.''

''Did he say where he was from?''

As frantic as she'd been at the time, Emily was surprised she even remembered. ''Chicago.''

Mrs. Clancy gave a nod. ''Thought he looked like big city.''

Speculation brightened Mrs. Clancy's pleasantly rounded features as she sat on the hay bale she'd selected for a chair. Emily sat on a bale beside her while Anna nursed, the cotton diaper she used for a burp cloth modestly shielding her from the men working beyond them.

''I'd say he's used to getting his way, too,'' the older woman observed, watching the man under discussion shoulder a heavy beam. ''I wonder if he's a firstborn? I can't remember if I saw it on Sally or Oprah. Or maybe it was *Extra*,'' she considered, pondering, ''but someone had a birth-order expert on a while back. A psychologist, I think. She said firstborns are the responsible ones. Used to being in charge and all.

''Junior is like that,'' she confided, lowering her voice as if someone might overhear her disparaging her own oldest, and only, child. ''Stubborn as the day is long. Just like his father.'' Settling back, Mrs. Clancy gave a sharp nod. ''As insistent as that lawyer was about you staying put, I'd say that he's just as set in his ways.''

''I don't know about birth order,'' Emily admitted. She'd never heard of such a thing before, but Mrs. Clancy watched all the talk shows and she was very informed. ''But he does seem quite sure of himself. Except with

Anna," she mused, contemplating his broad back. "When he held her, he acted like she was going to slip right out of his hands."

"Now, why would you be letting a strange man hold your baby?"

"So I could get out of the cellar after the storm passed." Her voice gentled, her expression turning pensive as she stroked her baby's downy little arm. The thought that she could have lost Anna tightened her chest, hinted at pain that went far deeper than any she'd felt before—and simply couldn't bear to consider. "He helped us, Mrs. Clancy. I don't know what would have happened if he hadn't come along."

For a moment, the older woman said nothing. She just pinched her lips and patted Emily on the arm.

"Well, he did come along," Mrs. Clancy allowed, looking as if she were thinking of the day help had come too late for Emily's husband. "And you and the baby are fine, so just push those thoughts right out of your head.

"I'll admit he did seem a little anxious when Anna started fussing," she observed, deftly changing the subject back to the man Emily was openly watching. "It could be that he's just never been around young ones before." She cocked her head full of pink curlers, her interest taking another turn. "I didn't notice a ring on him."

"A ring? Oh, you mean a wedding ring." Emily's glance automatically cut to the pretty little diamonds glittering on the woman's left hand. The custom of exchanging rings hadn't existed in her old community. In it, when a man married, he grew a beard which he never shaved. No one had worn any jewelry at all. "I didn't notice, either."

She hadn't looked at his hands. She'd only felt them. Watching him heft another board, studying the strong lines of his back and long legs, she realized she'd actually felt a considerable amount of his beautifully muscled body. He'd felt very warm, very...hard.

At the thought, her glance faltered, warmth touching her cheeks.

"I'd say you noticed something," her too observant neighbor murmured. "Of course, a woman would have to be drawing her last breath not to notice a man like that. But you can never be too careful around that sort, you know.

"You remember me telling you about that lawyer on *The Tame and The Wild*?" she continued, carrying the conversation the way she always did. "Handsome devil, that one. Charmed the sweet young niece of a client right into his bed. Seduced her in five episodes, then dumped her for his secretary's mother. I'm not saying this fella's like that and I'm not one to judge," she claimed, doing just that. "I mean he did offer you and my Sam a hand and I have to say that speaks well of him. But he is a lawyer. And he is from the *city*," she stressed, sounding as if the combination somehow diluted his more redeeming behavior.

"Sheltered as you've been, I know you haven't come up against his type. Smooth and sophisticated, I mean. And arrogant," she muttered, her expression turning to a glower as her thoughts shifted course. "Like those no-conscience weasels from SoyCo who spout statutes and clauses and time allowances instead of fixing the drainage problem by our land. We have crops being flooded because of their negligence and they keep telling us how much time they have to look into the problem. I can tell 'em what the problem is. That new drain tile they put in when they bought the Eiger farm is draining straight onto our land. All they've got to do is dig—"

"Mrs. Clancy," Emily murmured. A vein bulged by the pink tape holding a curl in place at the woman's temple. "Remember your blood pressure."

Connie Clancy glared at Justin's back for another moment then huffed a breath. "Well, I am of a mind to think they haven't a feeling bone in their bodies," she muttered, nowhere near ready to give up the subject now that she'd started on it. "They live their highfalutin lives and don't give a whit about common folk's livelihoods. Did this Sloan fella say what kind of lawyer he was?"

Actually, Emily thought, he had. He'd said he was 'corporate' which didn't bode at all well for ending the present course of conversation.

"A good one," she replied, because he'd certainly implied it.

"Sounds just like 'em."

The terse statement drew Emily's brow in a faint frown. The thought that Justin could be as coldhearted and presumptuous as the men Mrs. Clancy was so upset about disturbed her. For a twenty-four-year-old woman, she knew she was woefully unsophisticated, but that hadn't been her impression of him at all.

Dismissing the thought, and knowing the woman would go on forever if she didn't change the subject herself, Emily edged back the diaper to see how her little girl was doing. The nagging thought that maybe she was just being naive gave way to a more profound concern.

"Do you think Anna's grown any since you saw her last week?"

Bated exasperation softened the disgruntled woman's expression. It softened a bit more when she looked over to where the pink-cheeked infant had fallen asleep at her mother's breast. "Emily Miller, I know new mothers worry, but I've never heard of one worrying the way you do."

"But she doesn't seem to be getting any bigger."

"That's because you're with her every minute of the day. She's only a couple of months old. How big do you think she's supposed to be?'' She shook her head, looking vaguely amused. ''She's not some strapping boy like Paula Ferguson's grandson, you know. Why, that child must have put on a pound a week to be as big as he is now. Of course his mother isn't exactly dainty herself,'' she confided.

She pulled a deep breath, preparing to head off on yet another tangent, but the commotion from the barn had her clamping her mouth shut before she could even get started. A calf shot out of the rubble, its rust-colored rump bouncing as it headed for the flattened cornfield. Over the clatter of boards inside the barn, the bovine bellowing grew more insistent.

The men were nowhere to be seen.

Mrs. Clancy's hand flattened over her heart. ''What in the world…?''

Pulling the diaper from Emily's shoulder, she tossed it over her own and reached her weathered hands toward Anna. Even as she did, Emily was buttoning herself up and trying not to panic at the thought of what might have happened to Mr. Clancy—or to the man who knew far less than her husband had about the hazards on a farm.

## Chapter Three

Emily's panic was blessedly short-lived. Justin was fine. He assured her of that himself when she found him and Mr. Clancy glaring at the section of wall that had collapsed when the two of them had moved the beam trapping the calf. The old farmer grunted his assurances, too, then added his bulk to Justin's muscle when Justin started clearing away the new pile of boards.

The men did, indeed, appear completely unscathed, and for that Emily was most grateful, but it was clear enough that they needed help. Neither of them wanted her wading around in the rubble, though, so she left them to their task and did what she could by chasing down the animal that had bolted from the barn as if its backside were on fire. After staking the calf on a long rope near the hay bales, she headed up to the house with Mrs. Clancy and Anna to make sandwiches and a salad for the Clancys' dinner in exchange for the use of Mr. Clancy's little red chain saw and a can of gasoline.

She had a tree to cut up. She also had a bushel of beans waiting to be canned. With the sun slanting low on the horizon, she didn't have much of the day left to waste.

"I'll take those."

Justin's long shadow overtook hers on the rutted road a moment before she felt his hand close over the handle of the chain saw.

"Clancy will pick me up in an hour or so and jump my car for me," he said, leaving her to carry the can with the baby snuggled against her chest like a little papoose. "He said he needs to check his irrigation before he does anything else."

He'd wiped off a streak of dirt he'd had on his cheek earlier. But when he fell into step beside her, the saw between them, she noticed an angry red scratch on his arm. "I was going to watch for you. So I could thank you," she said, not wanting him to think she would let him leave without telling him how she appreciated what he'd done. "You don't need to carry that for me," she added. "I can manage."

"No thanks necessary. And it's either carry this back for you or sit here doing nothing until he gets finished. He didn't seem to need any more help.

"Actually," he muttered, as they moved between the rows of corn, "I think it was my help he didn't want. We were doing fine until he asked what I did for a living. When I told him I was an attorney, he turned as suspicious as the warden of a pen. He thought for sure that I worked for some corporation who bought a farm east of here and that I'd come to check the condition of his crops or something. I had to swear I'd only come here to fish before he'd let me past that cow." He shook his head, looking as if he weren't sure if he should be confused or insulted. "I've never even heard of the company he was talking about."

The furrows in his brow eased only slightly when he hoisted the saw. "You know how to use this thing?"

If the skeptical way he looked at the useful little device was any indication, he didn't appear overly familiar with it himself. What struck Emily more was his easy dismissal of her neighbor's suspecting attitude. He was either terribly forgiving or his hide was as thick as a buffalo's.

"I've borrowed it before. To cut firewood," she explained, searching for traces of the arrogance Mrs. Clancy claimed men like him possessed. "It's much simpler to use than an ax."

His glance swept over her face, past the tiny head resting between her breasts and down to her sneakers. "I have a little trouble picturing you swinging an ax."

"I had trouble doing it." Not arrogant, she thought. But definitely bold. "That's why I borrowed the saw. I've added one to my wish list."

"Of course you have." Wincing, he cautiously rotated his left shoulder. "It's what every woman wants. Flowers. Diamonds. A chain saw. I'll make a note of that," he muttered, a cornstalk snapping beneath his weight. "I'll have women falling at my feet."

The hint of sarcasm in his tone automatically stiffened her back. Yet, when she saw the faint smile tug at the corner of his mouth, she realized he wasn't mocking her as some people had been known to do when she expressed her admittedly simple desires. He was teasing her. From the way he flinched when he edged his left arm back, he also seemed to be rather uncomfortable.

"You speak as if you don't have a wife," she observed, wondering what he'd done to himself.

"I don't. I don't plan to ever have one, either."

"Never?"

Her luminous blue eyes went wide, her expression caught somewhere between amazement and incredulity. Justin wasn't sure when he'd ever seen anyone look so openly astonished. He wasn't sure, either, why he'd finally put voice to a conviction that had only solidified in the past year.

"I can't see any advantage to it," he admitted, figuring the bartender syndrome must be at work. He had never confided in one himself. He rarely confided in anyone for that matter. But he could see where it would be easier for a person to admit certain truths to a stranger than to someone he knew. Friends and family had their own expectations, their own agendas.

"Life is easier with a partner," she said simply. She gave a shrug, the gesture seeming to say her conclusion was nothing more than a plain fact. Snow was white. Birds had wings. Life was easier with a partner. "I read in *Newsweek* that studies show men even live longer when they're married."

He met her easy certainty with equal conviction. He'd heard about those studies, too. But he didn't get a chance to tell her that he'd prefer quality over quantity. He'd pulled his left arm in a little to move his sleeve from his stinging skin. As he did, her hand ceased its soothing motions on the back of the denim carrier and she reached for his arm.

Curling her fingers a few inches above where he held the saw, she peeked toward his opposite shoulder. "What is it that's bothering you? Did you hurt yourself back there?"

Justin's first reaction was to brush off her question. His second was simply to breathe.

She'd moved in front of him, setting the can of gas on the drying ground, and lifted the edge of his sleeve. Gingerly, she touched the skin below the abrasion on his biceps. Unguarded interest shadowed her exquisite face. But it was the troubled look in her eyes that hit him like a physical blow. No woman had ever looked at him with such open and honest concern.

"You are hurt," she accused softly. "What happened?"

There were flecks of pale silver in his pewter-gray eyes. Emily noticed them as his glance quietly searched her face. Feeling her heart catch at his scrutiny, she dropped her hand as she swung her glance back to the angry red abrasion emerging below the short sleeve of his shirt. What skin was visible looked raw and sore. The shirt itself was snagged, as if something rough had dragged across it, tearing and pulling its threads.

"The door hit it."

"What door?"

"The one to your cellar. Come on," he murmured, reaching for the gas can himself, "I could use something cold to drink."

She snagged the can before he could, her sense of indebtedness growing stronger as they cut toward the little house her husband had repaired. Logic told her Justin couldn't be hurt too badly. After all, he'd worked all afternoon hauling boards without a hint of hesitation or complaint. That she'd been aware of, anyway. But whether or not he'd been in pain before, he was now. And he'd hurt himself protecting her and her child.

"We'll have to go in the front," she said as they approached her house a few minutes later. "I have iced tea or lemonade. Which would you prefer?"

Leaving the chain saw by the can of gas near the back porch, Justin told her he didn't care as long as it was cold and wet, and followed her past a propane tank at the side of the house. He was pretty sure from her preoccupation that she was thinking about the tree she needed to clear from her back door. He didn't doubt that she wanted to get started on it.

All *he* wanted was to get his car running and get home. That was what he'd been telling himself, anyway.

He pushed his fingers through his hair as he took the steps up her front porch, the motion more habit than exasperation. He wasn't anywhere near as frustrated by the delays as he should have been. But then, he hadn't intended to accomplish anything today anyway, he reminded himself, pulling open the screen door Emily had already disappeared through. That was the only possible explanation for why he didn't feel like pacing out of his skin. Delays of any kind usually made him crazy.

The interior of the little house was dim. It was also cooler than it was outside. Drawn as much by curiosity as that coolness, he stepped over the threshold and let the screen door bump closed behind him.

Emily was nowhere to be seen. He could hear her, though. Her gentle voice filtered through a doorway to his right as she spoke to her baby. It sounded very much as if she were commiserating over how awful it must feel to be wet, and making assurances that she would remedy that situation in no time at all.

Figuring she must be changing her baby's diaper, he pushed his hands into his pockets and took another step into a room that smelled faintly of cinnamon and lemon oil.

The starched white curtains had been drawn to keep out the heat of the sun, but as his eyes adjusted to the dimness, he could easily see around the neat and sparsely furnished space.

To his left, a stone fireplace took up most of the wall. Across from it, a simple wooden bench was filled with embroidered pillows. Beside him, a rocking chair had a small quilt draped over its back.

The reds and blues in the quilt were muted in the pale light, but the exquisite workmanship in the beautifully crafted piece was evident. Resisting the urge to touch it, he glanced toward the old treadle sewing machine beneath the narrow front window. Judging from it and the oil lamps atop a crowded book case, it appeared that Emily was into antiques.

She also seemed to have an eclectic sense of philosophy. Two small posters lay on the braided rag rug that covered most of the wood floor, presumably waiting to be put into the inexpensive frames propped against the wall. The smaller one was of a secluded mountain stream cascading into an enormous waterfall. The flowing script across the bottom read Go with the Flow. The poster next to it, larger and presumably for her daughter's room, was of a teddy bear in a pink tutu looking out a window. It simply said Dream.

"She's happier now," he heard Emily say as she emerged from the bedroom and headed for the doorway across from him. "She wanted her bassinet. Please. Come in," she invited, only to come to a halt when she reached the doorway herself.

Over her shoulder he could see a large wood table graced with a bouquet of flowers. Other than that, he could see nothing in the roomy, Spartan space but the basics. An old stove, an older refrigerator and white painted cabinets. He couldn't even see a sink, but that was because the limb occupying her back porch blocked the early evening light—along with the sink itself. Part of that limb had punched through the window and was hanging like a bushy verdant waterfall nearly to the floor.

He heard her pull a deep breath, saw her slender shoulders rise. It didn't take a Rhodes scholar to figure out that the Fates were having a field day with this woman. In the past few months, she'd lost her husband, had a child and been shafted—whether or not she wanted to admit it—by an itinerant who'd split with a chunk of her hard-earned cash. Considering the way the Fates had jerked her around today, he wouldn't have been at all surprised if the broken window over the sink hadn't just supplied the proverbial last straw.

The thought had him reaching for her shoulder. Before he could touch her, she let out a sigh and stepped away.

Frowning at himself, wondering what he'd thought he was going to do, he shoved his hands into his pockets and watched her head for the window by the refrigerator. She pushed open the unruffled white curtains to let in what light there was, then took an oil lamp from the top of the refrigerator and set in on the table.

He was thinking that the electricity must be out here, too, when she stooped to pick up the bar of soap that been knocked to the floor and headed for the sink, picking her way through the glass on the floor as she went. As if she tackled a jungle of foliage in her kitchen every day, she rustled her way through the leaves until she found what she was looking for.

Metal squeaked over the rush of water as his glance slipped down her long, windblown braid. Life here was as foreign to him as life on Mars. But nothing he'd encountered so far puzzled him more than this woman's almost philosophical acceptance of what would have had anyone else he knew reaching for antacids, at the very least.

It was almost as if it hadn't occurred to her to be upset just now. Luisa, his long-suffering cleaning lady, would have thrown her hands into the air and railed at the litany of saints she evoked for everything from world peace to a lost sock had she been faced with this mess. His mother— along with nearly every other woman he knew—would have stared blindly at the disorder, expecting someone, any- one, to materialize from somewhere and tend to it, lest she wreck her manicure.

Emily simply worked around it.

"You might want to wash," she said, drying her hands with a towel she pulled from the refrigerator handle. The towel went over her shoulder as she reached into a cabinet. "The bathroom's through there," she said, nodding to a doorway on the other side of the refrigerator. "That would be easier than trying to get to the pump in here."

He'd barely glanced past her when his brow furrowed. "The pump?"

"The water pump. I don't have faucets."

Curious, he pushed aside the bough hiding the gunmetal gray sink and stared at the tall, upright and decidedly old-fashioned metal spout with its long wooden handle. "This place must have been here since the turn of the century."

"It has," she replied over the clink of ice in a glass. "Mr. Clancy said the building was here when his father bought the place years ago. They sold it to us along with these two acres of land in exchange for a year's work from Daniel. He worked for him for a wage after the land became ours."

"You didn't want to modernize?"

She'd wanted to. She'd wanted to keep the rose print wallpaper, too, tattered as it had been. She'd never had anything pretty on her walls before. But Daniel had stripped it and painted everything white.

"We were used to a simple house," she said, reminding herself that this winter, she would repaint every room. If she got up her nerve, she might even pick colors that were outrageously bold. The only room she had painted so far was Anna's and that was soft, shell pink. "The walls and the foundation were good, so Daniel only had to repair the roof and replace the windows."

Daniel had been a good carpenter. He'd learned from his father and his father had raised more houses and barns than anyone in Haven County. There had even been a man in

Hancock who would have hired Daniel to work in his cabinet shop, but Daniel had wanted to tend the land.

It had kept him closer to the old ways, made it easier for
him to keep himself separate from their neighbors.

"I'm sure you must be hungry," she said, refusing to let
her thoughts carry her back when she was trying so hard
to move forward. Ice cracked as she poured liquid over it.
"I'll put some antiseptic on those scrapes, then fix you
something to eat."

Soaping up after he'd given the handle a pump, Justin
eyed the golden pie sitting on the stove. His breakfast of a
large black coffee-to-go and two granola bars had worn off
hours ago. "You don't have to feed me," he said, marveling at the way she minimized her lack. She couldn't afford
regular plumbing. He wasn't about to take her food. "And
my arm's fine. It's just bruised."

"Your arm is not fine. You were out in that barn with
the sore open and unprotected. It needs to be cleaned.

"And you didn't have to help me, either," she continued, her voice suddenly quiet. "But you did." Gratitude
shifted in her eyes as she held out a towel. "I know you
said no thanks were necessary, but I'll never be able to
thank you enough for what you did for me and Anna today.
So let me do what I can." She lifted the towel a little
higher. "Please?"

The thought of the barn and what had been in it already
had him hesitating. Her unexpected plea had him hesitating
even more.

"You don't owe me anything." Whatever he'd done,
he'd done on instinct. When he'd dived for that cellar, he'd
been protecting himself as much as he had her and her kid.
"You gave me shelter. I'd say that makes us even.

"But I'll take you up on the antiseptic," he told her,
ignoring the disagreement in her eyes as he took the towel
she offered. She truly didn't owe him anything. But he

knew what it was like to feel obligated. If she hated the feeling as much as he did, he wouldn't deny her the satisfaction of evening the score. "Where do you want me?"

Emily looked up at the mountain of male muscle towering over her. She didn't know why he seemed so much bigger to her now than he had outside. But she didn't think it wise to stand there watching his glance move over her face while she tried to figure it out. "It would help if you'd sit down," she murmured and turned to gather supplies from the bathroom.

He'd drained the glass of lemonade she'd left for him on her well-scrubbed pine table and was leaning back in one of its straight-backed chairs when she returned and set everything on the table beside him. He was following her every move. She could feel it. But she didn't let herself meet his eyes. She focused only on the fabric covering his biceps. She'd noticed the snags before. What she hadn't noticed was the tear in the seam.

"I'll fix your shirt for you," she said, leaning over so she could lift his sleeve and see how far up the scrape went.

"Don't bother. I have another one in the car. Wait a minute," he muttered when he felt the sleeve scrape his sore skin. "I'll just take it off."

Before she could say a word, he'd bent his dark head and grabbed a handful of fabric between his shoulder blades. Seconds later, he dragged the garment over his head.

Emily swallowed hard as he dropped it to his knee. Until two years ago, Daniel had been the only man she'd seen in any state of undress. He'd worked hard and ate well, but his thin build had not been what one would call impressive. Justin's…was. His shoulders · were broad, every corded muscle in his tapering back and carved arms beautifully defined.

She'd seen pictures of statues depicting such beautifully

proportioned men. She'd even seen pictures of men themselves in ads for skimpy underwear, though the first few times she'd encountered them while flipping through magazines at Mrs. Clancy's and at the grocery store, she'd nearly turned pink with embarrassment.

The image of a half-naked man no longer startled her as it once had. Mary Woldridge, a checker at the market who'd become her friend, even said she was no fun to watch at the magazine rack anymore. The real thing, however, was rather disturbing. So was the four-inch-wide swath of bruised, raw and abraded skin that ran from Justin's biceps to the top of his shoulder. Little splinters were visible between the streaks of blood that had dried and crusted in places, any one of which could have caught on his sleeve with his movements and caused a fresh jolt of discomfort.

He would have been terribly uncomfortable working with Mr. Clancy. But it was the thought of how he'd been hurting while he'd shielded her and her child that had her reaching to touch the skin below his reddened flesh.

"You're already bruising," she murmured. "Does it feel like you chipped bone?"

"I don't think I did anything like that. It just feels a little sore."

She met his eyes, sympathy in her own as she straightened. She needed more light.

Justin watched her turn away, the soft fabric of her dress shifting against her slender body as she moved across the room. The dress itself was modest to a fault. *Demure,* he supposed, though it wasn't a word he recalled ever having reason to use before. The sleeves nearly reached her elbows and her delicate collarbone was barely exposed. But the memory of how she'd looked with the wind molding that fabric to her body had been burned into his brain. All too easily, he could picture the fullness of her high breasts, the curve of her hips, her long, shapely legs.

Thinking of how exquisitely she was shaped beneath that formless garment had his body responding in ways that were not wise to consider in such an intimate space. So he forced his attention to what she was doing as she turned back to the table and touched the match she struck to the wick of the oil lamp she'd set there. Moments later, a bright glow illuminated her lovely face. That light gleamed in her hair, adding shimmers of platinum to shades of silver and gold as she replaced the glass chimney and positioned the lamp near the jar of vividly colored flowers.

With the scrape of wood over scarred pine flooring, Emily tugged a chair next to his and sat down beside him.

"Are you hurt anywhere else?"

He held up the thumb of his left hand. "Just a couple of slivers. I can get them if you have any tweezers."

She reached toward a gauze pad. "I have a needle," she told him, pulling out the one she'd brought and sterilizing it in the wick's flame. "You have them in your arm, too. Here," she murmured, replacing the chimney once more. "Let me see."

His bare chest was terribly distracting. Trying not to think of how incredibly solid it had felt, she took his thick wrist and moved his hand closer to the light. With his hand resting palm-up on her table, she could easily see two fine slivers of wood in the pad of his thumb.

His hands distracted her, too.

They were strong, broad and long-fingered. Good hands. Capable hands. Yet, they were nearly unblemished. There were no calluses, no scars, no healing scratches. Only the fresh-looking scrapes and nicks he'd earned that afternoon.

Fascinated, she started to touch the smooth pad at the base of his fingers, only to pull back as if she'd touched fire the instant she realized what she was doing.

''What's the matter?''

With a sheepish smile, she ducked her head and went to work on his thumb, deftly slipping out a sliver with the needle and wiping it onto a gauze pad. ''Your hands are very smooth. I've never seen a man's hands that weren't scarred and calloused from years of work. Except maybe Dr. Fisher,'' she amended, thinking of the kindly old physician in Hancock who'd delivered Anna. The other sliver joined the first. ''But I can't honestly say I paid any attention to them. Yours are the only ones I've noticed.''

''Is that good or bad?'' He posed the question mildly, absorbed as much by her lack of guile as her brisk efficiency when she dabbed on peroxide with a cotton ball, then blotted at the bubbles. ''No calluses, I mean?''

''There are some who would say that soft hands mean a person is idle. But Dr. Fisher is a very busy man. And you work with your mind.'' She tipped her head, still looking intrigued as she finished with dabs of antibiotic cream. ''Your hands don't look soft, though. And they didn't feel that way at all.''

''They didn't?''

Emily kept her head down as she slowly wiped a bit of cream from her own fingers. ''No,'' she murmured, but she would give him no more than that. Her last observation had slipped out before she considered what she was saying. He didn't need to know she could still imagine how comforting their solid, masculine weight had felt against her back when he'd wrapped her in his arms. He didn't need to know how drawn she was by their strength. How drawn she was by him.

''I'm relieved to hear that.''

She thought he might be smiling—the way he had when he'd teased her about her chain saw. But he wasn't smiling at all. He was watching her as if he knew very well she was thinking of his hands on her body. And she was.

Though until his glance slowly wandered to her mouth, she hadn't considered that he might have been thinking of that, too.

She wasn't comfortable with the awareness shimmering between them. That was as obvious to Justin as the faint tremor in the breath she drew and the chips of sapphire darkening in her eyes. He wasn't all that comfortable with it himself. But it was there, thickening the air, snaking through his body and washing wariness over Emily's fragile features.

Pressing her hand to her stomach, she blinked twice and reached for the peroxide to continue with her task.

Clearly flustered, trying not to look it, she promptly knocked it over.

*"Oh, mein!"* She gasped, bumping the bottle again as she snatched for it. Solution spilled over the edge of the table. It pooled on the wood, splashed on his pants.

"I've got it." Catching the bottle before it went over the edge itself, he turned it upright and saw her grab a towel.

"I'm so sorry," she murmured, mopping at the wet spot on his thigh. "I wasn't paying—"

"It's okay. Really." Catching her wrist, he stilled her frantic motions. "It's okay," he repeated, ducking his head so he could see her eyes. "Honest. No harm's done."

"I'm not usually so—"

"Emily." Beneath his fingers, he could feel her pulse, its beat as frantic as a trapped bird's. Incredibly with her mouth inches from his, his own didn't feel much calmer. "You don't need to be nervous with me."

"I can't seem to help it."

His glance swept her guileless face. There wasn't an ounce of cunning in this woman. Nothing false or deceptive about her. She didn't seem to have any natural defenses at all.

Deliberately ignoring the urge to tug her closer, he

slipped his hand from hers. "What was that you said?" he asked, thinking she needed to protect herself better if she was ever going to make it on her own. "What language?"

All she'd said was "Oh, my." Emily told him that as she pulled back, handing him a towel for his pants, and made herself focus on wiping up the table. "It's Pennsylvania Dutch."

She must have been even more rattled than she'd thought to have reverted to the only language she'd heard spoken until she was six years old. She rarely spoke the old German dialect at all anymore. Except to Anna once in a while, so she'd know something of her heritage. She'd learned English in school and had spoken it most of her life, but she'd worked hard over the past two years to pronounce her words the same as her neighbors. She didn't want to be different. She wanted to belong.

Desperately.

Something like caution entered Justin's deep voice. "Isn't that what the Amish speak?"

"In their homes and to each other. In the Old Order communities, anyway," she said, returning her attention to his abraded arm. "But they speak English, too."

"How do you know that?"

"Because I was Amish," she said, gently wiping antiseptic over his scraped skin. "And we were Old Order."

She turned away, picking up her needle again. When she turned back, she frowned at his biceps. "You have one here that looks awfully deep." Apology touched her eyes even as she began picking at the stubborn splinter. "I'm sorry if it hurts."

He didn't get the feeling that she was avoiding the subject. She was simply concentrating on what she felt was more important—something he found oddly touching since what she was concentrating on was taking care of him.

With her wielding that needle, he didn't want to distract her, either.

She'd certainly distracted him, though. He knew next to nothing about the Amish. What he did know was limited to what he'd absorbed through the media, mostly in the form of an occasional newspaper article or magazine feature and one old movie. Mental images had already formed of bearded men in black suits and hats and women in dark dresses and white caps that covered their hair. The strictest of them, the Old Order, lived as they had a hundred years ago, driving buggies, plowing their fields with horses. They had no telephones, no electricity. And they had as little as possible to do with "the English," which he understood to be everyone who wasn't one of them.

Emily's simple dress had a row of little flower-shaped buttons down the front, utterly rebellious by Amish standards, he supposed. Unsophisticated and old-fashioned by his. But as he listened to the drip of the pump on a leaf in the sink and gritted his teeth against the sting in his arm when either the needle or the splinter made its presence felt, it now made sense to him why she was so comfortable working without electricity. There wasn't any. The refrigerator and stove were run on fuel from the tank he'd seen outside. It made a certain amount of sense, too, why there were no vehicles on the property—and why her husband had been so unfamiliar with machinery. She was living the only way she'd ever known.

She'd told him earlier that they had moved here a couple of years ago. But they would have arrived knowing only their own ways and, in a place as rural as this little corner of Illinois, they wouldn't have been exposed to anything startling in the way of change. Nothing startling to his way of thinking, anyway.

He couldn't believe how totally, completely different they were. Yet, even as that thought occurred, he was

equally conscious of the freshness of her scent and its subtle effect on certain of his nerves. He was aware of her
touch, too, the gentleness of it as she rested her fingers
against the side of his arm as if to hold his arm still—or
to soothe the discomfort she was inflicting.

It wasn't wise to be drawn by the way she flinched every
time she thought she hurt him. And he had no business
wanting to slip the rubber band from the bottom of her
braid and slowly unweave all that incredible hair.

"There," she finally said, looking enormously relieved
when she'd picked out the last of the splinters and bathed
the abrasion with antiseptic. Applying a couple of gauze
pads, she taped them in place with the efficiency of a field
nurse and gathered the supplies from the table. "Now, I'll
get you something to eat. Are you sure you don't want me
to fix your shirt?"

"Positive," he muttered, dragging it back over his head.
It was one thing to be intrigued by her. It was another
matter entirely to be as conscious of her as he was. He
couldn't deny his curiosity over how she had come to be
where she was, but he couldn't just sit there watching her
fluid movements while she waited on him. He needed to
do something. Anything to keep from wondering if she had
any idea what it did to a man to know he affected her the
same way she did him.

He figured he might as well go to work on her tree.

## Chapter Four

Emily swept the glass shards from the floor while Justin headed to the storage shed for a handsaw to cut off the limb hanging inside. He hadn't said much, other than that he might as well clear the sink since she'd need to use it, but he'd seemed edgy to her. Restless, perhaps, the way men got when a pouring rain kept them inside and away from their chores. Being stuck the way he was, she could hardly blame him for feeling tense.

Taking her cutting board and two fist-size tomatoes to the table, she started slicing. She was feeling a little unsettled herself. She had been ever since his hand had closed over her wrist and she'd found herself close enough to breathe in the scents of musk and citrus clinging to his skin. The crisp clean scent would have been his aftershave lotion, she supposed. The rest was just him.

She closed her eyes, drew a deep breath.

She'd been a married woman. She had a child. She'd

been raised on a farm, for heaven's sake, so she was far from naive about sex. Where she'd come from, the subject hadn't been spoken of with the casual abandon she'd encountered in magazines and on television in the past couple of years, but she'd still known long before she'd left Ohio about the concept of physical attraction.

Sarah Hostetler had turned the color of an inflamed cow udder every time Amos Beiler had spoken to her. And Emma Lapp had confided that she'd felt urges toward her Eli for a year before he started pairing up with her at Sunday evening singings. Emily supposed she'd felt that attraction with Daniel at one time, too.

She just hadn't ever felt it all that strongly before.

The knife barely missed her finger.

Muttering at herself, she pushed the meaty slices aside and snatched up the other tomato. There was something else she understood. She needed to pay attention to what she was doing before she did anything more embarrassing than what she'd done by dumping peroxide over the man's pants. And what she needed to concentrate on right now was what she was going to feed him before Mr. Clancy showed up and helped him with his car so he could leave. Justin struck her as a man with a hearty appetite. After all, it took a lot of fuel to sustain a body that big. And he had gone for hours without anything to eat.

Wiping her hands on her towel, she turned to her refrigerator. The best she could do in a hurry was prepare him something with the chicken she'd fried yesterday. There was plenty left. She'd been too tired last night to have much more than a drumstick and drink a glass of milk before she'd fallen asleep after nursing Anna. It would be good to use it now so it didn't go to waste.

She'd just decided to serve the chicken cold with a salad, since it was too hot for much else, anyway, when she heard Justin's heavy footfall on the front porch. A heartbeat later, the screen door groaned open and she heard him start inside.

From over her shoulder, she saw him glance toward her bedroom, then hurriedly reach behind him to catch the door. Anna was sleeping. Apparently, remembering that, he crossed the living room with little more than a squeak of old floorboards and walked into the kitchen carrying a three-foot-long handsaw.

"This should work," he said, sounding as if he were talking more to himself than to her. "It'll make a little bigger mess in here, but it'll be quieter than using the chain saw outside. The branch on the porch is too heavy to move without cutting it up first."

Leaves rustled as he shoved back the greenery and found the juncture of limb and branch. Propping one hip on the counter, he leaned toward the wall and dragged the saw a few inches out on the limb to score it before pushing forward to cut.

"You've done that before," she observed.

"Not in years. I used to hang around with the gardener in boarding school." With the grating sound of metal biting wood, he took a half-dozen strokes and angled himself to get a better line. "Every once in a while he'd let me do something other than haul his wheelbarrow around for him."

Emily moved automatically, pouring cream into a bowl, adding a bit of sugar and vinegar. Dividing her attention between her task and the concentration etched in Justin's brow, she leaned against the heavy pine table and began beating the mixture with a whisk. Beyond her, eggs boiled in a pan on the stove, steam rising in a cloud.

"You liked plants?"

"I liked the bugs in the plants." His left hand braced the limb, his right worked the saw. "We used to hide them in the counselor's desk. The gardener put me to work in exchange for not telling anyone what I was doing.''

Though it was hard to picture him so young, she couldn't help the smile that touched her mouth. Boys would be boys, it seemed, no matter where they were raised. "You must have lived a long way from the city. To go to boarding school, I mean.''

"Actually, Stanton Hall was ten miles from my parents' home.''

"In Chicago?''

"Boston. The Hall had educated three generations of Sloans. My parents wouldn't hear of sending my brother or me anywhere else before shipping us over to Harvard.''

She'd read of boarding schools. She'd read of Boston, too. And she'd certainly heard of Harvard. The combination conjured an image of something proper and wealthy, but she couldn't imagine sending a child away from their parents to teach them. To be away from the family would be so hard on a child. And a mother. "That must have been difficult, being away from your parents when you were young, I mean.''

Justin gave a shrug, catching the motion partway when his scraped shoulder reminded him he might not want to do that. He actually hadn't minded going away to school. It had been infinitely easier than listening to his well-bred parents' icy, horribly civilized arguments. To this day, he was sure the only reason they were together was because the other refused to cave in first and file for divorce. Tenacity ran strong in the Sloan family.

"It was tradition. My parents are very big on it.''

"Is it tradition in your family to do the same kind of work? I mean, are your father and brother lawyers, too?''

The blade stuck, drawing a quick, quiet oath and a scowl for the break in his pacing. "They are,'' he told her, getting his rhythm back. "But my father practices a different kind of law. He's in estates and trusts." Which was precisely why Justin hadn't chosen that specialty himself. He respected his dad. He just hadn't wanted to work with him. "My brother's a judge."

"Your younger brother," she prodded, more in conclusion than question.

"Older. I'm the youngest."

That seemed to perplex her.

"Mrs. Clancy thought you might be the oldest," she said over the steady tap of metal against the brown ceramic bowl. Dismissing the observation, she lifted the whisk to test the consistency of whatever it was she was concocting in the bowl. "What's the difference between what you do and what your father does?"

"He handles peoples' personal assets. I handle business matters for companies. Mostly mergers."

"Mergers?"

"Of companies," he explained, willing to keep up the conversation as long as she was. He'd wanted a diversion. Between the topics and his task, he'd gotten his wish. "Sometimes companies want to combine their resources to expand their market or purchasing power." Leaning in a little more, he worked the saw more quickly, the fresh smell of pitch scenting the air. "Sometimes one company is stronger than the other and they want to absorb the competition. Take them over, you know?" he asked, seeing her frown.

"I guess you could say that what I do is negotiate," he concluded, thinking he'd lost her. Her exposure to the world of business was probably even less than to the world beyond the farm. She'd told him herself that she knew nothing of law when he'd mentioned helping her turn in her crooked handyman. "That's basically why people hire lawyers to begin with. To get them what they want, or to make sure the other side doesn't get more than it should have."

Two more strokes of the saw and the limb gave a crack. One more and it broke away completely. When he looked over at her, she was still frowning as she lifted the wire whip again.

"It seems strange that people should have to hire someone to transact their business for them. Can't people just sit down and talk through what they want to do?"

There it was again, he thought. That innocence that bordered on naiveté. "It's not that simple," he murmured, shifting his weight to lower the thick, eight-foot-long branch to the floor.

"Why not?"

"For one thing, you're dealing with more than just people." He spotted a stack of neatly folded brown grocery bags wedged between the wall and the refrigerator. Snagging one, he returned to the sink. A few large pieces of broken glass were precariously wedged in the window frame. They'd become an exploding snowball of shards if they fell out and hit that galvanized gray sink.

"There are filings with regulatory agencies and government approvals to contend with. You have stocks that can take wild swings and sink a deal before the financing can even be put together. You're reorganizing an entire corporate structure.

"I just completed a case like that," he told her. He'd pulled his part of the huge megamerger together in record time, too. And timing had been everything because certain players could have caused the deal to fold at any point. "Something that involved couldn't have been accomplished without legal expertise."

She didn't looked impressed.

Not that he was trying to impress her, he assured himself. It was just that the enormously complicated transaction had been a real coup for him. It had also greased his way to becoming a partner a full year ahead of his personal schedule.

Glass clicked against glass as he dropped a couple of saucer-size pieces into the sack and added bits of twig. The satisfaction he should have felt with his accomplishment wasn't there. He kept waiting for it. Expecting to feel it. Since the day he'd left a much smaller practice and joined the firm six years ago, he'd kept his sights on his goal, paid his dues, bent his life to the firm's collective will and now, finally, he could begin to reap the rewards. He loved the challenges he worked with. There was no greater high than pulling off what others said couldn't be done. But even last night at the dinner the senior partner had given to welcome him into the inner circle, all he felt was the same restless sensation that had driven him from his condo a little after six o'clock that morning.

Moments ago, he'd been aware of the bubbling of the water on the stove and the soft padding of Emily's sneakers as she'd moved from fridge to cabinet to table. Now, he heard nothing but the boiling water and her silence.

She hadn't a clue what he was talking about. He was sure of it. He'd been talking about stockholders. She knew livestock. He'd talked mergers. She knew mulch. From the way she stood by the table watching him, he was dead certain she hadn't understood a thing he'd said.

"Your work doesn't make you very happy, does it."

He didn't know which confounded him more, the observation or the sympathy behind it.

"I didn't think it did," she said, before he could contradict her. "When you talk about your work, the muscles in your jaw jump.

"I suppose it stresses you," she concluded, sounding as if she didn't often use the term as she skirted the limb on the floor and headed for the sink with the pot of hard-boiled eggs. Concern clouded her expression. "Being tense all the time isn't good for a person, you know."

Steam rose in a plume when she dumped the hot water down the drain. Sawdust swirled down with it. Two squeaks of the pump handle and cold water filled the pan.

"I'm not stressed." Justin fairly muttered the claim as he watched her turn to get a couple of ice cubes from the refrigerator's freezer and toss them into the pan to speed the cooling process. "No more than anyone else is," he qualified. "And I'm perfectly happy doing what I do. It's what I've always wanted to do. And I just made partner," he told her, getting a choke-hold on the limb to move it before she had to step over it again.

"That's something important to you? Being this partner?"

She'd stopped beside him, her expression intent.

He was certain it was only her unexpected sincerity that caused him to hesitate.

"Yeah," he murmured. Turning from the other questions he could see forming, he dragged the long limb past the table and through the kitchen doorway. "It is."

It was more than important, he insisted to himself, leaving a trail of leaves as he rustled his way across her braided rag rug with the limb and down the steps of her front porch. It was the biggest thing that had ever happened to him. Beck, Wyler and Dunlap was one of the most prestigious general business law firms in the country. Being invited by that elite corp of attorneys to become an owner in the firm rather than an employee was huge. Of the sixty lawyers working there, only seven, now eight, had a say in its policies and goals. It meant his opinion was valued. It meant he'd accomplished something major.

Granted, it wasn't as big an accomplishment as his brother, Brad, being appointed Supreme Judicial Court Judge back in Massachusetts. But he did strive to keep up

the family tradition of judicial achievement. He just preferred to do it his own way—which also happened to include doing it seven hundred miles from Boston, where his
parents couldn't badger him into a bloodless marriage like
theirs and his brother's.

He tossed the branch to the ground at the side of the
house, forcing aside the thought that Kenneth Beck, the
senior partner of the firm, had pretty much taken over on
that score. Thinking about his very proper and quietly competitive family was more than enough to make his stomach
burn. Thinking about how Ken was pushing his daughter
on him was enough to set it on fire.

He could hear Emily's voice in the next room when he
walked back inside. Realizing that he must have awakened
her kid, he deliberately quieted his footsteps and headed
for the sink to finish his project. The restive sensation working through him was so familiar, he barely noticed it as he
started wiping up sawdust and tossing orphaned leaves into
the paper sack—and listening to the soothing tones coming
from the other room.

He wasn't sure when the memory had been etched. In
the cellar. As they'd walked along the rutted dirt road. At
Clancy's. But he could easily picture Emily running her
finger over her baby's downy-looking little cheek. He could
picture her, too, as she'd looked when the baby had been
fussing and she'd snuggled the infant closer. There was one
picture that wouldn't form, though. He couldn't even begin
to imagine her worried about mussing her lipstick or her
clothes by giving her child or her spouse a kiss or a hug.

"I think she just wanted to change positions," Emily
said on her way back in. "It must be frustrating not to be
able to turn over when you want to."

Seeing the set lines of Justin's strong profile, her quick
smile faded.

"Please stop thinking about your work for now," she

asked, assuming that to be the reason he was still frowning. Despite what he claimed, there was no happiness in him when he'd spoken of it. "I've never been to a big city, but I know life is very different there. And I know that it's sometimes hard to make the best of what we're given to work with. But for the sake of your digestion, you shouldn't think about what upsets you while you eat.

"Come. Sit," she encouraged, as she finished setting out bowls and dishes. "It isn't fancy, but it will fill you."

She'd piled a plate with cold chicken and some of the beets she'd pickled last year. Slices of bread, store-bought because it lasted longer than homemade, sat next to a dish of her blackberry preserves. The earthenware salad bowl held crisp lettuce and tomatoes from her garden, watercress she'd gathered from the stream and a generous dollop of cream dressing thick with diced egg.

She was adding a bowl of cucumbers and onion in vinegar, a combination her mother had always kept on hand when cucumbers were available for its digestive properties, when she saw Justin reach for the soap.

"How happy are you doing what you do for a living?" His tone was as deliberate as his motions as he scrubbed the pitch from his hands. "You're out here alone trying to make ends meet. I don't imagine you find a lot of pleasure in most of your days, either."

He sounded more critical than curious, and oddly defensive.

"Actually," she said, sitting down to wait for him, "I find some pleasure in all of them. I try to anyway," she qualified, seeing doubt cloud his chiseled features. "It's hard sometimes when I'm already tired from packing my produce and herbs for the produce man and I still have weeding or canning to do or Mrs. Clancy's house to clean, but I love seeing things grow. And I have Anna."

Justin's doubt grew to pure disbelief. The woman was a

widow. She lived alone. With a baby. And she'd as much as admitted that she worked her slender fingers right to the bone. Yet, she sat there, looking him dead in the eye and expected him to believe she found pleasure in her days.

The cynic in him rejected the idea outright. But his glance fell to the table just then and he found his train of thought completely derailed.

He didn't know what he'd thought she'd been building as she'd slipped back and forth behind him. But he hadn't expected the bounty on her generously spread table.

"I know the meal is light," she said, apology in her eyes. "But as warm as it is, I didn't think you'd want anything hot. I can heat the chicken, if you'd like and fry some potatoes. I have stock in the pantry to make gravy if you—"

"No. No," he repeated, amazed that she'd think he was somehow displeased. "This is…great."

It was better than that. Sitting across from her at her table a minute later, he sunk his teeth into a chicken breast so tender, the chef in his favorite restaurant would have wept. She'd fried it in flour and buttermilk, she said, when he'd asked. And she actually looked uncomfortable with his generous approval of her culinary skills when he told her he'd never tasted salad dressing so good.

"It's nothing," she claimed, her eyes on her plate when he repeated the praise. "It's just plain food."

"There's nothing plain about it."

"I mean *plain*," she stressed. "Amish."

She wasn't accustomed to compliments. As he took a bite of the sweet and savory beet, he was suddenly dead certain of that. He was pretty certain that had to do with being *plain*, too. People who did nothing to set themselves apart in any way from their peers, going so far as to dress with the same lack of adornment, wouldn't be very big on things like praise and verbal approval.

The woman who had progressed to wearing tiny, flower-shaped buttons, uncovering her incredible hair and quoting *Newsweek* was obviously adapting fairly well to her environment. But she still had a long way to go.

What he was curious about, though, was how far she'd come.

"Is this what you did before you came here…farming?" he asked, blatantly fishing.

"It is what we all did," she replied, buttering bread. "Daniel was a carpenter, but he tended our dairy animals and grew wheat with his brothers and I had my kitchen garden and chickens. Here, I grow organic vegetables and herbs for a company that supplies gourmet shops and restaurants. And I have my kitchen garden to grow what I need for Anna and me." Her glance flicked to his. "My produce goes to the Quad Cities," she said, backing up. "Have you ever been to them?"

She had grown what she'd served him. The thought piled on top of the other questions he wanted to ask, starting with why she'd left where she was from. But there was a hopeful look in her eyes as she waited for him to answer that made him think she wasn't terribly eager to talk about what she'd left behind. What she wanted was to change the subject.

The Quad Cities were another hour away. "Only on business," he replied, tempted to prod anyway.

"Can you tell me what they're like?"

Definitely trying to change the subject, he thought. "Not really. You've been here for two years?" he asked, giving it one more shot.

"Two years and two months. But I haven't been any farther west than Hancock, so I haven't been there yet myself. You must have seen something of the towns when you were there."

She wasn't biting. And he wouldn't badger her. Not while she was feeding him. "I remember a lot of industrial complexes and the inside of a couple of hotels, but that's pretty much it.''

He thought he saw disappointment flicker through her expression in the moments before he polished off the chicken and considered telling her again how delicious it was. But she'd looked genuinely discomfited with his compliment, and the last thing he wanted to do was embarrass her. Instead of saying another word about her meal, he helped himself to a little bit more of everything—which sent the same message—and saw a smile touch her lush, lovely mouth.

That smile was as soft as spring rain, warm, rejuvenating. And maybe a little grateful. It shouldn't have touched him as it did. It shouldn't have appealed as much. And it definitely shouldn't haven't resurrected the heat he'd felt when he'd seen her eyes go dark at his touch. There was nothing provocative about her. Nothing deliberately enticing. Yet, she aroused him with nothing but a smile.

The Fates were really on a perverse streak, he thought, stabbing another forkful of salad.

''I guess what I remember about the Quads is the river that cuts through them,'' he finally conceded, grappling for something, anything, to change his mental subject. ''The Mississippi is pretty impressive.''

She immediately told him she'd certainly read of the river, but she'd never seen it and wanted to know what had impressed him about it—a request he humored while wondering how she managed everything on her own. He even thought about asking her between comments about riverboats and sheer size, but he didn't trust the protective feeling that prompted the thought, so he let it go. Her business was none of his. And just so he wasn't tempted to butt in to it anyway, he left her alone a few minutes later to tackle her tree branch while she handled the dishes.

Doing something physical had definite appeal. And he'd feel like a louse leaving her to deal with the mess alone.

It took him thirty minutes to trim the outer limbs from the branch with the chain saw and cut the main section into chunks manageable enough to haul off the porch.

He'd never used a chain saw before. Never had a reason to. But the operating instructions were printed above the pull-cord and once he'd made it past the sputter-and-die stage, cutting wood was practically as easy as drawing a hot knife through butter. Wielding the saw didn't even bother his shoulder that much.

It was with a certain sense of disbelief that he realized nothing was bothering him at all when he glanced up after making his last cut and saw Emily push open the back screen door.

Beyond them, the setting sun reflected off the four green-house windows and streaked the wispy clouds above it with shades of salmon and peach. In the pale-pink light, he watched her glance from the wood chips scattered over the gray boards to where he stood ten feet away. She carried her daughter curled against the diaper draped over her shoulder, one hand under her baby's bottom, the other cupping the side of the little blond head as if to protect tiny ears from the scream of the saw.

Backing off the throttle, he killed the machine's throaty idle.

"I woke her."

"She was already awake. She just ate. I just wanted to see how much more there was to do. Let me put Anna down and I'll help."

"Just tell me where you want this," he said, walking over to her as he indicated the pile of leafy limbs he'd tossed beside the wide back porch. The broken kitchen window was visible now, as was the back door, whose window had survived, and a pine chair, which had not. "I won't have time to get the branch out of your cellar, but I can get this hauled off for you before I go."

"The little pieces can go in the compost heap. And I can use the logs for firewood. I'll take care of them in a minute."

"You don't need to do anything out here. I'm just about finished."

"But I want to help."

He noticed that she'd changed her daughter's clothes. The garment the baby wore before had been solid white. The little nightgown she was in now had lavender ducks and pink chicks marching over it. Looking from the impossibly tiny backside, he met the gentle smile in Emily's eyes.

"Emily," he said gently. "I'm sure you have other things to do."

"I do. But the work will be easier if we both do it."

"Look," he muttered, patience straining as he listened for sounds of a car or truck. "Clancy should be here any minute. If I get back to this, I might be able to get it all cleared before he does. Then you won't have to worry about it at all."

She was going to get stuck with a shattered post anyway, he thought glancing along the porch's roofline. The broken post was in the middle, so at least the roof wasn't sagging. Yet. He was no expert, but it seemed to him that it would if it weren't repaired soon.

He was thinking he'd ask Clancy if he'd be able to help her when Emily stepped back.

"I won't stay out here if you don't want me to," she said, her voice suddenly subdued. "I just thought it would be nice to work with you instead of working inside alone."

Her admission had him turning slowly back to face her. The light had vanished from her eyes as surely as if he'd just slapped a switch. Still, she tried her smile again and glanced toward the basket of beans and the flat of strawberries that had survived the carnage on the porch. "I got a little behind today. I guess I'll just get started on those."

Justin had no doubt that she was wondering which she could handle easiest with the baby when he saw Anna turn her head toward him. The little girl looked up, her blue eyes wide on his as her head bobbed, one arm waving like a maestro conducting Mozart.

If he hadn't been so concerned about Emily at the moment, he might have considered the child's incredibly perfect little face a moment longer. But his attention had already shifted to the lovely face of her mother.

All Emily wanted was his company.

He felt like a heel for denying her something so simple.

"You're right," he murmured, curling his free hand at his side to keep from smoothing back the wisp of hair looping toward her chin. "This will go faster if we work together." He glanced back at her baby, trying not to eye her with too much curiosity. Or uncertainty. "But before we do anything else, we'd better get some plastic over your window. If you'll tell me where it is, I'll get it while you take care of her."

He didn't question the relief he felt when he saw Emily's quick smile. Knowing he wouldn't be around long enough to have to worry about any of his reactions to her, he just watched her settle the baby in her carrier on the kitchen floor so she could keep an eye on her through the screen door and listened to her explain to the baby what they were going to do and that she'd be back to check on her in a minute.

He found himself checking on her, too. Not obviously. Just a glance every once in a while, something that seemed more automatic than planned—and which felt more like curiosity than concern. He'd never been as close to an infant as he'd been today. But the only conclusion he drew about the tiny child yawning in the carrier was that she didn't fuss as much as he thought a baby would. As they tacked plastic over the hole where the window had been, then cleared the debris from the porch, he concentrated far more on the evening silence, the lack of traffic of any sort on the road and the woman working beside him.

They seemed to have an uncanny knack for anticipating each other's moves as Emily tugged branches past her roosting chickens and he dragged off the logs she would eventually turn into firewood. But he felt certain she was as aware as he was of the encroaching darkness.

As the sun sank and the twilight dimmed, it was becoming more obvious by the minute that Clancy wasn't coming.

## Chapter Five

It had grown too dark outside to see.

Emily had already lit the lamp on the kitchen table. As Justin approached the back steps, he could see her moving past the bassinet she'd brought from her room then light another lamp and set it on a shelf above the drainboard.

A buttery glow filled the room, chasing away shadows, beckoning him inside. She looked familiar with the routine, comfortable with it the way people were with something they did night after night. Year after year. She tried to find a little happiness in each of her days, she'd told him. But he wondered how hard she had to struggle for those brief moments of peace. He knew fatigue when he saw it. He knew strain. If she'd take a look in the mirror, she'd see both.

The syncopated sounds of crickets melded with the quiet creak of wooden boards as he crossed the freshly swept porch. Rather than wondering if she even owned anything with a reflective surface, he should be thinking about what he was going to do for the night. As annoying as he found it when a flight was delayed, he should have been fuming at the inconvenience of being stuck a hundred miles from home with no way to get anywhere. But nothing about this day had been even remotely normal.

All things considered, he had no reason to expect the night would be, either.

Given that prospect, he decided he might as well throw caution to the wind and give one of Emily's poster-philosophies a test run. Going with the flow for one night took less energy than bucking the tide, anyway. He'd start by asking if he could stay. If she balked, he'd ask if he could borrow a pillow and head for his car. He was a practical man. He never entered a meeting without a contingency plan.

Stepping over the threshold, he quickly closed the screen door to keep out the bugs. "That was the last of it. Everything's off the porch."

"Thank you." The glass chimney snapped into place. A moment later, she glanced over her shoulder. "Still no sign of Clancy?"

"Not even a headlight. It's black as pitch out there."

"I think he forgot that he meant to help you."

"It looks that way."

"You're welcome to stay the night," she said, looking away as if she didn't know what he'd think of her for making the offer. "I keep Anna in my room with me, so you could sleep in her room. I don't have a crib yet," she explained, "and the bed in there is old and narrow, but it's comfortable."

She gave him a hesitant glance, then reached to close the room's starched white curtains. There was an uncertainty in her expression that belied the ease of her offer, an abruptness to her movements that hinted at either nerves, ambivalence or both.

He hadn't even had to consider Plan B. "Would my staying here bother you, Emily?"

Her hand faltered on the curtain before she turned with a soft smile. "It would bother me more if you didn't. I'd worry about you," she hurriedly qualified, "out there in the dark."

She really didn't want him to go. And for reasons that had to do with more than convenience, Justin realized he really didn't want to, either. It was just one night. He'd be gone tomorrow.

"I'll put hot water in the bathroom for you," she said on her way to the stove. "Would you like some milk and pie?"

She picked up the teapot, filled it and set it on to boil. Pushing her hair back from her forehead, looking as if she were trying to remember what she needed to do next, she skimmed a smile past her daughter cooing at the mobile clipped to her bassinet and eyed the basket of beans she'd set inside the back door.

"Emily," Justin muttered. "You don't have to wait on me. As tired as you are, why don't you just go to bed yourself?"

"I will. In a while. And I'm not that tired," she insisted, detouring to take glasses from the cupboard. "Is milk all right?"

He tried not to sigh. "It's fine." Intercepting her, he took the glasses from her hands. "I'll get it. You do whatever it is you'd normally do."

"I can do that any time. I'd rather listen to you." She slid him a cautious glance. "If you don't mind."

"Listen to me?"

"Yes. Please. Tell me what it's like for you out there. In Chicago," she clarified. "Start with the things you like best," she added, slicing pie as he turned to the fridge. "Chicago has libraries and theaters and wonderful restaurants. You must have favorites."

"How do you know the restaurants are wonderful?" he asked, finding that he actually had to suppress a smile at her enthusiasm. "I thought you said you'd never been there."

"I haven't. But I've read about them. And the shops. The little specialty ones. Ethnic, they call them. I didn't even know they had such places until I read about them in Mrs. Clancy's *Bon Appétit.*"

"The shops interest you?"

"Oh, yes. A little," she replied, deliberately curbing her own eagerness.

Frowning at what she'd done, he watched her set slices of pie on the table before she dragged the basket of beans to her chair and took a large bowl from a cabinet. "It sounds like more than 'a little' to me."

She gave a dismissing shrug, looking as if she knew she was being totally frivolous. "If I could have any kind of business I wanted, that's what I'd really like to have someday. A little shop where I could sell bright things for the kitchen and herbed oils and vinegars and my organic vegetables." After nudging the mobile to make it spin, she settled a bowl in her lap and reached into the basket for a handful of beans. "I read an article in *Newsweek* that said specialty stores in the country are doing very well right now. During the high season, anyway. People from the city come here to buy corn and to fish. Trudy at the hardware store says that both of the hotels and the campground are almost always full in the summer."

"And what would you do in the winter?"

"I haven't thought that far ahead." She smiled. "It's only a wish."

"And you got the idea from *Bon Appétit* and *Newsweek*," he concluded.

"I like magazines," she confided, snapping the ends off a bean. "There are so many wonderful things in them. Unusual things," she added, thinking especially of Mrs. Clancy's *Soap Opera Digest*. "I'd never even seen them before we moved here. Magazines, I mean. Except the farming one my father received. They weren't allowed in my parents' home. In the entire community, for that matter. They were *verboten*. Forbidden," she explained, when Justin's eyebrows merged.

"I can't think about a shop until after I've saved up enough money to buy a hot water heater, though." She continued snapping beans, her motions automatic. "That's on my wish list, too. And electricity. And a car. And driving lessons." She hesitated. "I should probably add the moon."

She glanced up, feeling faintly self-conscious when she saw him quietly watching her. She hadn't intended to talk so much. She wasn't even sure why she was, or why she'd told him of her little dream—except that something inside her told her he would understand about that. Becoming a partner with his other lawyers had been important to him. And finding security for herself and her daughter was important to her—even if all she could do was wish for it while she provided for them the only way she could.

"I'm sorry," she murmured. "I didn't mean to bore you with that. I want to listen to you."

"You're not boring me. In fact," he admitted, "I'd like to hear more about the community you're from."

"Now that *is* boring. Besides, I asked you first. Please. Tell me what you like best."

Justin leaned back in his chair, his hand wrapped around his glass as he watched interest light her eyes. He'd seen that expression before. It was the same hopeful look she'd given him when she'd asked him to tell her about the cities on the river. Only now, he couldn't tell if she wanted to avoid talking about herself, or if she was just eager to learn of what lay beyond Hancock.

"You must have seen cities when you came here from Ohio."

"All we saw were freeways and McDonald's. That's where the driver we hired would stop for us to eat. Have you been to a McDonald's?"

The woman would make an excellent hostile witness. She didn't give an inch when she didn't want to.

"I'll make you a deal," he said, trying to decide which impressed him more, her quick intelligence or the focus and drive that put his own to shame. "I'll answer your questions, but you also have to answer mine."

The one question he wouldn't have to ask was how she managed to do everything she did. Watching her protective glance move to her child as she rhythmically snapped beans, he knew. She simply never stopped. Her hands were never idle.

He'd bet his season tickets to the Bulls that her mind wasn't idle, either.

"I am answering your questions," she said, looking a little puzzled. "But if you have more, that's fine. So, what do you like?"

With the terms of the deal set, he settled back to consider what he'd never thought about before and told her he supposed the thing he liked best was the lake he jogged beside several times a week. That run along the shore of Lake Michigan probably saved his sanity at times. And there were a lot of restaurants he enjoyed, but his favorite was a little Italian place where the chef, who had come from Milan, broke into arias when he was creating something particularly inspired.

Emily wanted to know what an aria was. She'd never

heard an opera. It had only been in the past couple of years that she'd heard any music beyond that which was sung from a hymnal, she told him, and that was mostly country-and-western, what the Clancys and her friend Mary listened to. So talk drifted to composers, then to the countries those composers were from, and even though their conversation had moved a couple of thousand miles from Chicago, she seemed to absorb everything he said—while he simply absorbed the peace he felt in her presence.

Justin wasn't sure what it was, her quiet, nurturing manner or the simplicity of her needs, but he felt a totally unfamiliar sense of calm as he sat at her table. Considering how hard he'd worked all day, it could just as easily have been the physical fatigue that had him feeling so mellow. All he knew for sure was that the tiredness he felt now was infinitely different from the mental drain he normally experienced this time of night. Different and, oddly, far more satisfying.

He didn't concern himself with why that was. As he listened to the drone of crickets beyond the screen door and the quiet snap of beans, all he cared about was that, for once, he wasn't playing games, competing or clawing to stay in place. He was simply a man talking with a woman who seemed to appreciate his presence as much as she had his help.

A rooster was crowing.

The thought drifted through Justin's mind about two seconds before he became aware of light rudely beaming against his closed eyelids. He'd settled between sheets that smelled like fresh air and sunshine, wrestled the pillow into shape and fallen asleep. That couldn't have been more than sixty seconds ago.

Yet, he could swear he heard a rooster.

He could also hear the soft voice of a woman.

It was the familiarity of that voice that finally had him caving in to consciousness.

It had been nearly midnight when the baby had awakened and started fussing. Within a minute, the fussing had escalated to hiccupping little cries and Emily had gathered up the child, promising to feed her as soon as she reheated the water for Justin so he could wash up.

Emily hadn't argued when he'd said he would make do with cold. Looking grateful, she'd apologized for keeping him up so late, showed him his room and how to extinguish the oil lamp she left him and disappeared into her room with a quiet, "Rest well."

He could have sworn that had been only a minute ago.

Shoving his fingers though his hair, a gesture that reminded him of his shoulder's encounter with a cellar door, he pulled himself to his feet, dragged his shirt over his head and reached for his shoes. It normally took him forever to quiet his mind and get to sleep. Even then, he would wake in the early hours, wrestling with whatever it was nagging at his subconscious. Yet, last night, he'd lain down with his feet hanging over the end of a day bed in a pink room with a border of pastel building blocks and frilly pink curtains and the next thing he'd known it was morning.

He needed coffee.

He needed a phone.

He needed to get out of there.

The door creaked when he opened it. Not seeing her in the kitchen when he stepped into it, he figured she'd gone outside with her chickens or plants or whatever it was people in the country tended at the crack of dawn.

It was then that he noticed the partially open door of her room.

Through the two-inch gap between her door and the frame, he could see her sitting on her bed with little Anna in her arms. She was looking down at the child, her finger slowly stroking a rounded little cheek, the alabaster slope of her breast visible between the open sides of her pink bodice. One tiny fist rested against that fullness and the baby's eyes were closed.

Emily's expression looked utterly peaceful.

Justin wasn't sure what caused the odd tug in his chest just then. He wasn't a man easily impressed, much less easily moved. Yet, he couldn't seem to look away. Had he been standing before a painting, he supposed the eroticism was what would have caught his attention, the pure sensuality of soft light on skin, the gentle part of Emily's mouth, the suckling of the baby's. But there was an element far beyond that, a Madonna-like quality that made him feel as if he were witnessing something infinitely...precious.

The thought had his conscience kicking hard as it told him to look away. He was intruding here. But it was already too late. Emily glanced up, serenity slipping from her expression as her eyes locked with his.

He expected embarrassment. His. Hers. What he didn't expect was her small, self-conscious smile that flashed heat low in his belly.

"I've been listening for you," she said, seeming to explain why her door had been cracked open. "I put water on to heat for you so you could wash. It should be hot by now."

Thinking she looked more shy than chagrined, he murmured his thanks as he snagged the big pewter-colored pot and headed for the tiny bathroom. She was taking complete and unfair advantage of his caffeine-deprived mind. That was the only possible explanation for why he'd been standing there totally absorbed by something that was actually nothing more than a function of nature.

It's definitely time to get out of here, he mentally muttered, pumping cold water into the oval washbasin after he'd added the hot. The cabinet on the wall didn't have a mirror, but it had plenty of shelves. Opening it, he aimed low and grabbed the tube of toothpaste he'd found by the deodorant and baby powder last night.

The shelf above that held first-aid supplies, some of which she'd used on him. Next up were vitamins, a tin of something called bag balm, shampoo and lotion. The top shelf held makeup Emily apparently used on occasion, along with a little mirror she'd tucked behind everything as if she weren't comfortable with the fact that she possessed it.

Last night, he'd noticed it all. This morning, he was too busy telling himself that what he'd seen wasn't all that extraordinary to pay much attention to anything else. Women had nursed their children since time began. He'd just never come face-to-face with one doing it. He couldn't imagine any other woman he knew nursing a child, either. They were all too focused on their careers or themselves to even want children, and the few who did have them turned their care over to nannies and preschools.

In all fairness, he couldn't picture Emily as his date for the opera, the symphony or dining at L'Étoile either—even though he didn't doubt she would savor the experiences even more than she had his description of them last night.

He had no idea why he was making such comparisons. But by the time he'd used his finger for a toothbrush and done what he could with soap and his comb to keep from looking as derelict as he felt in clothes that were well past their prime, he'd admitted that the exercise was pointless. He would never see the woman after he left there.

"The coffee will be ready soon," Emily said as he walked into the kitchen. She stood at the counter, pouring grounds into the metal basket of a dented but serviceable aluminum coffeepot. She'd rebraided her hair, every strand woven neatly into place. Like the dress she wore yesterday, her loose pink shift skimmed the bottom of her calves and did nothing to reveal her very feminine curves. "I would have put it on earlier, but I didn't want to wake you. How does your shoulder feel this morning?"

"Not as bad as I thought it would."

"I'm glad to hear that." The lid to the coffeepot closed with a solid snap. "It will make your trip home more comfortable. Now that you're up, you'll want to tend to your car so you can get back to the city."

He caught her wistful smile before she turned the fire up under the coffee and started cracking eggs into a bowl. His own features folded in a frown. She made his life sound like something he should be in a hurry to rush back to.

Reminding himself that he did want to get back, he took two plates from where he'd seen her put them last night and set them on the table. "So, what will you do today?"

"I need to can those beans," she said, aiming a spatula at the bowls she'd filled last night. "It's best to can vegetables when they're fresh picked, but yesterday got away from me. And I'll make a batch of preserves with the last of the strawberries. Tomorrow isn't a produce day, so I don't have to harvest, but I do need to take down what's left of the laundry from yesterday and wash diapers."

Justin leaned against the counter, his arms crossed and his eyes following her as she moved about the neat little room. He'd seen her washing machine in the utility room off the back porch. It was an old wringer type that belonged in a museum. He assumed the wooden, accordion-style rack he'd seen folded up behind it was what she used to dry clothes indoors in the winter.

"Emily."

"Yes?"

"Why are you doing all this alone?"

Incomprehension touched her expression. "Because there is no other way to do it."

"Don't you have parents? Brothers or sisters?"

"I have parents," she replied, her voice suddenly hushed. With her back to him, she dipped bread in the beaten eggs. "And I have brothers and sisters. Three of each. I'm in the very middle." Fat sizzled as she dropped the bread into the pan. "What will you do today when you go back?"

"No. You're not doing that. We made a deal last night, remember? I answered your questions. Now, you answer mine."

She cut him a glance as she headed for the sink to hull strawberries while she waited for the toast to brown. He couldn't tell if it was resignation or reluctance shadowing her profile, but when she spoke it sounded like a little of each.

"What do you want to know?"

"Why you don't go home to your family."

"Because my life is here," she said, focusing hard on her task.

"But it would be so much easier if they could help you."

"They can't help me."

"Why not?"

"Because they're forbidden."

He paused. "Forbidden?"

Emily focused on her paring knife, making neat, quick cuts that removed the hull with little waste. "We were shunned," she explained, not totally sure why she was telling him what she'd told no one else. Maybe it was because he was just easy to talk to. Maybe it was because he was leaving and it didn't matter what he knew about her. It had always been easier to let people assume she and Daniel had left on their own, less shameful. To her, anyway. With the demands of her days, she rarely even thought of her old life. She really didn't want to think of it now, either. "First Daniel, then me."

She could practically feel Justin's hesitation.

"I don't understand."

She knew he didn't. No one could who hadn't lived with the prescribed discipline of the Old Order. Their lives were ruled by the *Ordnung,* the unwritten code of conduct understood by every Amish man and woman and passed down from generation to generation. It regulated every aspect of a person's life, the way they lived, the way they related to each other, their religious beliefs. That most of all, because being Amish was about church and religion. But strict as that life was, no one ever had to wonder what was expected of them. Emily had found great comfort in that. And great frustration. But the greatest comfort had been simply in belonging. And that was what she and Daniel had been denied. The right to belong.

"When a person is shunned, that means no one can eat with them, or speak to them, or buy their goods, or sell to them, or take anything from their hand. That means family as well as anyone else in the community."

"What did you do?"

"It's what I didn't do," she said quietly. "Daniel had been shunned for a disagreement with the church elders. There was no work for him in his father's cabinet shop," she explained, slipping off a green hull and reaching for another berry, "so he went to work for an English shop a few miles away. The owner wanted to promote him, to have him help with the installation of the cabinets in the city. Daniel wanted the job because the extra money he would earn would allow us to buy our own home sooner. But the elders said the travel was inappropriate, that such a job wasn't in keeping with the traditions and told him to decline the position.

"Daniel had always been a little headstrong. That was something he'd worked hard to suppress," she added, thinking it a quality Justin could appreciate. "He took the position anyway and told the elders he knew himself well

enough to know he wouldn't be unduly influenced by what
he encountered. That got him into more trouble because he
was being arrogant and prideful on top of everything else."

She drew a deep breath, her hands still busy. "He left
the church," she said simply. "And when he did, it was
my duty to shun him along with everyone else. But he'd
done what he had for us, and I couldn't bear the thought
of him out in the world all alone."

"What did your family do?"

"My father is dedicated to his beliefs," she replied, trying hard to focus on what she was doing rather than the
ache the memories brought. "He was a good Amishman
and very strict in his convictions. He reminded me over
and over that if I went with Daniel, I would be living with
a sinner and that they could no longer have anything to do
with me. He reminded me of the shame I would bring on
them and that it was his duty to protect his family if I were
to stray." With her forearm, she pushed an errant strand of
hair from her forehead. "I am no longer welcome in their
home."

Her tone was even, devoid of any hint of accusation or
anger. Justin marveled at it. But he didn't trust it. He
couldn't imagine such acceptance. But then, he'd never
lived with the sort of denial and obedience that would have
been required of her.

He should let it go, but he couldn't. He shouldn't want
so badly to know what all she'd left behind, but he did.
"And your mother?"

"My mom...my mom," she repeated quietly, "was
wonderful."

Her mother had said she'd known what Emily would do
from the moment the trouble had started. Known, and
feared it. Emily and Daniel had been like brother and sister
growing up, she always tagging after him, he always watching out for her. She had adored him and even though he'd

waited until long past the time their friends had paired up and married to ask her to marry him, it had seemed inevitable that they would be together. Just as it had seemed inevitable that she would choose to remain with him.

Her mother had said it was what she would have done herself.

There was no way Emily could describe the consolation her mother's words had given her. But Esther Beachy, a simple and obedient woman, had offered nothing else about the difficulty of the choice Emily had made.

"There wasn't much she could say without breaking faith with the *Ordnung* herself," Emily explained. "But when we left, she hugged me and gave me the quilt over there."

She nodded toward the rocking chair and the small quilt draped over its arm. "Mom has made dozens of quilts. We all have," she added, thinking of the hours her mom had spent with her and her sisters when they were young, teaching them how to make the tiny, even stitches prized by the older women. "But that one was special. Not the pattern," she explained, because there was nothing unique about the traditional nine-patch pattern her mom had created from blocks of red and blue cotton surrounded by squares of black. "It's special because of what it meant to her."

Emily picked up a berry, spotted mold and tossed it aside. "It was the first quilt she'd made as a young bride," she said, reaching for another berry. "She'd embroidered her name next to my father's on one of the blocks. Over the years, she'd embroidered the name of each of her children in a block of its own. When she gave it to me, she told me that she didn't have to see me to keep me in her heart…and that I was to add my own children's names to the quilt when they came along."

Anna had been three days old when Emily had added her daughter's name in the block next to hers.

There were some family traditions she would keep. She just couldn't allow herself to dwell on how much she missed some of the people who had been a part of them.

"I can't go back without being isolated," she finally told the man looming silently behind her. "Being that close to my mother and my sisters and not being part of their lives would be far more difficult than anything I have to do now." She glanced down at her pink cotton dress with its tiny fuchsia flowers and matching buttons. "I wouldn't be happy there even if I could go back. I've changed too much and I wouldn't fit in at all. Besides, I have nearly everything I need right here."

Justin would have argued her conclusion. Her latter one, anyway. But as she hurried to the stove to flip the toast, he couldn't get past her seeming acceptance of everything that had happened to her—or the enormity of what she'd done. She'd loved her husband enough to leave behind everything that was familiar so he wouldn't be alone in an alien and undoubtedly intimidating world. For her sacrifice, she'd been left alone in that world herself.

He couldn't begin to imagine caring that deeply about anyone.

The sound of coffee being poured joined the sizzle in the pan. Taking the cup she offered him when she turned around, he watched her head back to the sink.

"How did you wind up here?" he asked.

"When we left the community, we moved to the town where his job was. His boss helped us find an apartment there," she explained, wielding the paring knife again. "But it was all so...different."

It had been more than that. It had all been quite strange. But she didn't want to go into how the neighbors had gawked as they'd moved in their plain furnishings while wearing their plain clothes. Or how Daniel had been so fearful of her leaving the apartment without him. Or how she'd bounced between curiosity and being totally intimidated by her new surroundings. They'd gone from a community of three hundred to one of thirty thousand. Huge by their standards. Positively rural by the standards of someone who lived in Chicago.

"Daniel came home a month after we'd moved and told me he was taking us somewhere that would feel more familiar. He'd seen an ad in a farm journal and called the Mr. Clancy who'd placed it that very day."

"He quit the job that started all the problems?"

Emily started to nod. Instead, her head shot up, her eyes narrowing in concentration. In the distance, she could hear the chug of an engine and the faint crunch of gravel as a vehicle pulled up her long drive.

"That's Mr. Clancy. Please," she asked, looking back to where Justin leaned against the counter, watching her through the steam as he sipped the strong, rich brew, "don't tell him what I told you. If he tells Mrs. Clancy, everyone in Hancock—"

"I'm pretty good at keeping confidences, Emily. You didn't even have to ask."

"I didn't mean to offend—"

"You didn't." He reached over, curling his fingers around her arm, stilling her. "What you told me is no one's business but yours. But for the record, no one is going to think any less of you for what happened. Okay?"

Gratitude had barely entered her eyes when the engine idled to a stop. The slam of a truck's door echoed like a gunshot and pulled Justin's hand back like the snap of a rubber band.

"Just me, Emily," came Sam Clancy's gravelly bellow.

"I'm inside," she called through the open back door.

"I was expecting to see a tree lying on your porch." Beyond the milky plastic covering the window over her sink, she saw a wavering shape cross to the back steps.

Heavy workboots thudded on planks a moment later. "That lawyer-fella clean it up for you?"

He stopped at the screen door. Tipping back the bill of his green cap, he glanced from where Justin set his coffee on the counter, to Emily, who was moving toward the door, wiping her hands on a towel.

"Everything okay in here?" Clancy asked through the gray wire mesh.

No, she thought. It's not. I'm not ready for you to be here.

"Everything's fine," she insisted, wishing desperately for the numbness that had sheltered her the past several months. It had been there only yesterday, protecting her from the edges of whatever it was she felt. But the edges were there now, sharp with the deep pang of disappointment at knowing it would only be minutes before Justin was gone. "Please, come in. I'm just fixing breakfast. Would you like some?"

"Already ate." Eyeing the big man behind her, he motioned off her offer to step in and planted his hands on the hips of his overalls. "You stay here last night?"

"It was either that or walk back to my car. It was pretty late by the time we got the tree moved."

"I was wondering if you might not still be around," the old farmer muttered, looking far less interested in the situation than his wife would have been. "Sorry I didn't make it last night. I owe you for helping me out the way you did, and I don't want you thinking I didn't show up because I think you're working for that SoyCo bunch. You just caught me off guard when you told me what you did for a living, is all."

He pulled off his cap, scratched his spiky gray hair, plopped the cap back on. "I was going over my insurance policies last night and fell asleep in my recliner. Didn't wake up till nearly midnight. Last thing I wanted was to find that everything wasn't covered on that storm damage.

"Speaking of which," he said, apparently realizing he was losing track of his purpose, "I've got fencing to fix this morning. If you want me to jump your car, it's going to have to be now."

Justin looked toward Emily. She hadn't stopped moving since he'd stepped into the kitchen, though her motions as she wiped up the stove she was still cooking on now seemed more nervous than productive. He'd had no idea what he was tapping into when he'd asked about her family and he hated to just leave her there by herself after what she'd confided in him. But the wizened old farmer was his best chance of getting back to the city with the least amount of hassle and he couldn't let the opportunity slip by.

"I'm ready," he said, torn between an unfamiliar stab of protectiveness, the growling in his stomach and the man already walking away from the door.

Seeing Justin glance from the back door to the frying pan, Emily reached for the spatula. "Here," she said, piling preserves between two thick pieces of egg toast and wrapping them in a napkin. "You can eat on the way." He was leaving and she suddenly had a million things she wanted to ask him—and another million she wanted to say. "And Justin..." she began, only to find she couldn't say anything at all.

His glance skimmed her face, his dark eyes settling on hers as he took what she offered. "I'll be back in a while," he promised and left her so relieved that she actually sank against the counter.

They were back in less than twenty minutes. Clancy's battered blue truck came first, followed by a black sedan that, except for a coat of dust, looked as if Justin had just driven it off the lot. But Clancy didn't leave as Emily thought he would. And Justin didn't come in. The two men headed straight for her cellar where they hauled out the limb that had crashed through the doorway, then stood knee-deep in a conversation that had Clancy gesturing this way and that when he wasn't hanging on Justin's every word.

Emily had started water to boil so she could sterilize canning jars for the beans and had just finished feeding the chickens when she heard Clancy call out, "Thanks for the advice," and saw him head for his truck.

Before she could stuff the pail back in the burlap feed-sack and work her way out of the chicken yard, the chain saw sputtered to life and Justin was bent over the limb, lopping off yard-long branches and making little logs of the bigger section.

He'd changed his torn shirt. Aware of strong muscles shifting beneath beige cotton, she pulled her focus from his broad shoulders and silently carried off the pieces he cut much as she had last night.

She liked the way they worked together. She just didn't get to enjoy it for very long. Remembering the water she'd left to boil, she hurried inside to turn it off and to check on Anna, only to discover that Anna needed a diaper change.

By the time Emily washed her hands, changed the baby and washed her hands again, all she could hear outside were birds and Justin's solid footfall on the back porch.

He didn't come in, though, and the pang of disappointment she'd felt at Mr. Clancy's arrival hit again.

With Anna propped against her shoulder, she walked outside when Justin pulled open the door for her.

"Clancy said he'd try to get your cellar door back on," he told her, motioning her down the steps with him. "At least, I think this is yours. Does it look familiar?"

A slightly battered and peeling white door had been

propped against the side of the house. Rusty hinges were still attached to a strip of framing that had been ripped out with it.

"Where did you find it?"

"Lying down by the road. I didn't see the rest of your tree, though. Hard telling where that wound up.

"Anyway," he continued, moving to the boxy black BMW parked in the graveled drive, "I'm going to get him some information in exchange for his fixing your door. He said he'd try to get to the window, too, but it'll be a couple of weeks before he can do that. In the meantime, the plastic is tight and with the porch roof, you won't get any rain inside if another storm kicks up."

Justin hadn't asked Clancy about repairing the porch. It had become clear in a hurry that the guy was barely keeping up with his own crises. The older man wasn't in the best physical condition and his son, who worked the place with him, was in the middle of an emotional shoot-out with his wife and had been in Rockford for the past week trying to talk her into leaving her mom's and coming back to him—which had left Clancy especially shorthanded since the guy he'd hired to replace Daniel had just quit to go to work for the company that had bought out the farm behind his.

Wondering at how chatty the old guy had become, he narrowed his focus on the porch post. The support was nothing but a long four-by-four-inch piece of wood. It shouldn't take someone who knew what he was doing any time at all to replace.

"If you're thinking about fixing it," she murmured, seeing what he was pondering, "don't. You've done enough, Justin. More than enough. I especially appreciate last night. Just talking," she explained, looking as if that had meant more to her than anything. "You have a long ride back. You don't need to do anything else."

It wasn't that long a drive. Not to him, anyway. But he

didn't bother to point that out. He just stood beside his car watching her rub her little girl's back while the baby started wriggling against her shoulder. It had taken nothing more than his company to please her. No center seats at the opera. No expensive restaurant.

If he were to be honest with himself, he'd have to admit he couldn't remember the last time he'd enjoyed either of those things as much as he had the hours he'd spent at her table.

Anna's fussing turned to fretful whimpers.

"She's hungry," Emily said, her smile seeming to apologize for the baby's poor timing.

"How can she be? You just fed her."

"She usually goes a little longer, but she fell asleep during breakfast. Even when that doesn't happen," she continued, when his baffled expression didn't change, "she usually eats every three hours or so. Her tummy isn't very big, you know?"

There were times when it seemed that all she did was nurse. But Emily truly didn't mind. She just wanted Anna to get bigger. She was sure she wasn't gaining weight nearly as quickly as babies had back in Ohio. Her sisters' children had all been as plump as little dumplings by now. But Mrs. Clancy kept assuring her that every child developed at her own pace.

She was thinking that the baby books all said the same thing when Justin's glance slipped to the soft swells of her breasts. The puzzled expression had faded. Reflected in Justin's carved features was the same intense and stirring look she'd encountered when she'd found him watching her and Anna through the crack in her bedroom door.

When his eyes collided with hers a moment later, she felt the same bump behind her ribs that she had then, too.

There was no denying that her baby both intrigued and unnerved him. But as Emily watched his eyes darken and slip to her mouth, she had the feeling he wasn't thinking about her little girl at all.

"Emily, I have to go."

Disappointment pulled hard. She'd wanted a while longer to talk with Justin, to listen to his deep voice carry her to places she could only imagine. Talking with him was different from talking with Mrs. Clancy or the produce man or the ladies at the market. And being with him was different than being with anyone else. In her old life, she'd been regarded only as Aden Beachy's daughter or Daniel Miller's wife. In Hancock, even though she'd long ago come to look like everyone else there, she was still regarded by many of the small town's citizens as something of a quaint curiosity. But when Justin looked at her, when he talked to her, all he seemed to see was a woman.

It was probably prideful of her and she truly didn't want to be haughty or vain, but she'd very much liked the way that made her feel.

"I know."

She didn't know what else to say.

As he stood looming over her, it seemed he didn't, either.

"Take care of yourself out there," she murmured.

Justin looked to the baby busily sucking her tiny fist, then to the gentle woman holding her. He was a minute from heading back to everything that was familiar. Everything he'd worked for. Everything he wanted to avoid. And the urge to touch Emily was the strongest thing he'd felt in longer than he could remember.

Seeing no reason to deny something that could do no harm now that he was leaving, he lifted his hand toward her face. Aware that her breath had suddenly gone shallow, he let his fingers drift over her cheek. Her skin felt like warm satin, and her eyes were shot with sapphire. But when he would have let his thumb drift to the exquisite fullness of her bottom lip, her glance faltered and he pulled back before he could do something he had no business doing at all.

"You take care of yourself, too."

A minute later, he'd turned his car around in front of the greenhouse and was heading down her narrow graveled road. When he looked into his rearview mirror, he could see Emily holding her baby as she watched him drive away. He could still picture her little girl giving him a lopsided grin around her wet little fist, and the soft smile in Emily's lovely and tired eyes when she'd waved goodbye.

# Chapter Six

"Hey, Justin. Are you up for sushi at Ayoko? You're a partner now. You don't need to impress anyone by working through lunch."

Justin turned from his wide office window. Rob Dunlap, his fellow partner and jogging buddy, leaned indolently in the doorway, his arms crossed over his double-breasted jacket. The *GQ* stance could have been a pose. It could have been natural. With Rob it was hard to tell.

The smile was real, though. A good mood was something Rob couldn't have faked had his life depended on it.

"Thanks, but I just sent Rhonda down to the deli," Justin replied, speaking of his secretary. With his hands in the pockets of his suit pants, his vest buttoned over an impeccable white shirt and subtly patterned tie, he glanced toward the pile of documents waiting for him on his desk. For four days, he'd found his thoughts drifting to a woman who'd been naive enough to trust a total stranger with her hard-earned money. For those same four days, he'd been telling himself that her problems were not his problems. The weekend was over. It was history. Nothing more than a period of time that felt more like an out-of-body experience than a memory, but over and done with nonetheless.

He'd been doing fine until he'd heard the weather report on the radio on his way to work that morning. The announcer had cut in with a tornado alert for Davis County.

Davis County was where Emily lived.

"I have a deposition at one o'clock," he added, telling himself he wasn't going to check his radio again. He'd listened to the one on the disc player in his credenza just a few minutes ago. He'd been checking the weather on and off all morning. "The Carter brothers' matter."

The mention of the delicate negotiations between two warring factions of the Carter family for control of the family company had Rob unfolding himself and walking into the room. The sociable smile had vanished from his surprisingly boyish features. Without it, and with the overhead lights glinting off his receding hairline, he looked every minute of his forty-two years. "How's it coming?"

"Not bad," Justin replied, forcing himself to focus as Rob closed the door to block their conversation from the messengers and secretaries moving through the labyrinth of mahogany-paneled-and-red-carpeted halls. "It's pretty clear that our client kept things going after the father passed away. He pretty much kept his brother on for the ride. The sister we're deposing today is on the younger brother's side, but the statements from the employees all back up Maxwell," he said, speaking of the brother they represented. "It shouldn't be too much longer before he can buy out his brother's share and gain controlling interest in the company. A couple of weeks, I think."

"You think it will take that long?"

"I can't see it going any faster. The family is completely

divided. The younger brother won't cave in until he has to," he added, trying to keep his focus on the discussion instead of wondering whether Emily ever got her kitchen window and cellar door fixed. Especially the door. She needed a safe place to go with her baby if another tornado hit. "We're dealing with sibling rivalry as much as we are money."

"You'd know more about that than I would. The sibling thing, I mean." Rob shook his head, glanced at his watch. "I thank God every day that I'm an only child.

"Speaking of only children," he continued, blithely moving on now that he'd satisfied his interest in the former topic, "what's the deal with Cameron?"

Distracted, not wanting to be, Justin shook off the disturbing image of Emily huddled with her child in her cellar and shoved his fingers through his hair. "What?"

"Cameron," Rob prompted, a knowing glint in his eyes. "There's something going on with you two. I'm sure of it. You've been preoccupied all week."

Justin frowned. If he'd been preoccupied, it hadn't been because of Cameron Beck. "There's nothing going on. I haven't seen her since last Friday night."

"You weren't with her last weekend?"

"I told you when we were running Monday morning, I went fishing last weekend."

"And you stuck to the story Wednesday when I asked about it, too," Rob reminded with good-natured exasperation. "I thought you were just being a gentleman and keeping the details to yourself." Meeting Justin's droll glance, the glint disappeared. "Haven't you asked her out again?"

"No," Justin replied flatly, "I haven't."

Incomprehension knitted Rob's features. It wasn't often that he missed a guess. "Why not?" he insisted, clearly at a loss. "She's beautiful. She's intelligent. She's interested. Most men would kill to have everything fall into place the way it's happening for you right now. You play this right, you could be Ken's son-in-law.

"Hey," Rob muttered when Justin frowned. "With Kenneth Beck's name and influence behind you, there's no limit to where you could go. You're a natural for politics. You've even said yourself that you'd take a hard look at the right position if one were to come along. Don't you understand what she could do for your career? You could be a congressman or a senator in no time. The firm certainly wouldn't be opposed to the prestige that would bring us, either," he added with a chuckle. "Hell, that would have to impress even your family."

It was as clear as lead crystal that Rob thought Justin had hit the mother lode. In many ways Justin supposed he had. The political angle was just something he toyed with because he needed a new goal for himself now that he'd achieved partnership—something Rob had helped him accomplish by assigning him to cases that allowed his skills to shine. But now, if he played his cards right with Cameron, he held the potential to send his career soaring.

Rob was even right about his family, though the man really had no idea how insightful he was. Like everyone else in the firm, Rob knew of Justin's quasi-blue-blooded and accomplished family. Even his mother, a denizen of Boston society, was on the board of half a dozen charities and one major museum. But Justin had never confided in Rob—in anyone, for that matter—about how much he hated the quietly competitive nature of his relatives. They each seemed compelled to one-up everyone else, to impress them. Yet, no matter what a person did, what a person accomplished, it was always the lure of the next goal, the next achievement, medal award or title they talked about. Rarely could anyone be content with what they had. Rarely could anyone ever relax.

Yeah, Justin thought. Cameron would be exactly the sort

of goal his parents would approve. Cameron's parents had already endorsed the liaison. It had been no accident that he'd been seated next to her at the dinner they'd given for him.

He turned to the window, more to escape Rob's scrutiny than to seek escape in the view of other rats in other cages in the office building across the street. He'd first met Cameron at a reception at her parents' home nearly a month ago. They'd spent the evening talking about Madrid, where she'd just spent three years working for the American Consulate. He'd found her sophisticated, coolly beautiful and undeniably interesting. They'd had dinner once before she'd gone back to Spain for a couple of weeks. Now, she'd returned and, though her hints had been heavy last Friday, he'd yet to call her.

He'd been attracted to her, but he hadn't felt heat simply seeing her smile. He hadn't felt the sense of peace that was now little more than a distant memory. And he hadn't spent a moment wondering or worrying about her while she'd been gone.

Now, the thought of all that cool sophistication simply left him...cold.

Had he been alone, the restless feeling gnawing at him would have had him pacing a rut between the expensively matted and framed diplomas and certificates on one wall and the floor-to-ceiling bookcase on the other. With his business associate already trying to figure out what was going on with him, he opted for tackling the file on his desk instead. With any luck, Rob would take the hint and leave.

Rob never had been particularly sensitive to subtlety.

Justin had no sooner crossed to his wide mahogany desk and sat down in the red leather executive chair than Rob's glance narrowed. "What are you going to do about her?"

Who? Emily? Cameron? "Nothing."

"You're going to blow this."

At the flatness of Rob's voice, Justin glanced up. Despite the patience he schooled into his features, a muscle in Justin's jaw jumped.

"What I'm going to do is review this file before my client gets here. As for Cameron, she's a nice woman but she's also our senior partner's daughter. If I get involved with her, it has to be for more than fun and games or my name is worthless around here. The way I see it, I'm not interested in anything permanent, so it's best to cut my losses now and hope I don't offend her or her father in the process."

"Justin," Rob said in the same pedantic tone he would use with a first-year associate who was being particularly dense, "whether or not you're interested has nothing to do with it. I don't care what anyone says about equality. It's a fact of life that a married man goes farther in certain circles than a single one. You'll definitely get farther here with certain of our clients if you have a wife. Marriage is nothing but another career decision."

With that proclamation, he tugged the cuff of his shirt to the appropriate half-an-inch below the cuff of his suit jacket. "Take my advice and give this opportunity some hard thought before you do anything you'll regret. Unless," he added, his narrowed eyes belying his studied nonchalance, "you've met someone else who can do you even more good."

Justin said nothing. Aware of his tightened jaw, vaguely recalling Emily's remark about the muscles there and his work, he ignored Rob and opened a file.

"Who is she?"

"Rob," he growled, trying not to grit his teeth, "I have clients coming in less than an hour."

"I know you do. But PT Electronics," he said, turning his head as he read the label on the file, "has nothing to do with the Carter Brothers. What's going on with you, man? *Has* some woman gotten to you?''

''She hasn't gotten to me,'' Justin insisted, as frustrated with himself as he was with Rob at the moment. ''I'm just… No,'' he muttered, refusing to admit how concerned he was. The woman could take care of herself. She might look as fragile as glass, but she possessed an indomitable spirit and the tenacity of a pit bull. She'd survived long before he'd come along. ''Forget it,'' he told the man, deliberately closing the file to locate the one he wanted. ''It's nothing.''

''Right,'' Rob murmured, looking truly concerned. ''It's nothing.''

Justin shot him a level glance. ''It isn't. Just let it go. Okay?''

Dubious, Rob stepped back. ''Whatever you say. But whoever she is,'' he muttered, his tone dropping as a knock sounded on the door, ''just sleep with her and get it over with. She's wrecked the hell out of your concentration.''

The remark was typical Rob. But there was no time for Justin to inform the man that he wanted to believe he'd evolved at least one level above the Neanderthal. The door opened without invitation, something that intensified Justin's scowl—until he saw Kenneth Beck standing there.

''I hope I'm not interrupting,'' the tall, silver-haired gentleman said with the confident smile of a man who knew no one could openly object to his presence. ''Hello, Rob. Justin,'' he continued, authority radiating from behind the narrow silver rims of his lineless bifocals, ''I have the CEO of Deems-Wright Pharmaceuticals in my office. I'd like you to meet him.''

Rob was already moving toward the door, giving Justin a surreptitious thumbs-up and a veiled look of warning. Justin was being summoned for a command performance with one of the firm's top clients. Since the CEO of Deems-

Wright also happened to be one of Beck's closest friends, the invitation smacked heavily of an inspection.

"Mr. Beck—"

"Kenneth," the man interrupted with a benevolent smile.

"Kenneth," Justin corrected, feeling his frustrations knot neatly in his gut. "I appreciate the invitation, but I have a deposition in about—" he glanced at his watch, his hand as steady as his gaze when he glanced back up "—forty-five minutes."

"Here's your sandwich, Justin. They didn't have the curried chicken today, so I got you…"

Rhonda Swenson cut herself off as she swung around the doorway. His secretary was a small, neat woman with short, salt-and-pepper hair and an unflappable air. Justin didn't know what he'd do without her.

"Sorry to interrupt," she continued, smiling at both men as she placed a brown paper bag on the end of Justin's desk. She lowered her voice to nearly a whisper. "Turkey salad," she murmured, and was gone.

"Lunch at your desk, I see."

"I wanted to go over my notes."

There was approval in the distinguished-looking gentleman's nod. There was also a hint of favor that Justin knew wouldn't have been there had the man's daughter not taken an interest in him. That interest made him feel like a fraud.

"I like a man who knows his priorities. You can meet Ben some other time. Oh, and, Justin," Kenneth said, catching himself as he started to turn, "we're changing the monthly partnership dinner to the twenty-fourth. Mike and Stephen will still be lobbying in D.C. on the seventeenth," he added, speaking of two of the firm's other partners. "As we've made clear, it's imperative that we're all present for these dinners. Be sure to change the date on your calendar."

Justin reached for the calendar on his desk even as Kenneth walked out the door. Partnership dinners where the firm's business was discussed were sacrosanct. It practically took a note from the coroner to be excused from one. This would be his first. But even as Justin was thinking about how interesting the evening would be, he was rubbing the hot knot in his stomach and wondering what Cameron had said to her father about him. Justin knew Kenneth Beck doted on his only child. He also suspected that the man made sure his little girl got whatever it was she wanted.

Considering the detrimental effects mishandling the situation could have on his career, Justin figured the only graceful way out was to make sure Cameron didn't want him. There were only two ways to do that. He could ignore her and hope she or her parents didn't invite him anywhere. Or, he could ask her to dinner and casually mention that he couldn't understand why people ruined perfectly good relationships by getting married. She was a bright woman. A few comments like that should let her know he wasn't marriage material—if that was what she was after.

He'd take her to Nicolo's Trattoria rather than L'Étoile, he thought, liking the idea of the less-than-intimate atmosphere. But he'd no sooner made the decision than an image of Emily canceled it. He could easily picture the delight in Emily's eyes when he'd told her about Nicolo's tendency to break into song and he knew he didn't want to take Cameron there. After the way Emily had him describe every detail of the establishment, he doubted he'd be able to set foot in the place without thinking of how much she would enjoy it.

Emily.

He couldn't seem to get the woman out of his mind.

*Just sleep with her and get it over with.*

Frustrated with his inability to focus, he bit back an oath and glared at the closed door. Rob's tidy little solution had been no help at all. All week long, thoughts of Emily's small, slender body had been doing equal time with his disquiet at her naiveté and his concern about her and her baby. The feel of her slender thighs, the curve of her hip, the fullness of her breasts were all firmly etched in his mind. She would fit him perfectly. He was sure of that. So sure that the mere thought of sinking into her softness had his body going as hard as stone.

Preferring not to consider that particular form of frustration, he snatched up his phone and punched a button for an outside line. If he hadn't heard that damnable weather report this morning, he might well have only thought about her a half-dozen times today instead of every third minute. But he had heard it and the only way he'd get any peace was to prove to himself that there was nothing for him to be concerned about. He couldn't call Emily to find out if the storms had hit her area, but he could call Clancy. He had the perfect excuse, too. He'd told the guy he would see if there were any cases similar to the problem he was having with SoyCo's drainage tile. Since he'd planned to send him copies of what he'd found, he'd just tell him he'd lost his address and casually ask about the weather.

Unfortunately, there was no answer at the only Clancy listed in Hancock.

"This is basil," Emily said, clipping leafy stems from a foot-high plant. "It's best to harvest it just as it starts to flower. You know what a flower is. It's this part right here." With Anna facing her in the tummy-carrier, Emily held the small lavender-pink bloom on the tip of a stem so her baby could see.

Anna looked up with her big blue eyes, opened her mouth and blinked.

"I think it's pretty, too," Emily agreed. Dropping the stems in the basket beside her, she scooted the large container between the long bushy rows and kept clipping.

"And it tastes good," she continued, practicing what her baby book preached by engaging her child in what she was doing. "I didn't learn how to cook with herbs until I started growing them. We used spices when I was growing up, but never things like oregano or basil or savory like we grow here. It was just pickling spice like celery and mustard seeds and cloves and such.

"The Italians use a lot of oregano and basil, though," she added, tossing another handful of herbs into the nearly overflowing basket. "Justin told me that. Do you remember Justin? I think he knows more about everything than anyone else I've ever met."

Having filled her basket again, Emily wearily sank back on her heels and looked down to where Anna had grasped the sleeve of her pink T-shirt. With her little arms poking through the sides of the carrier and its quilted denim fabric forming a collar that supported the back of her head, she couldn't get her fist past the shoulder strap to reach her mouth. Emily knew she was getting hungry again. With her little mouth open as she impatiently rooted toward the strap, she could safely assume that she wouldn't be quiet for much longer.

Brushing a kiss over her soft little forehead, Emily told her she'd take care of her in a minute and rose to her feet. Despite her need to hurry, a faint smile tugged at her mouth. She could still picture Justin's look of disbelief when he'd realized how often a baby needed to be fed.

Justin.

She couldn't believe how often she thought of him. Having met him was almost like a fantasy to her now, like some fantastic dream that had been vivid enough to become a memory. A wonderful memory. For the most part.

As long as she ignored the odd sense of longing he'd awakened, she was fine. And she was fine now, she told herself, stuffing her clippers into the pocket of her denim

jumper. She was just a little thirsty and her back ached from
having spent the morning bent over the low bushes. But
she couldn't waste time thinking about that, either. She
needed to get this last batch of basil bunched before the
produce man arrived.

She'd started gathering and bundling herbs right after
she'd nursed Anna a little before 5:00 a.m. Except to nurse
her again and to feed the chickens, she hadn't slowed down
for so much as a minute, but she was still afraid she
wouldn't have the order ready. She was already on borrowed time. The produce man was usually here by now.

Snatching up the basket, she headed for the shade of the
apple tree where she'd stacked the dozen boxes of herbs
she'd gathered that morning and the baby beets, carrots,
parsnips and onions she'd picked yesterday. The morning
was glorious, the air crisp and clean, the breeze blessedly
cool. Since the storm had passed yesterday—mostly rain
and wind that, thankfully, had developed into nothing at
all—not a single cloud marred the crystalline-blue sky. But
instead of enjoying the reprieve in the weather, she was
praying that the produce man would be even later than he
already was. She had at least three more crates of herbs to
box and she needed every penny she could earn this week
to buy more plastic for the greenhouse and a new window
for her kitchen.

She'd spread one of her large quilts beneath the tree's
limbs. Lowering herself to sit Indian-style on the bright,
hand-stitched spokes of green and blue, she slipped the
denim straps of the carrier and her jumper from her shoulder and tugged up her T-shirt so Anna could nurse while
she bunched her basil. For now, she would ignore the fact
that another week had come and gone and the handyman
hadn't returned with windows for her greenhouse. Imme-
diate needs had to be dealt with first.

Emily had nearly a hundred, hand-size bundles of leafy

stems neatly banded with yellow twist-ties when the chug of a diesel engine and the crunch of gravel announced the arrival of the E and M Produce truck.

Figuring she had another fifty bunches to go, she hurriedly adjusted her clothes, eased her sleepy little girl over her shoulder to coax a burp and hoped the offer of cold lemonade would be enough to entice Ernie, the *E* of E and M, to give her another fifteen minutes. The taciturn produce man usually stuck to his schedule like a bug to flypaper, but he tended to bend a little where she was concerned. Not because he liked her lemonade, though he always seemed appreciative of it on hot days. But because he could always trust the quality of what she grew.

The driver wasn't Ernie, though. The burly blond man who climbed from the cab of the boxy truck and ground out his cigarette with the heel of his boot was new.

Seeing her beside the white and blue E and M Produce boxes, he stopped just shy of the shade.

"You're Mrs. Miller?"

"I am. Is Ernie ill?"

"He's on vacation," he replied, eyeing the baby in that dubious way men had before looking back to her. "I'm his nephew. My manifest says I don't have to check your produce for quality," he continued, obviously in no mood for pleasantries as he looked at the clipboard he carried. "That's a first."

His last words were muttered to himself as he sidestepped where she sat on the blanket and lifted one box then another to see what was inside. Poking around anyway, seeing row after row of tiny, perfect vegetables, his mouth tugged down at the corners and he gave a shrug.

"Guess not," he muttered, and started running totals on the calculator he pulled from his pocket.

"I have another fifty or so bunches of basil I can give you, if you're willing to wait a few minutes. I have cold—"

"Sorry," he interrupted, not sounding particularly apologetic at all. "I have ten rabid chefs waiting at their restaurants for this truck and I'm already running late. How many boxes do you have ready?"

"Four." Holding Anna to her with one hand, she held a handful of basil against the quilt with the heel of her free hand and tried to work a twist-tie around it with her fingers. There were twenty-five bunches to a box. "I have another ten bunches here," she said, working to get fifteen more as she nodded toward the pile of green on the blanket.

"No partial lots."

She hadn't needed the grumbled reminder. She was well aware of her buyer's requirements, which was why she eased Anna into the sling made by her skirt and tied herbs as quickly as she could while he carried everything else to the truck, weighed it all and propped a thick stack of flat cardboard by her greenhouse door.

"I only have a few more to go," she said over Anna's fretful whimpers when he held his clipboard out for her signature.

"They're not boxed. Come on, ma'am. I've already tallied your invoice."

She would have told him it would only take her a minute to fold one of the cardboard flats into shape and pack up what she had ready, but she didn't get the chance. The moment she opened her mouth, Anna's fussing turned to a full-blown wail and her little legs drew up hard against her belly.

The painful cry had the man looking more anxious than ever to be on his way. Emily scarcely noticed. She was too busy berating herself as she scooped up her baby, soothing her as she asked what was wrong even though she knew full well what the problem was. She'd been so intent on getting one more box together that she'd laid Anna down instead of taking the time to make sure she burped. Her baby was in pain from a trapped bubble of air.

"Oh, precious, I'm sorry," she murmured, rubbing her hand over the terry cloth romper covering Anna's little back. "It'll be okay," she promised, aching at the distress in the pathetic cries.

"Ma'am?"

Ernie's nephew waved the clipboard and held out a pen.

Emily sank back to the blanket, something tight knotting at the base of her throat. Swallowing past the odd constriction, trying to soothe the painful, syncopated sobs of the infant curling against her chest, Emily raised her knees to hold Anna against her and forced herself not to snatch the clipboard from his hand. After scrawling her name next to the total on the form, she pulled off the check under the metal clip and handed the clipboard back.

"Thank you," she said with as much aplomb as she could muster and lifted Anna to her shoulder again.

She didn't hear what the man said, something about having a nice day, she thought, but she couldn't be sure. She didn't care. As he walked away and started up his truck, she just wanted the discomfort in her little girl's tummy to go away—which it did after a minute of squalling, pacing, rubbing and one decidedly indelicate belch.

The sudden quiet drew Emily to a halt. Easing Anna back to see her tearstained face, Emily watched her little blond head bob as she lifted it and tried to hold it steady. The effort was valiant, but she couldn't yet quite manage the feat. She did, however, manage a smile that almost seemed to say "Thanks, Mom," and which for some unfathomable reason made the pressure in Emily's throat feel even tighter when she smiled back and hugged her.

*I'm just tired,* Emily told herself. That was all that was wrong with her. She hadn't slept more than three or four hours at a stretch since Anna was born, and she'd made herself get up earlier than usual this morning to finish the basil. She just wouldn't let herself think about the ten dollars' worth of herbs she hadn't had the chance to pack and which would be way past their prime long before the truck came through again on Tuesday. She wouldn't let herself think about anything distressing at all. Not now.

Not now, she silently repeated, and made herself focus on the chatter of birds flitting around the windmill and the cluck of chickens pecking around the henhouse. They were good sounds, peaceful in their way. But they were underscored by the deep-throated drone of a vehicle that drifted on the breeze.

She automatically glanced toward the sound. Even across the distance of her gardens and the soybean field, there was something terribly familiar to her about the shiny black car coming up the narrow ribbon of country road.

People in Hancock didn't drive cars like that. Folks around there drove utilitarian sedans and pickup trucks or big flatbed trucks that hauled hay and livestock. Except for television and magazines, she'd only seen a car like that once in her entire life.

When the car slowed as it neared her house, Emily felt her heart jerk in her chest. When the vehicle disappeared as it passed her house and she heard the crunch of gravel when it turned into the drive, she thought for sure that her heart had stuck to her breastbone. It didn't feel as if it were beating at all as the dark BMW pulled up next to her porch and the refined purr of the engine went silent.

Never before had she experienced the odd sense of anxiety and anticipation that ripped through her at that moment. The driver's door opened and Justin emerged, a mountain of lean, masculine muscle in a pale-cream polo shirt and worn denims.

She hadn't remembered him being so tall. She hadn't recalled the breadth of his shoulders, the leanness of his hips. She'd just remembered how solid he'd felt, and how safe she'd felt in his arms.

She remained rooted by the quilt in the dappled shade of the sprawling fruit tree. In that broad shadow, she didn't think she would be noticeable. Yet, his glance arrowed to her like a dart drawn to a target.

He stood with his hand on the top of his door, hesitating a moment before closing it with a heavy thud. Seconds later, he walked toward her with his hands jammed in his pockets and his glance narrowed on the porch with its broken post and the plastic still stretched over the kitchen window. Most of his attention fixed on the cellar door.

"I see Clancy got the new hinges," he said, sounding as if he might have requested them himself. "When did he get the door back on?"

Emily moved toward him, stepping into the sunlight that caught a hint of silver near his temples.

"Tuesday." She was glad she'd taken the time to braid her hair this morning instead of winding it into the familiar knot at her nape that was so quick and easy. But she wished she were wearing something other than the old denim jumper she loved for its big pockets and practicality. "He mentioned the trade you made with him. Thank you for that."

"It was nothing. I just got him some information." He stopped in front of her, his attention shifting from her baby falling asleep on her shoulder to her upturned face. "How are you, Emily?"

Confused. Anxious. Desperately glad to see you, I think.

"I'm fine," she replied, totally unprepared for what he caused her to feel. She had no frame of reference for the improbable range of reactions he elicited. She'd never felt them before. Certainly not with her husband. Daniel had been...Daniel. With him she'd simply felt...comfortable.

"How about you? How's your shoulder?"

"My...? Oh, it's fine. No problem at all."

She took a deep breath, willing the flutter in her stomach to ease. "Good. I'd wondered about it."

Justin's silver-gray eyes narrowed as his glance swept her face. "Are you sure you're okay?"

"Do I not look sure?"

No, he thought, watching the corners of her lush mouth curve. She didn't. Despite that welcoming smile, she looked tired and troubled. But he wasn't going to push the point. As he took in the pile of neatly bundled herbs on the quilt, her bare feet and the baby asleep and drooling against her shoulder, he had the feeling the sky could be falling and she would deny that there was anything wrong at all.

With her attention on her daughter as she shielded her little face from the sun, Emily barely caught the faint tightening of his mouth.

"What are you doing here?" she asked, looking back up at him.

"Finishing up." He'd planned to spend the day coming up to speed on Deems-Wright Pharmaceuticals since Ken Beck wanted his input on their acquisition of a smaller company. Now, because he couldn't stop worrying about her even though last night's news had eased his mind about the storm, he would spend Sunday working instead.

"There were a few things I didn't get around to here last week," he explained, nodding in the general direction of his car. "I brought you a window. For the kitchen," he explained, because she suddenly looked utterly baffled. "I knew Clancy had a lot to do at his place and with the storms this time of year he'd said he'd be sure to get the cellar door fixed for you. But it didn't sound like he'd have time to help you with the rest of it."

"You brought me a window?"

He might as well have said he'd brought the Hope diamond. Disbelief washed over the delicate lines of her face.

It was followed rapidly by pure delight—and a fair amount of hesitation.

"Justin, I...how much—?"

"It's a gift."

"But I can't accept—"

"Sure you can," he murmured, fighting the urge to soothe the little lines from her forehead. "If it'll make you feel better, we'll work a trade. You can feed me in exchange for parts and labor."

The depth of his concern for this woman didn't make a whole lot of sense to him. He barely even knew her. And he wasn't at all familiar with the sense of protectiveness she elicited. But there had been no way he could leave her with the damage from last weekend. Just as there had been no way in Hades that he could show up just because he was worried.

The window had seemed like the perfect excuse—until he'd realized he wouldn't have a clue what to do with it once he got it there. That was why he'd spent an hour last night getting installation instructions from an amazingly patient guy in an orange apron at the home improvement center. He figured he'd need equal time with Clancy to figure out how to fix the porch.

"It might not even fit," he told her because she still looked so dubious. "I remembered the aluminum casing and what the lock looked like and the guy at the home improvement center identified the brand from that. I can exchange it at a place called Gerritsen's Feed and Hardware in Hancock, if I have to. I'll have to go there anyway to get the stuff to repair the porch.

"Don't," he said, stalling what he was sure was protest. "Let me do this. You'll actually be doing me a favor."

The claim sounded ridiculous to Emily. As busy as he was, she couldn't imagine that he'd find benefit in spending time she doubted he could spare wrestling with tasks he'd clearly never tackled before. She didn't question him, though. She needed a window and he seemed to have a need to give her one.

Not that it was his job to do, she thought, watching him rub at the muscles in his neck as they headed for his car to check out his gift. But he seemed to be a man who didn't question responsibility. When the situation called for it, he simply took it on. She could sympathize with that. She did it herself, all too well. But with him, there seemed to be more than that demanding compulsion prodding him.

It wasn't long before she began to suspect what that something was. And it had little to do with her.

## Chapter Seven

Emily stood at the sink, openly watching Justin pace a trench in her lawn through the mesh screen of her newly installed sliding window. The late afternoon sun slanted low in the still cloudless sky, throwing the shadow of the house across the backyard and reflecting off the windmill blades like arrows of orange fire. Behind her, canning jars boiled on the stove. The familiar clink of glass blended with Anna's occasional coo at the mobile suspended over her bassinet.

All Emily really noticed was the tension that snaked through Justin as his agitation carried him between the porch and the far end of the clothesline.

He was on his cell phone, his brow drawn, his jaw rigid. The little black instrument had rung a few minutes ago, earning a frown even before he'd answered it. But once he had, the change in him had been unmistakable. One minute he'd been working on her new porch post, as relaxed as she'd ever seen him. The next, he'd started pacing like a panther in a cage.

She couldn't hear what he was saying at the moment. Not with his back to her as he headed for the clothesline again. She wasn't deliberately trying to eavesdrop. It was just that, with the window open, every time he turned around and came back toward her, she couldn't help but catch his conversation. She just couldn't catch enough of it to figure out why he looked so displeased.

"Let me see if his attorney is still in," she heard him say when his stride carried him back to the porch again. He glanced at his watch, his expression darkly determined. "If I can't track him down, there won't be anything we can do until Monday.

"Right," he muttered, then pulled the phone from his ear to punch at the buttons on the small keypad.

A moment later, he had the phone pressed to his ear and had pivoted again, leaving her to turn her attention back to the task she'd started when he'd left for the Clancys' and the hardware store in Hancock shortly after he'd arrived.

Canning a year's worth of food wasn't nearly as big a project as it could have been. With only herself and a baby to provide for, she didn't have to put up a thousand quarts of vegetables, fruits and chow-chow as her mom and aunts had done year after year. A few hundred pints would certainly suffice. Still, canning went on all summer and fall because it had to be tackled as the vegetables ripened and, in the past couple of days, the tomatoes had gotten ahead of themselves again. After putting up a dozen quarts to use in soup later, she'd decided to get creative with what was left.

She'd never made spaghetti sauce before. Since Daniel had insisted on eating only what was familiar, she'd had little opportunity to venture far from her culinary roots. She'd ventured today, though. Having dug through the box full of recipes she'd clipped and collected over the past two years, she'd found three for marinara sauce. Now, the scent of fresh tomatoes spiced with onion, oregano, thyme and heavy on the basil, filled the kitchen. With her ten-quart stockpot nearly full of the thick concoction, she would have enough sauce on hand this winter to open her own trattoria, but at least she'd been able to use some of the herbs she'd cut that morning.

She was wondering how close she'd come to seasoning her creation properly when she heard the pounding of a hammer.

Realizing that Justin was off the phone, she spooned a little sauce into a custard cup. After a quick check on Anna, she pushed open the back screen door and glanced to where Justin knelt on one knee at the far end of the porch. His broad back was to her as he secured a metal bracket to the end of the raw wood post lying across scuffed gray boards. Between his preoccupation and the racket he made, he didn't seem to notice the arthritic groan of the screen door's hinges—or the fact that she stopped by the sawhorse three feet behind him.

The corded muscles in his arm bunched as he brought the hammer down with enough force to dent wood.

An instant later, seeing that he'd just bent the nail, he muttered something short and shocking.

"Justin?"

He turned abruptly. Realizing she'd heard him, his mouth thinned, but he said nothing as his glance slid impersonally from her face to what she held in her hand. Curiosity suddenly flickered in his storm-gray eyes, but it did little to dilute the tension that seemed to radiate from him in waves.

Feeling as if that tension had just knotted itself in her stomach, she set the cup and spoon on the sawhorse he'd taken from the shed. "Something is wrong."

There was no question. No query. Just the flat pronouncement that slammed Justin's eyebrows into a single slash.

"Why do you say that?"

"Because of what you're doing."

"Hammering nails?"

"I believe the object is to drive the nail into the wood. Not through it. Why did your phone call make you angry?"

"It didn't," he muttered, looking as if he couldn't imagine why she thought it had. "It was just a business call."

She tipped her head, studying the tightness around his mouth, the taut set of his jaw. "Then, you're not upset?" she ventured. He certainly *sounded* calm enough to her. But then, he'd sounded that way on the phone, too. Authoritative. Controlled. It was his actions that gave him away.

"No," he insisted, still sounding more convinced than he looked. "I'm not upset. That kind of thing happens all the time."

With a tight shrug, he hooked the claw of the hammer under the nail he'd just bent and yanked it out. Tossing it aside, he took a new one from the box by his knee. Apparently deciding he didn't like the looks of that one, he pitched it aside and reached for another.

She didn't care what he said. He was upset. She could tell by the way his jaw was working. "What kind of thing?"

"A snag. A complication in a negotiation," he added, setting the new nail in place. "I learned long ago never to be surprised when the current changed direction midstream."

"Then that is what's wrong. You feel like a salmon now. Swimming against the current, I mean."

Justin's attention shifted from the dent he'd put in the heavy pine. Emily's head was tipped thoughtfully to the side as she studied him, her hands in the pockets of her loose denim jumper.

# Here's a **HOT** offer for you!

## Get set for a sizzling summer read...

with **2 FREE ROMANCE BOOKS** and a **FREE MYSTERY GIFT!**

## NO CATCH! NO OBLIGATION TO BUY!

Simply complete and return this card and you'll get **2 FREE BOOKS** and **A FREE GIFT** – yours to keep!

Visit us online at www.eHarlequin.com

- The first shipment is yours to keep, **absolutely free!**
- Enjoy the convenience of Silhouette Special Edition® books delivered right to your door, before they're available in stores!
- Take advantage of special low pricing for **Reader Service Members only!**
- After receiving your free books we hope you'll want to remain a subscriber. But the choice is always yours—to continue or cancel, any time at all! So why not take us up on this fabulous invitation, with no risk of any kind. You'll be glad you did!

**335 SDL C26R**

**235 SDL C26M**
(S-SE-OS-06/00)

Name: _____
(Please Print)

Address: _____ Apt.#: _____

City: _____

State/Prov.: _____ Zip/Postal Code: _____

## The Silhouette Reader Service™ —Here's how it works:

Accepting your 2 free books and gift places you under no obligation to buy anything. You may keep the books and gift and return the shipping statement marked "cancel." If you do not cancel, about a month later we'll send you 6 additional novels and bill you just $3.80 each in the U.S., or $4.21 each in Canada, plus 25¢ delivery per book and applicable taxes if any.* That's the complete price and — compared to cover prices of $4.50 each in the U.S. and $5.25 each in Canada — it's quite a bargain! You may cancel at any time, but if you choose to continue, every month we'll send you 6 more books, which you may either purchase at the discount price or return to us and cancel your subscription.

*Terms and prices subject to change without notice. Sales tax applicable in N.Y. Canadian residents will be charged applicable provincial taxes and GST.

"I guess you could say that," he murmured, speculation in his glance as he leaned back on one heel. "I'm in the middle of negotiating a buyout of a party's interest in a company. It started out as one party anyway. Now an uncle has decided to back the opposition by throwing his hat into the ring."

"I don't understand. The company is owned by a family?"

There was no mistaking the interest in those innocent blue eyes. Or the intelligence. He'd never met anyone who picked up nuances as quickly as Emily did.

Were he a trial attorney, he thought, watching her gather her skirt as she sat down below her new window, he'd hire her in a heartbeat. She'd be a real ace at jury selection.

Intrigued by that thought, and more annoyed than he wanted to admit that this latest development had waited until five o'clock on a Friday to present itself, he couldn't help but wonder how she'd treat a hostile buyout.

"The company is now into its second generation," he told her, offering her a little background. "The father died and left his half of the business to his three adult children. Two brothers and a sister.

"The two brothers work in the business. The father's brother owns the other half as a silent partner. The oldest brother...my client," he explained, "has been running it for the past two years and wants to buy out his siblings. He'd cut a deal with his sister, but the younger brother has his own ideas about expanding the company and doesn't want to let go. Now the sister has decided not to sell so baby brother can keep his job."

"What kind of business is it?"

"Manufacturing plastic products."

"Can't they work together to expand it?"

The question didn't surprise him at all. Not coming from her. But it did make him consider how impossible it was for her to relate to his work. There was no way he could make her comprehend the intricacies of running a million-dollar corporation, either. It would be like explaining the mechanics of space flight to Betsy Ross.

"They aren't even speaking to each other anymore. It's not as if stockholders are involved," he muttered, placating himself with the thought. Things with the Carters could easily be worse. "If it were that sort of situation, we'd want the issue resolved before the stockholders got wind of trouble in the management and the company started losing some serious money. This is just a family operation."

Distractedly, she smoothed the ragged cuticle on her thumb. "You mentioned these stockholders before. I assume they aren't men who hold on to cows and horses. What are they?"

Anyone else would have offered the assumption with a hint of wryness in their voice. Or, at least, a tongue-and-cheek smile. Emily simply offered it as an observation based on what she knew of the world and patiently waited for him to answer.

Charmed by that candor, he eased himself against the wall and sat back. "A stockholder?" he repeated, thinking her interest had turned more general.

Crossing his long legs in front of him, he cast her a sideways glance. She sat with her arms looped around her upraised knees. The denim of her skirt puddled over the tops of her bare feet. He had no idea what he found so appealing about her running around without shoes.

"They're also called shareholders," he told her, just so she'd know. "Basically, it's someone who acquires a share, or a percentage, of a corporation. You could buy shares in a company yourself and hope to share in the company's profits. Depending on the company and how it's doing, you could just as easily put your money in and lose it."

She gave a little nod, still rubbing her nail. "And keeping stockholders happy is important?"

"Very."

"And 'serious money' is important?"

The woman was definitely quick. "Even more so."

"And people aren't?"

She glanced toward him then. There was more than simple curiosity in her question; more than a basic need to understand the world beyond her little farm. He just wasn't sure he trusted whatever it was.

"What are you getting at?"

"You told me before that there's more involved in the negotiations you handle than just people. But isn't your client's brother important?"

"Not to the company," he replied, thinking her interest hadn't been so general after all. "The older brother wants to stick to the old way, which has made remarkable profits. The younger brother wants to tinker with products that have been surefire sales for them for years. He's spent so much time perfecting his new ideas that my client has been stuck doing all the work."

"So you're helping the older brother get rid of him?"

"I don't think I care for the way you put that. But, yes."

"And the other sister and the uncle are on the younger brother's side?" she clarified, ignoring his disclaimer.

"Yes."

"And they all agree with the younger brother's way?"

"Not totally. It's my sense that the sister agrees with the older brother's business philosophy, but she feels the younger brother has a right to be in the family business, too."

"So the family is divided and the business will be harmed if they don't resolve the matter soon."

"In a nutshell."

"That doesn't bother you?"

"Of course it bothers me. The company has been solid for forty years. It's also one of the firm's oldest clients."

"I'm not talking about the business, Justin. I'm talking about what's happening to their family. Isn't that important to you?"

She posed the question quietly, her eyes searching his as if she couldn't imagine how he'd overlooked that element. He knew family was important to her. He'd heard it in her voice when she'd told him of her people; seen it in her eyes even though she'd tried to remain so matter-of-fact about all that had happened to her. But at the moment, he was more aware of how the reflected sunlight burnished her hair, and the fact that she hadn't grasped the situation at all.

"My concern is the business, Emily. Not personal relationships. I appreciate that you're thinking in terms of the people involved, but preserving their family isn't what I was hired to do."

"You were hired to think only of the company."

"Exactly."

"Then it doesn't matter to you that you're helping to tear the family apart," she concluded.

"I didn't say that."

"But isn't that what you're doing?" she asked, sounding more confused than accusing. "That's being like the lawyer who doesn't care about the Clancys' crops. That company doesn't care what it does to people, either."

He wasn't sure he followed her logic at all. But he was dead certain he didn't like being lumped in with counsel for the corporation that was so cavalierly stonewalling her neighbor.

"Emily," he began, wanting very much for her to understand that his handling of the Carter matter had nothing in common with the Clancys' problem. "I know this rift must be hard on my client. And I understand the complications of being related to people who think their way is the only way. I come from a very opinionated family myself and, believe me, they add their own brand of stress to my life.'' He couldn't imagine them going as far as the Carters had gone, though. And the total banishment Emily had suffered was unimaginable. The Sloans didn't always agree with each other, but they'd never stopped speaking. His parents were a prime example of that.

''It's not that I don't care about the family,'' he added, though he really couldn't say he'd given that element much thought until she'd brought it up. ''I'm just trying to protect my client's best interests.''

''But that's not what you're doing,'' she gently insisted. ''If you care about people, you try to help them, not divide them the way you're helping divide their business. Isn't it in your client's best interests to protect his relationship with his relatives?''

There was no accusation in her tone, no censure in her expression. All he sensed in her was a genuine desire to understand his reasoning. The only problem at the moment was that he couldn't easily explain his rationale even to himself.

''I don't expect you to understand,'' he defended, not liking that he felt the need to defend himself to begin with. He'd never considered his actions to be anything but totally ethical. And they were. Yet, she almost made him feel as if he were some sort of hypocrite. He did care about people. He just wasn't anyone's keeper. ''You come from a place where things are simpler.''

With a blink of her long, silken lashes, she glanced back to her thumb. ''That's true.''

She offered the concession easily, the slight twist of her mouth making her look as if she felt certain she'd never get a handle on the world she wanted so badly to understand.

"In Ohio a family disagreement like that would be rare because no one would take more than their share or try to outdo the other. It would be wrong to be selfish or to stand out in any way. Except in virtue, of course. But a person who is truly virtuous would also be humble and that would make them not stand out."

She glanced sideways at him, her nose wrinkling like her daughter's did sometimes. "Trying something new wouldn't happen, either. Like what the younger brother wants to do by changing the product your client sells. Change comes very slowly to the Old Order. Before something new can be used, the bishop and the elders would have to decide whether or not it speeded life up too much or if it would still be in keeping with the old ways.

"Anyway," she continued, sounding as if she might be working her way around to a point. "In larger communities there isn't always enough work for men on a farm and some of the sons have to develop other skills. Some don't want to farm to begin with. Some are blacksmiths or carpenters or shopkeepers. Some are all three. But everyone is still part of the same community. If the company is like a community and if the company is big enough, maybe the brother could use his ideas in a separate part."

In the past few minutes, the shadow of the house had stretched to reach the chicken yard. Justin was watching the rooster herd his chickens inside their neat little coop when Emily's comment caught him by the throat.

"You mean start a new division?"

"No," she muttered, clearly looking as if he'd misunderstood. "The idea is to keep them from becoming more divided. I mean—"

"Not *division* as in *dispute,*" he clarified. "*Division* as in *department. Section.* You mean, have him start a new line with his modified products and manage that department?"

He couldn't tell if she'd taken her thought that far, but he was certain from her hesitation that she didn't know if he liked the idea or not. He wasn't totally sure what he thought of it himself. But as she gave him an uncertain little nod, the part of him that loved a challenge wondered if, just possibly, he couldn't keep both the family's business and their relationships intact.

With that charming uncertainty in her eyes and the fullness of her bottom lip taunting him, he figured it couldn't be any harder than keeping his hands off her.

"I'll think about it," he murmured, shifting to rise. "The idea might have potential."

A smile slipped into her expression as he rose and held out his hand. She took it without question, letting him pull her to her bare feet, then reached behind herself to brush the sawdust from the back of her skirt. But whatever she'd been about to say froze in her throat. When she turned back to him, her braid slipped over her shoulder. Without thinking, he reached to move it back.

His fingers closed around the satiny length, his knuckles grazing the top of her breast. She went still at the contact. For a moment, he wasn't sure he moved himself. He was aware only of how firm she felt beneath his fist and the heaviness in his hand.

He felt her heart bump a moment before he let the braid slip a few inches over his palm. There was more weight to it than he would have thought, more softness to the feel of it than he'd imagined. Fascinated, he slowly drew his thumb over the twining shades of ash and pearl and pale wheat. He had no trouble imagining how it would feel to loosen that mass of silk and gather it in his hands. The trouble was that he wanted to do far more than that. He wanted to cradle her face in his hands, tip her mouth to his, then systematically work his way down her alabaster throat

to the ripe swell he'd just brushed. It was where he wanted
to go from there that had him cutting off the thought.

Without a word, he eased the braid over her shoulder to
let it swing down her back. Her breath had stalled and her
eyes held as much hesitation as invitation, but he couldn't
let it matter that she had made no attempt to move. He
couldn't let it matter, either, that the restlessness that
seemed so much a part of him lost its claws when he was
with her.

The only reason he was there was to ease his mind about
her. That and to get her window and porch fixed so he
didn't have to worry about her struggling to get them fixed
herself. Anything else he felt toward her, he'd just have to
ignore.

"I need to get back to work."

Emily swallowed past the pulse skipping in her throat.
"I'd best, too," she murmured, telling herself that what
he'd done had meant nothing. Though her insides had gone
jumpy and warm when he'd touched her, he was still preoccupied with his work. That had to be why he'd looked
so edgy when he swiped up the hammer. "My jars should
be sterilized by now."

"What are you canning this time?"

"Spaghetti sauce. That's what it's supposed to be anyway."

The spoon resting in the custard cup rattled when she
picked them up. Hesitating, not sure she should ask, she
gingerly held it out. "I was wondering if you'd mind tast-
ing it for me. I've only had it once. At Mrs. Clancy's. But
you've had real Italian food at that restaurant you like, so
you can tell me if I have it right.

"There are a couple of ingredients the recipes called for
that I don't have," she admitted, as he took the cup and
sampled. "But I'd like for it to be as authentic as I can
make it."

He took a second spoonful, concentrating. "If you want authentic, you'll need garlic."

"That's one of the ingredients I don't have."

"Olive oil?"

"That's the other."

"Sorry."

Disappointed, trying not to show it, she took the cup when he held it out.

"Hey," he murmured, ducking his head to catch her eyes. His smile came easily now, deepening the lines around his eyes, smoothing his edges. "I still wouldn't turn it down if you fed it to me. You are going to feed me again before I head for Hancock tonight, aren't you?"

"For Hancock? You're not going back to Chicago?"

"There's no way I'll get all of this done today. The lady at the hardware store recommended the Hancock Inn, so I stopped there and reserved the only room they had left."

He was staying until tomorrow. The thought lit Emily's face before she even realized how thoroughly her expression betrayed her. But she really didn't care if he knew how much his staying pleased her. As she assured him she would never allow him to leave hungry and he went back to hammering on her post, she had the feeling that his being there pleased him, too.

"I hear that lawyer from Chicago was out at your place again last weekend. You got yourself a boyfriend, Emily?"

Mary Woldridge grinned as she hauled a ten-pound bag of flour across the grocery scanner at the Hi-Way Market. Mary was a few years older than Emily and knew everything worth knowing about everyone in town. That was what Mrs. Clancy had said, anyway. Emily just found the woman to be very likable and friendly. With her curly brown hair held back with bright little butterfly clips, her perfectly applied makeup and poppy-red nails, she also thought Mary quite stylish.

Smiling back, Emily reached past Anna, who blinked up at her from her tummy-carrier, and added six packets of pectin to the conveyor belt. "He's just a friend. He was over to see Mr. Clancy, too."

"How many weekends has he shown up here now. Is it three?"

As informed as Mary was, Emily was sure she knew exactly how many weekends Justin had been there. And it had been three, if a person included the weekend the tornado had come through. "He's helping Mr. Clancy with that water problem, remember? And he's been meeting with some of the other farmers about it now, too."

Mary's eyes twinkled. "Lawyers don't make house calls, Emily. He could call them if that was all he was up to. His car's mostly at your place. Denise Gerritsen said she's seen it coming back from her mom's. And Ike," she continued, speaking of Denise's husband and the owner of the hardware store, "said he was in last weekend to buy paint so he could finish the post he'd put in the week before. Since he couldn't find the same gray, he bought enough to paint the whole thing."

It was as clear as the engagement diamond on Mary's enviably smooth and feminine hand that she thought something was going on between her and Justin. Since Justin had been spending weekends at her place, and coming into town to spend nights at the Hancock Inn, Emily could see where other people might be getting that idea, too.

But he truly was just being a friend. They worked together and talked of their respective worlds. Except for those few moments on her porch when he'd moved back her braid, he had been very careful not to touch her.

"Really, Mary, he's just helping me with repairs."

The loquacious checker gave her a look of utter patience.

"I know you don't get out much," she said, not unkindly, "but a man like that doesn't drive all the way from the city to a place like this unless he's found something here that he really likes."

"He has found something," Emily agreed, hefting a large bag of sugar to the belt. "He's found a way to work with his hands. He doesn't get to do that in his line of work."

Her smile was soft, her tone mildly preoccupied as she pulled her list from the pocket of her lavender print dress to make sure she hadn't forgotten anything. She only came into town every other week with the Clancys. Anything she didn't get now, she'd have to do without until next time. "I think he likes spending time in the country, too," she added, trading the list for the bills she'd acquired when she'd cashed her produce checks at the bank. "It sounds to me as if a city is a very hectic place."

The conviction vanished from Mary's friendly eyes as she ran baby lotion, baby powder, laundry soap and bleach across the scanner. Emily was relieved to see the woman's certainty falter. She wouldn't trade a moment of the time Justin had spent with her for anything in the world, but she meant what she'd said about the reasons he'd been coming to see her.

She could practically watch the tension drain from him as he worked around her little farm. There was always a restlessness about him when he first arrived. That same restlessness crept over him when he was getting ready to leave again, too. But while he was helping her with her chores or sitting at her table, he seemed far more at ease with himself, far more relaxed.

As intriguing as his world was to her, she had the feeling there was little peace in it.

"He's really just helping you?"

"I'm afraid so."

The twinkle leapt back into Mary's bright hazel eyes. Over the call for a price-check at checkstand two, she murmured, "Did you ever get around to practicing with that makeup I gave you?

"You haven't, have you," she chided at the flash of guilt in Emily's eyes. "I know you're busy, Emily. Heaven knows if I was running that place all by myself and with a little one at that," she added, reaching over to tug back the side of the carrier so she could smile at the baby yawning inside it, "I wouldn't want to do anything with my spare time but sleep. But, trust me, I've seen that guy and, honest to Pete, if I wasn't wild in love with my Tyler, I'd be giving you a run for your money.

"Now," she pronounced, lowering her voice because nosy old Ella Mae Issac had just jockeyed her cart into position behind Emily's, "after you put that precious little thing down for a nap, get yourself comfortable with that makeup-tips booklet that came with the mascara. Practice with the eyeshadow and lipstick, too. You want everything to look subtle. Okay?

"The next time he shows up, you have your makeup on and your hair down and see if he doesn't make a move." She swept Emily with a critically appraising glance. "Could be he's just waiting for a cue from you."

Pulling back, Mary gave her a wink, hit the Total button on the register and started bagging groceries. Since Ella Mae wanted to hear what they were talking about, she sidled up under the pretense of taking a peek at Anna, but there was nothing to hear except Mr. Clancy calling from down by the automatic double doors that they needed to hurry and pick up Mrs. Clancy from her checkup at the doctor's office.

The conversation with Mary hadn't lasted but a minute. Yet, the woman's last comment had rooted in Emily's mind as stubbornly as the ragweeds that flanked the road. All the way home from town, while Mr. Clancy drowned out Mrs. Clancy with the weather and crop reports on an AM radio station out of Cedar Rapids, and while she put her groceries away and fed Anna, Emily wondered if Mary could possibly be right. If, maybe, Justin did care about her just a little more than he was letting on and that he was waiting to see how she felt about him.

She wasn't sure she even knew herself. She truly didn't understand the strength of her reactions to him. She wanted to believe what she felt was just gratitude for his help, his company and mostly his getting her and Anna out of harm's way the fateful day they'd met. Gratitude was safe. It was understandable. But gratitude didn't explain the fluttery feeling in her stomach when his glance would linger on her mouth, or when she would lay awake at night, remembering how it had felt to be held in his arms. And it certainly didn't explain why he was on her mind nearly every moment of the day.

She was standing in front of the cabinet in her bathroom, putting her hairbrush in it after scrubbing out the chipped porcelain sink, when her glance fell on the zippered cosmetic bag Mary had given her.

It had been a baby gift, along with the frilliest pink baby dress Emily had ever seen. Mary had said she'd noticed her looking at the cosmetics at the store and knew she was curious about trying them. She'd then proceeded to show her how to use the items she'd tucked into the pretty little case and transformed her into what she quite immodestly called "a vision."

What Emily had seen in the mirror was simply herself, only more finished. "Polished," the nurse who'd shown her how to braid her hair had called it.

She removed the bag, running her fingers over the satiny fabric. Justin hadn't said he'd be back this weekend. But he hadn't said he'd be back the weekend before that, either. Both times, he'd simply shown up.

She could feel the hope rising before she could stop it. He'd told her he wanted to replace the plastic that had been torn from the greenhouse—tactfully avoiding mention of the windows she'd paid for but would probably never see. He hadn't said exactly when he would tackle the project, though. And he definitely hadn't specifically said he would come this weekend.

Still, just in case he did come and because she couldn't quash the hope, after she bathed Anna on Saturday morning, she put on a blue dress because Mary had pronounced it "her color" and the faintest touches of mascara and lipstick. She couldn't bring herself to wear her hair unbound as Mary had suggested. She had been raised to believe that a woman's hair was her glory, the single most beautiful thing about a woman and meant only for her husband's eyes. Since it had only been in the last few months that she'd worn it in anything other than a bun, to leave it loose would be like greeting Justin in her underwear.

The anticipation lasted until noon. That was when she heard the rumble of a vehicle and the crunch of gravel in her drive. But it wasn't Justin. It was Clancy. He'd come to tell her that Justin had called last night and asked him to tell her that, just in case she was expecting him, he wouldn't be there. He'd forgotten to mention last week that he had a prior commitment.

It didn't help that she knew she had no one but herself to blame for feeling so let down. Mary had only been trying to help, after all. And Emily had already known that Justin Sloan was far too worldly a man to ever want a simple woman like her.

Justin watched the light from The Hunt Club's chandelier reflect off his wine goblet. The refined clink of silver on china punctuated the conversations of other members and their guests. In the bar, the last strains of the pianist's latest effort met with distracted applause.

"...would never have considered it myself, but you know how parents are. Not that Daddy isn't usually right," Cameron added with the elegant lift of one perfectly arched eyebrow, "much as I used to hate to admit that. We did have our moments."

He hadn't a clue what she was talking about.

Lifting his goblet, he merely smiled.

"I prefer to make my own choices, though. I'm sure you do, too. You strike me as the decisive type."

"Thanks," he murmured, and sipped.

"But now that I'm back in the States, I think I'm ready to settle down. I've been everywhere I've wanted to go. Seen everything I want to see. I'll be thirty next month. Time for a reality check."

It was a pity not to savor the nuances of the wine, he thought. It was truly one of the greater vintages. But he'd already resigned himself to the sacrifice. Cameron's impression of him would be carried right back to dear old dad. That was why he'd brought her to the club, why he'd ordered the wine with his usual care, why he was trying to be as tactful as humanly possible with the words he chose next. If he'd heard correctly, Cameron had just told him she had nothing left to discover and was ready to get serious about finding a mate.

"You're lucky," he said, lowering his glass to study the sultry sweep of her dark lashes. With her sleek, dark hair swinging against the shoulders of her elegant black dress, the finishing school grace of her moves, he couldn't argue her attractiveness. Poise. Polish. Breeding. She had them all.

What she didn't have was a smile that seemed to warm his soul.

"I'm thirty-four and I still don't know what I want."

From the wry look she gave him, she clearly thought he was teasing.

Emily would have known he was dead serious.

"Right," she murmured, running her finger around the rim of her own goblet. "You graduated magna cum laude from Harvard, clerked for a supreme court judge and made partner at Daddy's firm in record time. I've grown up around men like you. You're the sort of man who has to have goals. You live, eat and breathe them." She dipped her finger in her wine, touched it to her tongue. "I'm sure you know exactly what you want."

The woman was sending signals a blind man couldn't miss. Justin was sure she meant her words to be complimentary, too. But all he seemed to hear was that he was a type, that she felt she knew him because he fit some sort of mold.

He could play games as easily as the next man. Crossing his arms on the cleared table, he leaned forward. "Then, what would be my next goal?"

She mirrored his position, her voice dropping as she tilted her head. "Probably the one you've been avoiding. Marching up the aisle, starting a family." She smiled, her glance narrowing playfully. "Why is that, anyway?"

With anyone else he would have tossed off some innocuous response and edged the subject to less bothersome ground. But Rob's admonishments kept ringing in his head, reminding him of what was sensible, practical. This woman could move him years ahead in his career, open doors he might have to beat down otherwise. Pursuing an alliance with her would be most advantageous.

But his gut kept reminding him of the more subtle messages Rob sent. He continually implied that his family was little more than a prop, something he used when it was convenient, useful or necessary. Justin remembered, too, the emotional deep freeze his brother lived in, and the icy disagreements between his parents that had finally thawed to benign indifference. But what he truly couldn't get past was how empty it had felt growing up in a house with parents who had lived such distant and separate lives.

"Frankly," he finally said, "I suppose there's nothing about marriage that's ever appealed to me."

The casualness faded from Cameron's skillfully made-up face. But he barely had time to realize that the sophisticated woman might have taken his confession as a challenge when he saw her glance up at the couple who'd just approached their table.

Within seconds, he was being introduced to friends of the Beck family, a prominent stockbroker and his wife, who asked if they'd like to join them in the bar for a nightcap. Justin figured that Rob would have been proud when he'd said they would be happy to. After all, the broker had major connections. Justin had simply welcomed the interruption. He could think of a hundred other things he'd rather talk about than marriage. But even as he went through the motions of enjoying himself that evening, he was wondering what Emily's marriage had been like.

He was still wondering when he turned down Cameron's obvious invitation to come in when he dropped her off at her apartment and, with his hands in his pockets, thanked her for joining him.

He knew from the way she glanced at his stance before she said good-night that she understood there wasn't going to be anything between them. But when he turned from her vaguely disappointed smile, he wasn't thinking of the opportunities he'd just kissed goodbye. He was still wondering what, if anything, Emily had found appealing about wedlock.

## Chapter Eight

Emily tried not to moan. She didn't know what was worse. The heat. The humidity from the heavy clouds building on the horizon. Or the fact that Justin had just pulled up to her house and she had to look like something the cat had dragged in and attempted to bury.

Stepping back from the long section of irrigation pipe she'd just moved, she wiped the back of her hand over the dampness on her forehead, and glanced across the long rows of her vegetables and herbs. From beneath the shadow of her wide-brimmed straw hat, she could see Justin walking from his car at the far side of the house.

He carried two large sacks. He set one on the back porch. The other he dropped off by the bassinet in the shade of the apple tree and continued toward the garden.

"Can you take a break?" she heard him call.

A pale-blue polo shirt stretched across his broad chest. Worn khakis hugged his lean hips and powerful thighs.

What she noticed most was the smile that revealed even white teeth and deepened the masculine creases bracketing his mouth.

"I still have four sections of pipe to move," she called back, watching him work his way through rows of potatoes. "We haven't had any rain this week. Clouds. And wind to dry out the plants. But no rain."

His smile faded when he stopped in front of her. She wasn't sure what he saw as his gray eyes scanned her flushed face, but she knew what she was trying to hide. The disappointment she'd experienced yesterday had lingered, making her reluctant to fully acknowledge the surge of pleasure that had spiked through her the instant she'd realized he was there. Still, she couldn't help the way her heart did a little flip when he touched the back of his hand to her cheek.

"You're hot," he bluntly informed her, looking thoroughly displeased with that circumstance. "Let's get you something cold to drink. I brought lunch."

"The plants need water."

His displeasure intensified as his inspection moved from the wet handkerchief she'd tied around her neck to the perspiration soaking the front of her long lavender tank dress. She'd thrown on one of Daniel's old white shirts over it to keep from burning her bare arms and rolled the sleeves to her elbows. The thing hung on her like a sack.

"So do you," Justin informed her when his unapologetic scrutiny ended at her bare feet. "Come on. I'll help you move everything later."

Without another word, he took her hand and hauled her toward the yard. She'd left a clean towel over the pump in the middle of the lawn. Pulling it off, he handed it to her and reached for the handle

"How long have you been out there?" he muttered, the pump handle squeaking as he cranked on it. In seconds, blessedly cool water splashed and pooled at her feet. A few seconds more and she'd soaked one end of the towel and pressed it to her face.

"Only a couple of hours," she replied, her voice muffled. "I had a break in one of the lines and had to fix it before I could start moving anything."

"Of course you did."

She lowered the towel to see him heading for the quilt. Not at all certain what to make of his odd manner, she turned back to the pump and bent her head to drink.

From the corner of his eye, Justin watched Emily push her long braid over her shoulder before she washed off her feet and hands and untied the old white handkerchief from around her neck. It wasn't that unpleasant in the shade. But in the sun, the heat was intense. The woman could get heatstroke working outside the way she was.

The thought had no sooner formed, than he reminded himself that she was far more accustomed to being out in such weather than he was. She had, in fact, survived all the summers before he'd come along.

The reminders were becoming as familiar as the streak of protectiveness that invariably prompted them. Not sure what to make of the vaguely proprietary feeling she also elicited, he reined in the troublesome tendency and picked up the sack he'd left on the quilt Emily had spread in the shade. As he did, he glanced into the wicker bassinet beside it.

Mosquito netting lay over the top, but he could see through the fabric easily enough. He just couldn't imagine how Emily's baby could sleep so peacefully with her legs crossed at the ankles and her little bottom sticking in the air. But the position seemed to be one that she liked. He'd noticed that she liked being held against her mom's shoulder, too, so she could look around. Except her head tended to wobble when she did that. Even with Emily's hand supporting her neck, she'd almost banged her nose on her mom's collarbone a couple of times.

What he couldn't get over, though, was her feet. They weren't much longer than his little finger.

From the corner of his eye, he caught the flutter of dark fabric and a glimpse of bare toes in the grass.

Emily stood a yard away, running the wet end of the towel around the back of her neck. She'd dropped her hat to the quilt and the rosy flush had been cooled from her face, leaving her flawless skin sun-kissed and glowing. He knew she was aware of who had held his attention. But all she did was give him a curious little smile and nod toward the large brown paper bag.

"Did you really bring lunch?"

"I did," he replied not wanting to admit how anxious he was to see her reaction. "I called Nicolo's when I got home last night and asked him if he'd fix us something 'authentic.'"

There had been an unfamiliar restraint in her welcoming smile when he'd first seen her. Now, as she sank to the quilt in the dappled shade and he pulled out containers of antipasto, focaccia, and iced cantaloupe wrapped with prosciutto, the restraint was gone.

"It's the real thing?"

"He even used flour from Tuscany. It's as authentic as you'll get without going there yourself. The only thing that's missing is a bottle of Chianti. I didn't know if you should drink wine since you're…nursing."

She didn't seem to notice his faint hesitation, or his consternation with himself for the telling pause. He was perfectly comfortable with sex. The whole man-woman thing was pretty straightforward as far as he was concerned. On a physical level, anyway. The only thing complicated about it was how it could complicate a relationship with expectations of commitment. But the mother-and-child aspect that occasionally resulted from the fun and games was something else entirely. It seemed to command more... deference.

The ground he mentally treaded was as unnerving as it was unfamiliar. Yet, amazingly, he didn't leap back from it and change the subject. He just let his comment ride while Emily distractedly said she didn't know if wine was all right or not because she'd never had reason to look it up in her book, and broke off a piece of bread. After thoroughly studying the golden, herb-and-cheese dusted crust, she asked him what it was and sank back to savor the flavors she'd never encountered before.

When she bit into the juicy ham-wrapped melon, closed her eyes and smiled, his only thought was that her reaction easily made up for the outrageous price he'd been charged by the chef for opening the restaurant early on a Sunday morning.

Justin leaned against the bark of the gnarled old apple tree. He and Emily talked as they ate. First, of the food. Then of how relieved she was that her regular produce man was back and about Justin's annoyance with the temporary filling in while his secretary was on vacation. Finally they talked about the Carter brothers, who were now considering a new division of their company.

Justin felt good about the way that case was leaning. Better than he had about anything he'd handled in a long time, including the merger that had secured his partnership. He had Emily to thank for that. And he had. He would have mentioned that he was sure the Carters were grateful, too, but Emily wasn't allowing herself much of a break. Within moments of declaring herself stuffed and making sure he'd had his fill, she was brushing crumbs from the quilt and snapping closed the foam containers so she could get back to work.

She was on her knees, reaching for the bag to put the

containers into when he caught her wrist and moved the bag out of the way.

"Leave it. We'll clean up in a while."

"I need to get back to the field, Justin."

"You will. Just give yourself a couple of minutes to rest first."

"What?"

"Rest," he repeated, thinking he should spell it for her since she seemed so unfamiliar with the word. "That's where you sit and just do nothing. Give yourself a half an hour."

"I'll have time to rest when the fields are fallow and the snow is keeping Anna and me inside. Winter is when everything rests on a farm. Right now, my plants need water."

"Nothing's going to curl up and die out there in the next thirty minutes, is it?"

"You said you'd help."

"I will," he promised as she determinedly pulled back. "But there's something else I want to talk to you about."

For a moment, he thought she might ask if they couldn't talk about it while they moved irrigation pipe or whatever it was they were going to do in her field. But she fell back to her heels again, interest and concern knitting her exquisite features.

He truly did want her to rest just a little longer. Knowing her, she'd been up since dawn and hadn't slowed down since. With the leaves rustling in the gentle breeze and the shade sheltering them from the sun that peeked through the billowing clouds, he couldn't have imagined a more restful place to be, either. But there really was something he needed to talk to her about.

"I want to know how you're going to keep up with all of this," he said, figuring it as good a time as any to shake the concern that had nagged at him all week. "You said the bulk of the crops don't come on until late August, and you're running yourself ragged now. Are you going to hire someone to help you? Work a trade or something?" he asked, since the people around Hancock seemed to do a lot of that sort of thing. "You can't do this all by yourself."

Puzzlement shifted through her eyes. "I don't see why not. That's the way I did it last year. And the years before that in Ohio. The garden is always woman's work. The women usually got together to help each other and that made chores a bit easier, but this is a small garden compared to those."

"But when you came here," he pointed out, thinking she had a definite talent for avoiding the issue, "you didn't have those women around and you weren't bound by your old customs. Didn't Daniel help you?"

"When I came here," she countered, "I was still very much an Amish wife. It didn't take long to make my clothes more modern and convince Daniel that he'd have to wear blue jeans and T-shirts if he didn't want to stand out like a sore thumb, but that was all the change he could handle." She motioned toward the sack. "Will you give me the bag now, please?"

When he didn't move, she reached for the sack herself. Again, he stopped her, flattening his hand over hers on a strip of green stitched into the quilt. "What do you mean about Daniel not being able to handle change?"

He watched her glance falter. Seconds ago, his only thought had been to assure himself that he didn't need to worry about her any more than he already did. Now, he was thinking only of the question that had accompanied him last night from Cameron's door.

He leaned forward, refusing to give Emily time to withdraw as she'd done moments ago. He knew he should keep his hands to himself. But the need to touch her seemed to be overriding his common sense today.

Or maybe the need was just becoming stronger than he was.

The thought made him go still a second before he pulled back on his own.

"Were you happy being married, Emily?"

The faintest of frowns tugged at the delicate wings of her eyebrows. "Daniel was a good man."

"I'm not asking you to defend him. I asked if you were happy."

He wished she'd look up. He wanted to see her eyes. He didn't nudge her chin up himself, though. There was something self-protective about the way she sat there, her legs tucked under her, her head bent as she ran her finger along a line of impossibly tiny stitches

"There are degrees of happiness, Justin. But basically, yes. For a while."

"For a while?"

Emily gave a small, tentative nod. The empty sensation that lurked under her breastbone suddenly felt a little more hollow. It was so rare to feel it when she was with Justin. "He...we," she quietly corrected, "adjusted differently to our life here. I think it was all much more difficult for him."

She toyed with a loose thread, refusing to pull on it and destroy the delicate handiwork. She wasn't accustomed to speaking of the feelings she hid or held in her heart, and the sadness she'd felt over losing Daniel had been there for so very long. Long before the accident had taken his physical presence from her. His spirit had started dying the moment they'd left Ohio. Within months, she'd been living with a man who'd become almost a stranger to her.

"I would have thought it would be more difficult for you." Justin offered the observation quietly, his deep voice soothing, encouraging. "With that job he'd taken, he'd been around a lot more than you had, hadn't he?"

"Much more," she conceded.

"Then, I don't understand why the transition was harder for him. You would have had to deal with more that wasn't familiar."

"I think it was because it was more of an adventure to me. Or maybe it was because my curiosity had always been so much greater than his.

"I remember when we were teenagers," she mused, marveling at how easily Justin could draw her past her reticence. "We would sit up in the haymow after chores and I'd ask if he ever wondered what made an airplane fly, or what it would be like to drive a car or wear fancy clothes. He would look so worried about me, and warn that I wasn't supposed to question such things. The Rule said I wasn't even to think of them lest I be led from the Old Way and if that happened I could never be his wife.

"I don't think we could imagine not being together," she confided, wondering at how long it had been since she'd felt so certain about her place in the world. "I don't think anyone else could, either." Her finger halted its tracing. "I couldn't have imagined him withdrawing so much."

He should let it go.

The thought occurred to Justin as he'd watched her retreat into her memories. He'd never known the sort of discipline she'd lived with, never cared about anyone the way she obviously had the man she'd married. He had no way at all of understanding how deep her grief had been. But he recognized emptiness when he saw it. And he hated what he'd uncovered.

"I'm sorry," he began, wanting to reach for her, not trusting the reasons prompting the desire.

"Me, too." She drew a deep breath, her expression suddenly more contemplative than somber. "It wasn't as if he changed all at once," she said, looking as if she wanted him to understand how things had been. "He hadn't wanted us to join any of the more lenient communities because he didn't want to have to explain why we'd left where we were. And he didn't want us associating with the English because their ways were so foreign and he was sure we'd be taken advantage of somehow. He just started going more and more inside himself. The more interested I became in our neighbors and our new life, the more he clung to the Old Ways."

"And you weren't wary?"

"Of course, I was. I was scared to death."

He had the feeling that she still was. Alone, with nothing but a couple of acres of land to support her, she was probably more frightened now than she'd ever been in her life.

"But you didn't let that stop you." He doubted it had even slowed her down. As fragile as she looked, as small as she was, he could pretty much picture her rolling up her sleeves, swallowing her trepidation and doing whatever needed to be done. But it sounded to him as if Daniel had been afraid to move beyond his comfort zone, as if he'd found refuge in clinging to the familiar.

All that had done was hold the guy back. He'd never made it past what had gone wrong in his life and moved on the way his wife was so bravely doing.

"You know, Emily," he said, wondering how far she would push herself before she broke, "you say Daniel is the one who changed. But it sounds to me as if he stayed the same as he'd always been. You were the one who changed. Who grew," he amended, because to him, that was what she had done.

She slowly shook her head. "I'm talking about in here." She pressed her hand to her heart, her quiet voice becoming quieter still. "It didn't matter that he didn't want us to use electricity or buy a car. I was used to living without those things and a person can't really miss what she's never had.

"I'm talking about the contentment he used to have inside him," she explained, though she had the feeling that Justin had no idea what she was talking about. He didn't have it, either. What he had was ambition. But without contentment, not a thing he accomplished or possessed would make him truly happy. "That's what changed about Daniel. He was forced to struggle in a world he was never meant to live in and it robbed the joy straight from his soul."

The breeze rustled the leaves, the gentle sound blending with the call of birds and the soft stirrings coming from the bassinet. Despite the hollow feeling that lingered in her chest, her heart smiled at the thought of how her little Anna would be stretching her arms above her head and making the little scowl that pleated her forehead.

When the stirrings became a small squeak, that smile made its way to Emily's mouth. Rising to her knees, she lifted back the mosquito netting and reached into the white wicker bed. "Now this little girl," she murmured, the lilt moving back into her voice, "would have brought some of his joy back.

"Hello, sweet pea," she murmured, smoothing a spike of blond fuzz on Anna's head. "How was your nap?"

Justin gave Emily a considering look as she lifted the little bundle of bare arms and legs in a pink T-shirt and a diaper and eased back to the quilt once more. He couldn't help the relief he felt seeing the light slip back into her eyes. He didn't even question his relief at knowing that she wasn't still in love with the man who'd been her husband. What bothered him was the odd empathy he felt for a man he'd never met—and the uneasy feeling that he had more than a little in common with a displaced Amishman. But he wasn't about to consider that he was holding himself back by clinging to a life that sabotaged his potential the way Daniel Miller had done. He had quite deliberately spent his life getting himself exactly where he was.

Not liking the trapped sensation that came with that thought, Justin promptly dismissed it and focused on the baby. Emily had the yawning little girl on the quilt in front of her and was unpinning her diaper.

"Did he know he was going to be a father?"

"Yes, he did," she replied, reaching into the bassinet for the clean diaper she'd left there. "We'd thought for the longest time that we weren't going to be blessed with children and he'd thought it a blessing itself that we didn't have any when we moved. When I told him we were expecting, he worried about not having our extended families to teach me about caring for her, but the nurses at the hospital were wonderful. Two of them took turns coming by for the first couple of weeks to make sure we were doing all right. One of them even spent the first couple of nights with me, since I was by myself. My friend, Mary, spent a few nights, too."

It had to be hard having a baby all alone.

The thought hit Justin as something of an understatement as he stared at the smallest little legs and belly he'd ever seen.

Emily glanced over at him and smiled. "You've never been around babies before, have you?"

"Never."

He knew nothing about children. And he couldn't begin to imagine being responsible for one. Especially one who couldn't communicate, get around on her own or feed herself. He didn't know a soul he could talk to about them without raising eyebrows and speculation, either.

Except Emily.

"How could you tell?"

"You always look at her as if she's as fragile as an egg."

"She is. Isn't she?"

"Not quite. You have to be careful with them when they're this young," she agreed, graciously refraining from looking at him with amusement. "Support their neck and be careful of their soft spot. But baby's won't break if you're careful with them."

"Soft spot?"

"Right here."

She brushed her finger over the top of Anna's head. Looking closely, he could see a faint pulse beating in a quarter-size spot beneath the wispy corn silk hair.

"The bones are soft so they can make it through the birth canal," she said matter-of-factly. "There's another one farther back, too, but it's much smaller."

With her fingers gently wrapped around the baby's ankles, Emily made short work of the diapering process, tucking and snapping while he was still trying to figure out if the head of the big safety pins were ducks or chicks. Since they were yellow, it was hard to tell.

"Wouldn't disposable diapers be easier?"

"Sure they would. But they're too expensive. They're not environmentally sound, either." Seeing his arched eyebrow, she smiled. "A woman is entitled to her causes," she informed him. "I raise organic vegetables, remember. Here."

"Here what?" he asked, frowning as she shifted to kneel closer to him.

"Hold out your arms."

His eyes widened at the little blond head moving in front of him. "Emily, I don't—"

"Like this," she said, and before he could say another word, she'd placed the featherlight little girl in his arms.

"You can breathe, Justin. It's all right," she assured him, touching her hand to his shoulder. "I'm right here and you're sitting down. You won't drop her."

It barely registered that she'd just read his mind. Gradually releasing his breath, he glanced down at the baby staring at the logo embroidered on his pocket.

He'd held her once before. In the cellar the day of the storm. And he'd watched her when he'd been here before. But he'd never looked closely enough to realize just how perfect she was.

She looked up, eyes as blue as her mother's focusing on his before glancing away. Her eyelashes were long and so fine they were almost invisible. And there was a tiny cleft above her sharply carved upper lip. Her pink mouth was drawn in a faint pout.

"Getting in some practice, huh?" he murmured, thinking how effective that pout would someday be for getting what she wanted.

*She's going to be beautiful,* he thought, getting brave and brushing her downy cheek. Her skin felt as soft as air.

*She already is beautiful,* he corrected, pulling back when her mouth opened and she turned her head toward his stroke.

Drawn by the miracle in spite of himself, he touched her little hand, amazed when her tiny fingers gripped his.

"I've never seen anything so small," he mused, checking out the diminutive fingernails and a tiny pink thumb.

"She was even smaller." Emily's glance moved from the concentration etched in Justin's features to the child turning her open mouth toward his shirt. "But I wish she'd grow a little faster. At her last checkup, the doctor said her weight gain was a little slow, but not to worry as long as she's eating. Some babies just take a while to really get started. That's what everyone tells me." She tipped her head, considering. "Does she seem bigger to you than when you first saw her?"

"I'm the wrong person to ask about this, Emily. To me, little is little. You're not a very big woman," he added, seeking to alleviate the concern in her face. "She probably just takes after you."

The hand gripping his finger suddenly pulled away and Anna poked one leg into his side. She kicked again, trying to shift position. Or, maybe, just to get a little exercise.

Justin regarded the movements as a definite threat to his hold. When Anna's head jerked back and forth as she tried to get her fingers into her mouth, he could feel his muscles stiffen. "You'd better take her," he muttered. "I'll try again when she's bigger. Right now, she's just too small."

He didn't care if Emily knew the baby intimidated him. His ego wasn't as important as making sure the little girl didn't hurt herself because of him. Not wanting to lose his grip, he remained still while Emily edged closer and slipped her hand between his arm and the baby's back.

"Careful," he said.

Emily couldn't help but smile at the warning.

"I will be." She offered the assurance as she tucked her hand between the baby's side and the rock-solid wall of his chest. It was a shame to move her, Emily thought, terribly aware of the feel of heat and hard muscle as her arms tangled with Justin's. Anna actually looked quite content right where she was. But then, she knew herself how secure it felt to be cradled in those strong arms.

The thought had barely registered when she glanced up and found Justin staring at her mouth. A heartbeat later, his eyes met hers.

He looked as if he'd been about to say something. Perhaps ask if she had a hold on Anna. But he said nothing at all. He just let his glance drift back to her mouth, lingering there long enough to make her throat go dry before easing back to watch the baby again.

Anna had finally found her fingers. She had three of them in her mouth and was noisily sucking away when Emily rose to her knees and settled her in her bassinet so she could kick to her heart's content. Behind her, Justin pulled himself to his feet, seeming oblivious to the effect he had on her.

She was trying very hard to act as unaffected as he was when she glanced up and saw him hold out his hand.

He was offering to help her up, something he'd done any number of times before. But he'd no sooner drawn her up in front of him than he lifted his hand toward her face and she went perfectly still.

"Bend your head," he murmured. "You have something in your hair."

She felt his fingers at the back of her crown when she did as asked, and the slight tug at her hair when he pulled out a bit of leaf. Thinking he must have noticed it when she'd stood, she glanced back up. "It must have fallen from the tree."

"Probably."

He said nothing else as he flicked the leaf away. He just stood towering over her, looking as cautious as she suddenly felt when he reached back to smooth the strands of hair he'd loosened. His motions were slow, almost tender, and when his eyes met hers once more, she had the feeling he hadn't even considered what he was doing.

Seeming to consider it now, he reluctantly lowered his hand. He only made it as far as her cheek before he skimmed his knuckles down it the way he had in the field. Only this time, instead of pulling back once he'd felt the warmth of her skin, he carried his touch to the curve of her jaw.

His voice grew husky. "We should probably get to work."

"Yes." She barely breathed the word. "We should. Anna will need to be fed soon."

He gave her a little nod. Agreeing. But he made no attempt to move. He just stood there, letting his thumb graze the fullness of her bottom lip, his eyes following the gentle motion.

She couldn't seem to move herself. It was all she could do to breathe. The air felt faintly electric, the way it did before a storm when the wind had been blowing and everything suddenly stopped. That was exactly how she felt, as if her whole body had just gone utterly still. Except for her heart. It was beating double-time when his free hand curved at her waist.

Something like resignation slipped into his eyes as he lowered his head. He brushed his lips over hers. Once. Twice.

His lips were warm, firm and far softer than she'd thought they would be. "Kiss me back, Emily."

He breathed the words against her mouth, tugging on her lower lip with his thumb. She'd scarcely realized what he wanted her to do when she felt the touch of his tongue to hers.

She wasn't prepared for the tremor that darted to her breasts, pooled in her stomach and sucked the strength from her legs. Needing to hold on, she curved her fingers around his biceps and felt herself sag toward his rock-hard chest. This was exactly where she'd wanted to be, though she'd had no idea how badly she'd wanted to be there until she felt his breath filling her, his hands touching her body. He felt so big. So solid. And as he angled her head, deepening his kiss, he seemed to be slowly filling her with a warmth that crept deep inside, taking away a chill she hadn't even realized was there.

Suddenly craving that warmth, she dared to lean closer.

Needing her closer yet, he took her arms and curved them around his neck.

She tasted like warm honey. Felt like pure heaven. Justin shaped her to him, drawing her slender body against his, letting his hands roam over her narrow back, the inviting curve of her hips. If there was any hesitation about her, it felt more like shyness than uncertainty. So he kissed her gently, deeply and all but gritted his teeth against the raw desire that ripped through him when he slipped his hand up her side and skimmed his fingers over her breast.

The heavy fullness fit his hand perfectly. She would fit him perfectly everywhere. He was certain of that. But the thought had no sooner sent a jolt of fire straight to his groin, than he became aware of the dampness around the hard bud growing beneath his palm.

He wasn't at all sure what he felt just then. The desire to slip his hands beneath the soft cotton covering her and feel the silk of her skin slammed squarely into the realization of what he was doing. His stimulation was causing that warm moisture. But it was the thought of what that moisture was and who it was for that had him slipping his hand back to her waist and slowly lifting his head.

His heart felt as if it could pound right out of his chest when he pressed his forehead to hers.

Mistake, he thought, willing his breathing to calm. Big, big mistake.

There was a reason he'd been keeping his hands to himself. There was a reason he hadn't caved in long ago and done exactly what he now knew he definitely should not have done. Emily wasn't just a lovely, intriguing woman. She was a widow, the mother of a nearly three-month-old infant and absolutely the last person on God's green earth he had any business getting involved with or leading on.

Now he knew how she tasted, how trustingly she responded to him and it wasn't enough. He wanted more. He wanted to feel her body moving beneath his. He wanted her long, taut limbs wrapped around him. He wanted her. Pure and simple.

But there was nothing simple about it.

Drawing a deep breath, he eased his hands up her arms.

She was definitely not the sort of woman a man could have an affair with, then guiltlessly walk away.

And he was feeling the guilt already.

It took all the willpower he had to lift his head and gently unclasp her hands from behind his neck. Holding her by the wrists, he slipped their hands between them. He wasn't a masochist. He wasn't going to torture himself with something he wouldn't take.

"This isn't getting your chores done."

Emily heard what Justin said, but she couldn't respond. She was too busy trying to calm the erratic beat of her heart, still the heaviness of her breathing. Confusion had joined the assault of sensations that had her feeling strangely disoriented, but there was no mistaking the edge in Justin's deep voice. It was as obvious to her as the tension snaking through him and the deliberate way he avoided her eyes.

He slowly lowered their hands. A moment later, he let her go.

"If Anna's going to need you soon, you might as well stay with her now. I'll take care of the irrigation pipes."

"I'm sure I have ten minutes or so—"

"So use them to rest. I need to get busy anyway. It's going to take a while to tack the plastic up on the greenhouse."

Emily had no idea what she'd done. But something felt very wrong. He was acting as if nothing had happened. Yet, there was a distance about him that had never been there before, a shuttered look to his chiseled features that was at once familiar and totally unknown.

He stepped back, nodding toward the field. "What do I do out there?"

It only took her a moment to explain that she needed the two forty-foot-long sections of pipe moved twenty feet to the west and where to find the coupling that brought in her irrigation water. If he thought it odd that she didn't insist on helping, he didn't let on. He just gave her a distracted nod, assured her that he could handle it, and left her with her hand pressed over the hollow little ache in her stomach.

That ache was still there when she saw him walking toward the house three hours later. He'd just put away the tools he'd used to tack up the last of the plastic and she'd taken Anna out to the porch with her to ask if he wanted something cold to drink. But she knew the moment she saw his strides slow when he noticed her that he wasn't planning on staying any longer than he already had.

The air felt suffocatingly still as she took the stairs and met him ten feet from his car.

"I put on double layers of plastic," he said, his expression guarded as he nodded toward the greenhouse. "And I used redwood tack strips instead of pine. Ike at the Feed and Hardware said redwood would weather better and I want them to last until that guy shows up with your windows."

"I won't be getting the windows." Lifting Anna to her shoulder, she tried for a smile. The effort didn't work. "You were right about the carpenter. He's not coming back."

The admission weighed heavily on her. Letting go of the hope was harder than letting go of the money. And hope was what she felt fading now.

"No," he agreed. "He's not."

Neither was he. Justin had the feeling she knew that, too. She'd tried as hard as he had that afternoon to pretend everything was the same as it had been. But it was like trying to ignore a ticking time bomb. It was only a matter of time before it would go off and everything would be over.

He was trying to do the right thing. For both of them.

He knew she was totally confused by how quickly he'd cooled after that bit of spontaneous combustion under her apple tree, and he would try to explain himself to her. Still, between what he'd done and what he was doing, he couldn't help feeling like as big a louse as her crooked carpenter.

"It's all finished now. The work you wanted to do here," she said, holding Anna close. "Thank you for that, Justin. For the window and for asking Mr. Clancy to fix the cellar door—"

"Emily—"

"And for fixing the porch and the greenhouse—"

"It wasn't just the work bringing me here."

"Promise me that you'll take care of yourself out there."

Something snagged at his heart, something painful and totally unwanted. "Emily. Don't do that."

"Don't do what?"

*Don't make me miss you. Don't make me wonder if I'm doing the right thing by walking away.*

He stepped closer, his hand cupping her face as he memorized the crystalline blue of her eyes, the poreless texture of her skin. It no longer mattered whether or not he kept his hands to himself. The damage had been done. If he hadn't crossed that line already, he could have kept coming back, he could have pretended friendship was all he wanted. But that pretense was gone. He'd never had a friend who had him thinking about babies, or whom he wanted so badly he ached.

"I don't think you have any idea how hard it is for me to keep my hands off you." He was touching her even now, his actions proving just how impossible it was to resist her. "If I keep coming back here," he said, wanting her to understand how impossible a relationship was, "I'll be trying my damnedest to get you into bed. But you're not the kind of woman who sleeps with a man unless she believes he'll be there for her.

"I can't make those kinds of promises," he admitted, ruthlessly checking needs clamoring to be felt. "You're home and family and commitment, and I don't have a clue how to make any of that work."

He skimmed his thumb over her cheek, his eyes searching the depths of hers as his blunt admissions sank in. She deserved far more than some guy who wanted to sleep with her because he needed to get her out of his system. She needed someone who could take care of her.

"Tell me if I'm wrong about you."

He couldn't believe how long she hesitated before she slowly shook her head. "No," she whispered. "You're not wrong."

"I didn't think so," he murmured, and slowly lowered his mouth to hers.

It was only a kiss goodbye. But the desire that strafed though him was fierce. If she hadn't been holding Anna, he would have pulled her closer just to feel her small, soft body against his one last time. But with the baby between them, he settled for what contact he had.

When he lifted his head, she glanced away, her features drawn and pale.

He couldn't think of a thing to say to take the sting from what he was doing. Wanting only to get it over with, he reached toward Anna, allowing himself to touch her soft little cheek. The baby turned her Cupid's-bow mouth toward his finger, a smile crooking up one corner when she blinked up at him.

He was falling for the kid, too, and that made him more certain than ever that he should get out before he got in over his head.

Though he hesitated for a moment, when he turned away and reached for his door, he never looked back.

## Chapter Nine

He'd stop thinking about her eventually.

Justin turned off the CD player in his credenza, silencing Jackson Browne, and picked up his empty coffee cup. The corporate annual report he was wading through was as boring as watching paint dry and he needed the stimulation of music and caffeine to stay with it. It didn't help that his mind kept drifting.

It had been over two weeks since he'd seen Emily. Two weeks and a day to be exact, though the fact that he was aware of just how long it had been probably didn't bode well for forgetting her anytime soon. He knew that forgetting her was the only rational thing to do, too. There had been no place for the relationship to go. It made no sense that he couldn't get her off his mind.

Annoyed with himself, annoyed with the project he couldn't focus on, he ignored his ringing phone and stepped out of his office.

Rhonda, who'd come back from her vacation with skin that looked a bit pinker and considerably smoother than he remembered, picked up the call from her desk with a crisp, "Mr. Sloan's office," and held up her neatly manicured hand to have him slow down.

He didn't want to slow down. He wanted coffee. Telling himself he'd find out what she wanted on the way back, he hoisted his red Chicago Bulls mug to let her know he was going to refill it and kept moving past her cubicle.

"I'm sorry, Mrs. Miller," he heard her say from behind him. "He's not available at the moment. May I ask what this is regarding?"

Justin stopped dead in his tracks. Abruptly, he turned. "Who?"

Looking every bit as efficient as she was, the woman with the stylish salt-and-pepper bob asked the caller to wait a moment, put the call on hold and glanced up at her boss. "Emily Miller. She didn't say what it's about. And I have a message from Mr. Shuman," she continued, speaking of one of the partners. "He wants to know if you can join him and Mr. Dunlap before the partnership dinner Thursday night."

"Probably. Find out where and what time." He motioned to her phone. "I'll take that call."

With a shrug she replaced her handset. "Do you want me to get coffee for you?"

Looking as distracted as he sounded, he told her he'd appreciate it, left his mug on her desk and headed back into his office. He couldn't imagine why Emily would be calling him, but he didn't waste any time trying to figure out what she might want. The door had no sooner closed with a solid click behind him, than he reached across his desk to snatch up the phone.

"Emily. What's wrong?"

As greetings went, his was hardly the most cordial. His

demand didn't even make a whole lot of sense, considering that he had no concrete reason to think she had a problem.

She didn't seem to think it extraordinary at all.

"I'm not really sure yet," she replied, a faint but discernible tremor in her soft voice. "I know you're busy and I'm sorry to bother you at work, but I'll only keep you for a minute. Our bus leaves in half an hour.

"I'm at Anna's pediatrician's office," she continued quickly. "We're on our way to University Hospital in Chicago and I need the name of a hotel. I've never been there before. To Chicago, I mean. Do you know of a place that's close enough to the hospital for me to walk? And that doesn't cost very much? Dr. Fisher said there are liaison people at the hospital who might be able to help with accommodations, but I can't talk to them until I get there and I wanted...I hoped..."

He didn't know if she ran out of air or courage, but her voice suddenly trailed off, leaving him straining to hear something in the silence.

"You hoped what?" he coaxed, hearing her release a shaky breath.

Several more seconds passed before she said, "...that you could help me."

She wanted the name of a place to stay. Someplace close. Someplace cheap. That was all she was asking.

All he considered was that she had to be frantic if something was wrong with her baby.

Uneasy himself, his tone grew more abrupt. "What's the matter with Anna?"

"Dr. Fisher isn't sure. He said I'm not to panic...and I'm trying not to," she claimed, valiantly attempting to sound calm despite the fact that the tremor was still there, "but he's concerned about her weight now, too. She's not doing some of the things babies should be doing at her age, either. All he'll say is that something isn't right and that he doesn't want to wait for it to go wrong before we figure out what it is. He took some blood tests the other day and he said the results could mean any number of things. He's just not saying what.''

Justin didn't care for the sound of that at all. The woman deserved to know what the doctor suspected. He didn't much care for the thought of her being in Chicago on her own, either. She'd been taken to the cleaners on her own farm. She'd be eaten alive in the city.

''You can stay with me,'' he told her, far more comfortable with taking charge than with the protectiveness he felt. ''I'm not that far from the hospital myself.''

''Justin, I can't—''

''You don't have time to argue, Emily. What time does your bus get in?''

The bus scheduled to arrive at 1:50 from Hancock via Sterling, DeKalb and a dozen points in between pulled in at 2:20. Watching for her, Justin saw Emily before she saw him. She appeared in the doorway of the gleaming silver bus in a white shirt and a long beige skirt and struggling with the baby carrier, a purse and a blue denim bag the size of a small suitcase. Her flaxen hair was drawn in a tight neat knot at her nape.

She didn't look up until she reached the bottom step. The instant she did, she went as still as Lot's wife.

A sea of people swarmed ahead of her. Other buses were debarking, their passengers spilling into the terminal. Baggage lined the walkways. Porters jockeyed carts loaded with more suitcases, duffel bags and boxes toward the baggage area. Above it all, loudspeakers broadcast a steady, echoing drone of departures and arrivals, only half of which were audible over the rumble of diesel engines.

Feeling like the salmon Emily had once mentioned, Justin slipped through the wave of people moving toward him and edged between the two women who'd disembarked ahead of Emily.

He reached the parted doors of the bus just as someone behind her gave her a push. Already visibly disconcerted by the confusion, she didn't seem to realize she'd been shoved on purpose.

"Take it easy back there." Justin growled the warning, aiming a quelling scowl at the green-haired teenager impatiently waiting for her to move. He reached for the carrier, infinitely more concerned with Emily than with the gesture the kid started to flip him before catching the deadly glare in Justin's eyes.

"Give me the baby," he said, taking Emily's arm as she grabbed a handful of calf-length beige denim and stepped to the concrete. "What other luggage do you have?"

She looked as pale as snow. "I only brought this."

She started to hoist the denim bag higher on her shoulder. As she did, Justin caught it by the strap, swung it onto his instead and flattened his hand at the small of her back.

He'd nudged her toward a revolving door, careful to avoid bumping the carrier, when he glanced down at the peacefully sleeping baby. Tucked securely in soft yellow and white blankets, Anna looked as sweet and perfect to him as she had the last time he'd seen her. The thought that something could be wrong with her was incomprehensible. "Are we going straight to the hospital?"

"Please."

"Do you know where you're supposed to go when you get there? It's a pretty big complex."

Emily pulled the piece of paper she'd written the directions on from her bag while he guided her into the elevator in the parking garage. She started to read them to him, only to press the paper to her stomach when the elevator began its ascent. He suddenly realized she'd probably never been in an elevator before, but encumbered by the bag and the baby, he couldn't reach over to offer reassurance. The best he could do was tell her to hold onto the rail behind her if it would make her feel more secure.

All she did was nod, seeming too overwhelmed to appreciate the new experiences the day was bringing, and too disquieted by him to pay much attention to anything she didn't have to—including the sights outside his car once Anna's carrier had been belted into the back seat and Emily had crawled in beside her so she wouldn't be riding back there alone.

Justin had expected her to be a little uneasy with him. Heaven knew, he wasn't feeling terribly comfortable himself. But it still surprised him that she didn't even seem to notice the tall glass buildings rising on either side of the street, the hot dog vendors and flower carts on nearly every corner, or the midday bustle of people and traffic that would have once enthralled her. It was only when he told her they were getting close to the hospital that she even bothered to focus on any of the buildings at all.

When she did, he could have sworn he saw her go even more pale than she already was.

The hospital was an enormous structure of glass and steel and interconnecting buildings. The complex of inpatient and outpatient facilities and parking garages seemed to go on for miles. Sky bridges joined everything, their arching windows reflecting blue sky so perfectly that they sometimes seemed to disappear.

Following the directions she read to him, he pulled up in front of a plazalike area leading to a series of automatic doors. "This is the admissions entrance," he told her. "I can either let you out here or park and help you inside."

"We'll get out here. I don't want to impose any more than I have."

"You're not imposing, Emily."

She'd needed his help. There was a huge difference be-

tween that and bothering someone with an unnecessary in-
trusion. But he didn't bother explaining that. Leaving the
car running, he just helped her out, waiting until she pulled
her purse strap over her shoulder before handing her the
carrier with its thick mauve liner. Anna was waving the
edge of the pale-yellow blanket she gripped in her fist.
When he touched the little dimple in her chin, one corner
of her mouth kicked up in a smile and she waved the blanket even harder.

He hadn't hesitated to touch her. He did, however, feel
oddly hesitant about pulling away.

A moment later, aware of Emily watching him, he
reached inside his jacket and withdrew a slim gold case.
"Here are my home and cell phone numbers," he said,
scrawling them on the back of his business card. "Call me
when you want me to pick you up. Do you have change
for a pay phone?"

She glanced up, her expression momentarily blank. "I
don't know if I do or not," she replied with a hesitant
glance toward her purse. "I hadn't thought about it."

Pulling change from his slacks pocket, he started picking
out quarters and dimes. "Take these."

"That's not necessary, Justin. I'm sure I can get change
somewhere."

With the tip of his index finger, he opened the slash
pocket on the hip of her skirt and dropped them in. "Now
you won't need to. Is there anything in your travel bag that
you need now?"

He wasn't sure if she frowned because of what he'd done
or because she was thinking. Since she finally met his eyes,
he tended to think it was because he'd ignored her claim.
She was just too preoccupied to call him on it.

"I don't think so."

"Then there's no reason for you to have to mess with it
in there. I'll take it with me."

Suddenly looking uncertain, she glanced from him to the doors and back again. There was no mistaking her ambivalence. He could see it in her clouded expression as her concerns for her child battled the awkwardness of staying with him. But he was a known quantity. Faced with so much at the moment that wasn't familiar, he was the only port in the storm.

"Thank you," she said quietly. "Thank you," she repeated and, needing to get her child inside, she turned away.

A moment later, she'd straightened her shoulders and she and Anna were heading inside alone.

Emily would have felt more at ease with a total stranger. Having been surrounded by them for the past seven hours, she knew that for a fact as she stood beside Justin in the wood-paneled elevator that swept them from the parking garage to his fifty-second floor condominium.

Her stomach lurched as the elevator slowed to a stop. The sensation was interesting, similar to what she'd experienced as a child in the first second of a free fall from the hayloft to the hay below. Having been in the conveyances no less than half a dozen times today, she thought she should have been accustomed to the feeling by now.

"So how long do they want to observe her?" he asked as the doors silently opened.

"Dr. McLeary said a couple of days. Some of the results from the tests they ran today will be back tomorrow, but he said they might need to run more depending on what they find."

Emily stepped out ahead of him, kneading the ache in her temples. She couldn't shake the image of her little Anna hooked up to the monitors that would record everything about her for the next couple of days. Despite the nurses' gentle insistence that her baby was perfectly comfortable, and even though Anna had been sleeping quite peacefully when Emily had left the nursery, she found the whole ordeal so awfully fearful.

It had been so hard leaving her there.

"It's a genetic problem they're looking for?"

"That's what Dr. McLeary said. Dr. Fisher called him because Anna had two Amish parents and sometimes Amish children can have certain genetic disorders. Dr. McLeary said one of those disorders is a problem with absorbing nutrients and they think that might be what's wrong with Anna."

"Why would Amish kids have genetic problems?"

"Because the Amish are descended from only forty-seven families. The doctor said that concentrates the gene pool. He said there are similar problems in other groups with…what did he call it?" she asked herself, rubbing her temple again. "Genetic uniformity, I think."

What she knew about modern medicine wouldn't fill a teacup. But the people at the hospital had been wonderfully kind. She'd had a thousand questions, and they'd been most patient with their answers. In return, they'd taken her blood for some sort of comparison with Anna's and asked what seemed like a thousand questions of their own.

"Dr. McLeary also said it might not be that at all."

"Did they say what they think the problem is if that isn't it?"

"No," she murmured, the word sounding every bit as weary as she felt. It was after nine o'clock and the day had already been forever long. "They didn't."

She felt his hand brush the small of her back as he led her to a door at the end of the hall. He was probably just guiding her, something he seemed to do out of manners as much as necessity. But she took comfort in the contact, anyway.

"How long do you have before you need to go back?"

He posed the question as his hand fell and he slipped a key into the lock. When he swung the door open and motioned her inside, she was still rubbing at the dull ache.

"I'd like to be there early in the morning. One of the nurses said there's a train, the 'L,' she called it, that stops a block from the hospital. And there are buses. Which is best to take from here?"

"A taxi," he muttered, flipping on the light. "Or I can take you. But what about Anna? Don't you need to feed her?"

"They had me leave milk for her. I hope she'll take it," she murmured, vaguely aware of his uncomprehending frown as she dropped her hand and looked up. His concern struck her as very sweet, even if he did look rather formidable to her at the moment. He was still in his charcoal-gray suit, though his tie was now loosened and the top button of his collar undone. "She's never taken milk from a bottle before."

Justin closed the door with a quiet click. A couple of weeks ago, he might have worked around to asking how she'd managed to fill the bottle to begin with. Considering the intimate nature of the question and the awkwardness of their silences when they weren't talking about Anna, he settled for changing the subject.

"Come on in. Get comfortable."

He shrugged out of his jacket as he crossed the marble entry floor, his footsteps going silent when he hit the dove-gray carpet. Directly ahead of him, a long iron sofa table stretched along the back of a pearl-gray leather sofa. The sofa faced a glass table and a ten-foot-high wall of windows with an obscenely expensive view of the Chicago skyline.

Draping his jacket over the sofa back, he turned to see that Emily hadn't budged. She stood beneath the small art deco chandelier in the mirrored foyer, her pale hair restrained and gleaming in the reflected light and her expression strangely puzzled.

"Is this your lobby?"

"My what?"

"Your lobby. That's what they called the area like this inside the main entrance of the hospital."

He glanced behind him, taking in the clean, uncluttered lines of the open area. Emily had been waiting for him just inside the main doors of the new, ultramodern hospital when he'd picked her up, so his attention had been on her rather than the interior. If he'd had any impression of the lobby at all, it had only been of stone walls and floors and echoing space.

"It's my living room," he replied, thinking the hospital's reception area had seemed rather...sterile.

His brow pinched at the thought.

Emily caught his quick frown. But he was already moving away and by the time she'd opened her mouth to apologize, he'd disappeared behind the wall to her right.

It hadn't been her intention to offend him. She'd just expected that his home would be something enormously grand and she'd spoken her first impression when she'd looked up. But as she followed him, it quickly became apparent that his home wasn't much bigger than hers. It just had a higher ceiling and fewer walls.

A raised tile walkway ran along the far side of the main area. The open doorway toward the middle revealed a room with a smaller leather sofa and a desk. In the doorway farther down, she glimpsed an enormous bed covered in royal blue.

It was apparent that she'd been wrong about the size of his personal space. And there didn't appear to be much in it. As she stepped around the wall, however, it became clear that the size of the objects he'd chosen to live with leaned toward massive.

A breakfast bar separated the kitchen from the dining area. The dining table was a huge slab of peach-colored granite. The black-framed painting that took up the entire wall next to it was an indecipherable swirl of blues and purples that looked like something a child could do with a few buckets of paint.

"He's a very popular artist," she heard Justin say, when he saw what had caught her eye. "His colors are supposed to evoke memories, so each viewer sees something different."

"What do you see?" she asked, skeptical.

"Blue and purple. I needed something for the wall and I liked the colors. A friend of mine talked me into buying it." *You are what you own,* Rob had joked. *The man's paintings are famous. Go for it.* "What do you see?"

She tipped her head, relieved by the distraction. The colors were pretty. They'd look quite beautiful in a quilt, actually. But the way they flowed together looked almost like a tornado to her. Something violent. Angry. "A storm," she said, still studying the whirlpool of blue and purple with an admittedly unsophisticated eye. "Or a bruise."

"I should take you with me the next time I buy art."

He muttered the conclusion, sounding more as if he were talking to himself than to her as he tossed his tie onto the upholstered back of a narrow gray dining table chair. With the tie gone, he opened another button of his pristine white shirt. "Are you sure you're not hungry?"

"Positive. But thank you," she murmured. "If you don't mind, I'd just like to go to bed."

He stood on the opposite side of the table, the slab of stone less of a barrier than the undercurrent of tension each was trying to ignore. With the bright overhead lights it was easier to see the caution his manner lacked. That masked reserve shielded him as surely as her reticence guarded her.

She had the feeling he was relieved by her request. He

didn't hesitate but a moment before he gave her a nod and turned to the tiled walkway.

"I put your bag in here."

He turned into the room with the desk, walking in ahead of her to flip on the light.

Stopping behind him in the doorway, Emily spotted her denim bag on the far side of the black enamel desk. The desk itself was painfully neat, the blotter centered, the pens and pencils all sitting points down in a silver cup. A large framed photo of him in a skinny red boat emerging through a cloud of white water hung next to a photo of him with his arm slung over the shoulder of a man who looked very much like him. His brother, the judge, she thought wondering how they'd reached the top of the huge rock where they stood overlooking a majestic valley.

Justin had headed straight for the sofa. It was a darker gray than the one in the living room and had only two cushions instead of six. He picked up those cushions, stacked them beside the wall and nodded to a door to his right.

"The bathroom's through there," he told her, motioning toward a closed door. "We'll have to share." Grabbing a metal handle in the middle of the small sofa, he stepped back, pulling out an already made-up bed. "There are clean towels in the cabinet under the sink. And you'll have to let the shower run for a minute to get hot water." He hesitated, turning to where she stood just inside the doorway. "Should I show you how the knob works?"

From the cautious way he watched her, she had the feeling he knew she'd spent most of the day facing one unfamiliarity after another. But he didn't treat her as if she were mentally deficient the way some people did when she didn't know what something was or how to use it—like the young mother with two small boys in the waiting room who couldn't believe she knew nothing about the care and feeding of electronic pets. As Justin had in the elevator, he treated her lack of worldly experience as a simple matter of fact. Since he knew her background, and that she only had an old-fashioned claw-foot tub at home, he had every reason to suspect she wasn't familiar with showers at all.

"The apartment in Ohio had a shower," she told him, speaking of the place she'd lived for a month. "And the hospital where I had Anna had them. Is yours different?"

"Probably not." He reached into the closet for a pillow, glanced at it, and decided to take out two. "If you need anything else, the other door in there is to my room."

"You're going to bed now, too?"

"Not for a couple of hours. I have a ton of reading."

He already looked preoccupied to her. Knowing he still had work, feeling guilty for keeping him from it, she walked over and took the pillows from his hand.

"I won't need anything else," she told him, hugging the pillows to her. "Please, go do whatever it is you need to do."

Justin's glance swept her face. Worry etched itself in her brow. The blue of her eyes was clouded with concern for her child. She looked pale and tired and he could swear she hadn't met his glance for more than a second at a time since he'd picked her up from the bus.

And since the moment he'd picked her up, he'd been telling himself that all he wanted to do was make sure she got where she needed to be and that she was safe while she was in the city.

That was still all he wanted when he reached for the doorknob to keep from smoothing the strain from her brow.

He'd turned to the door and was about to tell her he'd see her in the morning, when he heard her take a step toward him.

"Justin," she said, hesitantly. "Have you ever done something that you can't explain?"

The unexpected question had a frown touching his brow. "What kind of thing are you talking about?"

"Calling you. I can't explain why I did it." She needed him to know that. She needed him to know, too, that the need to talk to him had simply been instinctive, a response she hadn't even questioned at the time. "When Dr. Fisher told me something was wrong with Anna, all I could think…

"I couldn't think," she amended, hating how weak that must sound to someone who handled crises for a living. But it was the truth. When the doctor had told her Anna needed to be hospitalized, it had felt as if the ground had been torn from beneath her feet. She'd needed something solid to grab on to, something to keep the world from pitching any farther out of control than it already had. Her first thought, her only thought, had been of Justin.

"I shouldn't have bothered you. We both know you never intended to see me again, and I called before I thought of how uncomfortable this would be for you. For both of us. When you said I could stay with you, I should have just thanked you and waited to see what arrangements the hospital could help me with. I'll check with the liaison people in the morning about staying somewhere else. I'm sorry I put you in such an awkward position."

*We both know you never intended to see me again.*

Of everything else she had just said, those were the words that seemed to echo across the four feet of pale gray carpet separating them. Justin had been bluntly honest about why he wanted out of her life. He'd made it clear, too, what would happen if he'd kept coming back.

As his glance fell to her mouth, it was apparent he hadn't forgotten that, either. She just didn't know what aspect of making love with her he was thinking about when his darkened eyes lifted back to hers.

"You have nothing to apologize for. I didn't question

why you called and neither should you.'' A muscle in his jaw jumped. ''As for making other arrangements, there's no need to do that. You didn't ask to stay here. I offered.''

Actually, she thought, he'd told her she was staying. But the point seemed less important than the fact that he wasn't letting her make the situation any easier for them. She wasn't going to worry about it now, though. As he turned his dark head with a quiet good-night and closed the door behind him, she had enough to worry about with Anna.

Emily didn't know how long she'd slept. Four hours. Maybe five. It seemed she'd tossed and turned for at least that long before she woke with her breasts tender and leaking milk.

The instant she'd awakened, her first thought had been that something was terribly wrong and her feet had hit the floor before she'd realized where she was—and why Anna wasn't fussing to be fed. Now, the panic of that moment had long subsided. She'd used the pump a nurse had given her to alleviate the discomfort and filled the bottle she'd just put in the refrigerator, but she couldn't shake the aching need she felt to hold her child.

She'd never gone so long without nursing her baby—or just simply holding her. She was worried about Anna trying to take a bottle at the hospital, too. If she didn't like it, she wouldn't eat enough. And she definitely wouldn't get enough to eat if the nurse didn't remember to hold her high on her shoulder to burp her. That position worked best. She'd mentioned that to all three nurses in the nursery and she hoped they didn't forget.

The clock on the microwave glowed 2:26 in bright pea green.

It was the middle of the night. Long hours stretched between her and the sunrise. Beyond the curtainless windows dominating the living room, the sky was as black as pitch.

The only other light in the place came from her bedroom. Pale as it was, that buttery beam slanted through the partially open door, lighting a path behind the dining room table and chairs where it faded to little more than shadows. Dim as it was, she could easily make out the shapes of the furniture as she made her way to the window.

Any other time, she would have been spellbound by the breathtaking view. The city below seemed composed of nothing but blackness and a million pinpoints of light that rivaled the stars in the sky.

The view barely registered as she crossed her arms against a chill that came more from within than without.

She'd felt lost before. She'd felt alone. But always before there had been something familiar to ground her. At the moment, there was nothing. She was separated from her child. And she was in a place where the only person she knew really didn't want anything to do with her.

"Emily?"

Justin's voice was deliberately subdued, but she turned with a start anyway, her hand flattening at the base of her throat as she turned to where he stood behind the sofa. With his back to the light, she couldn't see his expression. She wasn't even aware of how little he was wearing until he walked over and lifted his hand to run his fingers through his hair.

When he stopped an arm's length away, she could clearly see his bare shoulders and the corded bulge of his biceps. He looked sculpted of shadows, all hard angles and planes.

His hand fell, drawing her glance to his broad chest, the rippling muscles of his stomach and the low waistband of his dark boxer shorts.

"Couldn't you sleep?"

"No. I...no," she concluded, hurriedly turning back to the window. "I didn't mean to disturb you."

"You didn't. I was already awake when I heard you come out here."

His glance moved from her tightly crossed arms to skim her elegant profile. She'd pulled her hair into a ponytail and braided it, presumably so it wouldn't tangle in her sleep. The silken rope hung down the back of the virginal white nightgown that covered her from her neck to her toes.

"This is what I do when I can't sleep. Look out at the lights," he explained, though he doubted that much of the diamond-on-black-velvet vista even registered. Her thoughts seemed light-years away. "How long have you been up?"

"I'm not sure. A while."

"You're worried about Anna."

At his flatly delivered conclusion, she tightened her arms. She didn't just look worried to him. She looked frightened. And desperately in need of reassurance. If she held herself any tighter, she'd break.

She'd barely nodded her head when he turned away and picked up the portable phone from its base on the end table. A moment later, he held out the faintly glowing instrument. He couldn't give her the kind of reassurance she needed, and the kind of comfort he could offer, he wasn't sure she'd want. Not from him.

"You might feel better if you call the hospital and find out how she's doing. If you hear that she's sleeping, maybe you can get some rest yourself."

"I can call now?"

"You can call a hospital anytime. Do you know the number?"

She had the number in her purse. Telling her not to bother getting it, he called directory assistance and punched in the number for her. In less than a minute, she'd reached the nurses' station for the nursery and was asking if Anna had taken her bottles or if she'd had trouble with them. She

also wanted to know how much she'd eaten, if she was
fussy or if she was sleeping.

Justin had moved back, giving her space. He didn't have
to see her hand to know that she was clutching the telephone like a lifeline. He didn't have to see her face to know
it was lined with concern. He didn't want to be affected by
her fears or cares or worries. He didn't want the sharp pang
of need he felt at the thought of gathering her in his arms
just to comfort her. He didn't want to be affected by her at
all.

She'd ended her call and turned to face him. Seeming a
little hesitant, she moved toward him. "Thank you," she
murmured, holding out the phone.

He took it, turning the instrument off as he did. "How
is she?"

"The nurse said she's doing just fine. She wasn't too
happy with the bottle at first, but she finally got the hang
of it. She's sleeping."

"How about you?" He was affected anyway. "How are
you now?"

She tried to smile. Tired, still worried, the effort failed
miserably. "Better. Thank you," she added, her glance faltering as it skimmed his bare chest. "I think I could get
used to having a telephone."

There were a lot of conveniences she could get used to,
Justin thought, and reached over to pick up her hand.
"Take the phone with you. If you wake up again, you
won't have to lie there worrying. Just push Redial. You'll
get right through."

Emily thought she nodded. She wasn't sure. She wasn't
sure she even understood what he'd said. With him standing little more than a foot away, she was conscious only
of the deep rumble of his voice, the heat of his hand on
hers and the nearness of his big body.

He was much too close. Yet, he wasn't anywhere near close enough.

The empty sensation inside her opened to a gaping void.

There had been times in the past couple of years when uncertainty had plagued her, when the unknown had loomed large and intimidating and she hadn't been entirely sure what to do. But only one other time in her life had she felt the sense of helplessness that had been with her since she'd left Dr. Fisher's office. That had been during the tornado. But during the storm Justin had been there, his strong arms protecting her, protecting her child. And somehow, just being held by him, the fear had gone away.

Heaven help her, but she desperately needed that sense of safety now.

He stepped back, slowly dropping his hand.

"You should go back to bed, Emily."

She gave him a nod. "You, too."

He motioned her ahead of him, letting her pass. But she only made it to the door of her room before she turned back. "I'm sorry," she murmured. "What button do I push? I've never used a phone like this before."

He reached toward the phone, the lean lines of his face totally unreadable. "That one. You push here," he added, indicating the Power button, "to turn it on and off."

"Thank you."

She wondered if he had any idea how thoughtful he was as she glanced back up at him. She wondered, too, if she had the courage to ask him to hold her, just for a minute. Then, she saw his eyes glittering hard on her face and her only thought was of the tension she could feel radiating from the carved muscles of his body.

His jaw hardened an instant before his big hands settled on her shoulders. But her heart had barely caught at the thought of feeling his arms around her when he turned her away from him.

"Go to bed, Emily." His voice was tight, the rough sound of it totally at odds with the gentle brush of his thumbs over her nape an instant before he pulled his hands away. "Please."

Swallowing hard, she moved into her room and quietly closed the door.

## Chapter Ten

Justin's shower was finally running.

Emily stood at the counter in his kitchen, listening to the rush of water through wall pipes as she opened a loaf of bread she'd found in his pantry. She'd been awake since dawn and desperately needed something to do. She'd already called the hospital to check on her baby, showered, dressed in a lavender jumper that she'd made last year and rebraided her hair.

If she had been home, she would have been outside working by now. Had the weather kept her from her outside chores, she could have canned or cleaned or sewn or quilted or read—though she truly wouldn't have had time for the last luxury.

Time, however, was all she had here.

Yesterday, she'd spent hours with nothing to do in a waiting room full of magazines she'd been too preoccupied to read. Justin had magazines, too, though the ones on his coffee table were about sports and law. The bookcase at the end of the hall was crammed with more novels than she'd ever seen outside of a library or a bookstore. But even surrounded by that wealth of material, she was too restless to sit still. What she'd needed yesterday, what she needed now, was something to do with her hands.

She opened his refrigerator, trying not to be too curious about the lack of anything but the eggs and milk she carried to the counter and an assortment of condiments and white cartons with wire handles on them. It felt good to be doing something productive, something normal. Relatively normal, anyway. She'd have to go without coffee. The coffee beans she'd found were whole and the sleek black-and-chrome automatic coffeemaker bore no resemblance at all to the aluminum pot she used to boil her morning brew. Since she had no idea how to use it, she would focus only on the things she could handle.

She'd found a bowl and was searching for his utensil drawer when the electronic warble of the telephone she'd left on the dining table cut through the relative silence. Before she could decide whether Justin would mind if she answered it in case it was the hospital, the sound stopped. Seconds later, the low drone of a male voice nearly sent her out of her skin. It was only an instant before she recognized the deep rich tones as Justin's, but Justin wasn't there. The disembodied sound was coming from the phone base on his end table.

She'd just realized she was listening to an answering machine when the instrument clicked and another male voice piped in.

"Just me. You must be on your way down," came the terse message before she heard the click again.

Lowering her hand from her chest, she wondered if the odd message was something Justin needed to know about now or if she could wait until he appeared to mention it.

Considering where he was, she opted to wait. The man was much easier to take fully dressed. And technology, she decided, would be far easier to handle if she wasn't coping with nerves stretched thin from worry and surroundings that were a far cry from familiar.

What she needed to do was fix her attention on her task. She'd discovered long ago that she could handle just about anything if she concentrated only on what she had to do at that very moment. When that task was finished, or that moment had passed, she would then deal with the next. There had been times yesterday when she'd concentrated simply on putting one foot in front of the other.

She had beaten eggs in a shiny stainless steel bowl and placed slices of bread on the top rack in the oven when she felt an uncomfortably familiar tightening in the pit of her stomach. She knew Justin was there even before she turned around. He hadn't made a sound. Yet, she could feel his glance moving the length of her back. Or maybe what she felt was the bridled tension that was more a part of him than she'd ever realized.

He couldn't have been out of the shower for more than a couple of minutes. He stood at the end of the breakfast bar rubbing the back of his dark damp hair with a royal-blue towel. A trickle of water snaked down his neck. It curved to the center of his impressive chest before disappearing into the low swirl of hair that arrowed beneath the terry cloth anchored around his lean hips.

"Morning," he muttered, taking a swipe at his neck before slinging the towel around it. Snagging the ends in his fists, he skimmed a guarded glance down the row of tiny buttons on her T-shirt and the tinier violets printed on her loose jumper. "I thought I'd get the coffee going."

Despite the air of tension following in his wake, he seemed as comfortable walking around half-naked as he did in a tailored suit. Trying to ignore how precarious the tuck looked on the lower towel, she attempted to look comfortable, too.

"I would have done it," she told him, "but I've never used one like that before." She stepped aside when he passed in front of her, forcing her attention from the taut muscles of his tapering back. With her nerves already jumping, it seemed wiser to focus on the way his hair spiked up on his head, or the fact that he'd dripped on his clean marble floor. "I couldn't find ground coffee, either."

"I don't have any. I grind it myself."

Without another word, he plugged in the black-and-clear plastic appliance next to the coffee maker and dumped in whole beans from the bag in the refrigerator. Seconds later, the grinder was slamming beans around with enough noise to wake the dead. Emily jerked at the unexpected racket. All Justin did was frown at the slightly open oven door.

"What are you making?"

"Toast."

"Just regular toast?"

"The kind with butter and jam," she said, because she'd made different kinds for him before. He'd especially liked her egg toast. "French," he'd called it. But just because she'd cooked for him so many times before didn't mean he wanted her invading his territory by doing it now. "You always have such a big appetite, so I thought you'd need breakfast before we left. I knew you liked scrambled eggs because I'd fixed them for you before, but if you—"

"You don't need to explain," he insisted, looking annoyed that she thought she had to. "I just wondered why you were using the oven. I have a toaster, if you want to use it." Taking the glass pot to the sink to fill it, he nodded toward the jet-black appliance on the far side of the counter. "It's over there."

She hadn't even thought about using the appliance. Preoccupied, she'd simply been doing what she'd always done.

Realizing he'd been prompted more by curiosity than disapproval, she felt her shoulders drop. ''I've never used one. I've cleaned Mrs. Clancy's before,'' she added, wanting him to know she wasn't totally unfamiliar with the contrivance. ''But I've never seen one like this.'' Removing the bread from the oven, she dropped it in the parallel slots and stared at the line of digital settings. ''After I put the bread in, what do I do?''

''Push the button on this end. It'll lower it automatically.''

She could handle that. ''How about a frying pan for the eggs?''

''Cleanup is easier if you do them in the microwave.''

It was his kitchen. She'd do it his way. ''I haven't used one of those before, either.''

''There's a book that tells you what setting to use and how long to cook them. It's in that drawer by the stove,'' he said and left her to search it out while he dumped water into the coffeemaker and pushed the button that made things start to hiss and bubble.

With the coffee on, she prayed that he would go back to his room. She needed for him to leave, to go put some clothes on, to let her breathe. It wasn't just his very male presence that disturbed her, though she couldn't begin to discount the effect of a well-built man in a towel. It was the uneasiness he'd brought in with him. It didn't matter that they were talking about something as mundane as breakfast. Beneath the polite and painfully cooperative conversation, the strain between them was as thick as the morning fog outside his window.

She thought she'd heard him turn away when she pressed the latch on the door of the microwave to open it and set the bowl of eggs inside.

''Don't!''

Justin's fingers closed around her wrist like the jaws of

a trap, stilling her hand on the door and slamming her heart to her throat. Behind her, she could feel his hard torso branding her from shoulder to hip.

"You can't put that in there," he said, his warm breath brushing her ear. "It's metal."

She opened her mouth to ask what that had to do with anything. With his heat searing the strength from her voice, it was all she could do to drag in air.

Beneath his fingers, Justin felt the wild flutter of Emily's pulse. He hadn't intended to touch her, much less jump at her the way he had. And he definitely hadn't intended to get so close when he'd been trying so hard not to think about her taut little body at all. It was just that he'd seen what she'd put in the microwave and a vision of sparks and a major meltdown had him grabbing her before she could close the door and start pushing buttons.

"I thought...I mean, I know I've seen Mrs. Clancy use bowls in her microwave oven. I'm sure I have."

"You've seen her use plastic or glass," he said, cursing himself for rattling her so badly. The scent of his soap lingered on her body, the familiar perfume of sunshine and wildflowers clung to her hair. Whether she knew it or not, she was rattling him, too. "You just can't use metal ones."

"Any metal?"

He heard a subtle quiver in her voice, felt it in the fine bones of her wrist. He'd caused her to tremble like that before. When he'd kissed her.

The thought alone was enough to arouse him. Breathing in her scent, feeling the delicate sharpness of her shoulder blades, the gentle roundness of her hip, was enough to make him groan.

All he'd have to do was turn her around and she'd be in his arms.

The fact that he wanted her there, that he'd lain awake

half the night wanting her in his bed, was something he was doing his level best to ignore.

"Most." He forced himself to ease away. "It causes electrical arcing."

The moment he drew back, he saw her fold her fingers over the wrist he'd just released and clasp her hands to her chest. The stance was decidedly protective. So was the way she edged from the stove when she turned to face him.

"Like lightning?"

"Yeah," he agreed, marveling at how gamely she attempted to overlook the decidedly electrical charge snapping right there in the room. "Like lightning."

Caution clouded her expression, warring with the incredible innocence in her fragile features as she gave him a little nod. She still held her wrist clasped between her breasts, but as he watched the delicate cords in her neck convulse as she swallowed, a frown pulled at his forehead. She was holding her wrist for a reason.

The thought that he might have grabbed her harder than he'd thought had him canceling the distance she'd put between them. "Did I hurt you?" he demanded, reaching out to curve his fingers around her forearm.

Puzzlement darted through the caution. "No. I...no."

"Let me see."

"There's nothing—"

"Emily," he said flatly, ignoring both the denial and the way her breathing shorted at his touch. "Let me see your wrist."

He gave a gentle tug, his eyes challenging hers in the moments before her hand fell from what she seemed to be protecting. But there were no marks on her soft skin and when he tested the delicate bones with his fingers and gently moved her hand in his, she simply stood watching him.

There wasn't a trace of physical discomfort in her clear blue eyes. But there was no mistaking the bated awareness.

"You didn't do anything," she quietly told him, pulling her hand away. "I tried to tell you that."

She touched her wrist again. Catching herself, she looked away as she slowly crossed her arms.

It was then that he realized what she'd been doing. She hadn't been reacting to discomfort by curling her fingers where he'd grabbed her. She'd been holding in his touch.

"I'll find a glass bowl," she assured him. "How long before you'll be dressed?"

The need for physical distance grew even stronger. "Five minutes."

"Breakfast will be ready."

Had he not already showered, he might have considered a cold one as he rounded the breakfast bar and left the kitchen. But calling himself ten kinds of fool for getting that close to her had pretty much the same effect before she stopped him three feet from his bedroom door.

"Wait," she called, hurrying around the counter to grab the phone from the table. "You had a phone call. I don't know who it was, but he spoke into your machine." She held out the phone, not totally sure how he went about hearing the message himself. "Whoever it was said something about you being on the way down."

Justin had barely closed his eyes with a grimace and muttered a terse, "Damn," when a heavy, five-beat knock sounded from behind her. A second later, his jaw set in stone, he was moving past her to head for the entry.

The man at the door was the man who'd called. Emily recognized his voice within seconds of Justin swinging open his front door.

"Hey, buddy, what's going on? I've been waiting in the lobby for ten minutes. Did you oversleep?"

Justin shoved his fingers through his hair. As he did,

Emily saw the shorter, stockier man look from the towel wrapped around Justin's hips and dart a glance over his bare shoulder.

Immediately, he caught sight of her. His high forehead reflected the overhead light and his thinning hair was the same bay brown of her Grosmutter Hochmeier's old plow mule. But what she noticed most about the man in the gray Lakeshore Country Club T-shirt and running shorts was the quick interest in his blunt features.

"Hi," he said, his glance raking from her head to her toes.

"Hello," she replied, offering a smile.

"Look." Apology joined Justin's exasperation with himself. "I forgot all about running this morning. I can't go. Something's come up."

"I can see that."

"You don't see anything," he grumbled, deliberately blocking the speculation his colleague aimed over his shoulder. "I'll talk to you at the office."

"I can hardly wait." Rob sniffed the air, shifting the other way to catch another glimpse of the unexpected guest. "Coffee's on. Is she cooking you breakfast?"

Justin's voice dropped like a rock in a well. "I'm not having this conversation right now. Take an extra lap for me," he said, wanting only to be rid of the man running another curious and critical inspection from Emily's braid to the white sneakers below the hem of her flower-print jumper. "I'll be in by nine."

He hadn't given his normal routine a single thought with Emily around.

The only thought he gave it as he shut the door on his colleague's beady-eyed scowl was that his routine at the office would now be shot, too. As sure as Lady Justice was blind, Rob would be camped at his desk when he got there.

"He's the man who called. I'm sorry," she murmured,

cautiously watching Justin walk over to the answering machine. "I should have told you when you first came out."

Preoccupation creased Justin's features as he pushed the Play Messages bar. After a faint screech while the tape did a quick rewind, the clipped message replayed itself.

Emily felt her stomach tighten as the muscle in his jaw jumped. She had no way of knowing for sure, but he looked very much as if he wished he'd intercepted the call himself.

"We better hurry up," he said, heading for his room once more. "I know you're anxious to get to the hospital and the traffic's only going to get worse the longer we wait."

"Justin, I'm—"

"Don't worry about it, Emily. Let's just get going. Okay?"

There was an edge to his tone as he spoke. Or maybe, Emily thought trying to pull breakfast together without blowing anything up, the edginess was simply in him. Though he hadn't said another word about the fellow who'd come to the door, she'd have to be as dense as mud not to know he was upset that the man he'd called Rob had seen her. The way he'd tried to block the man's view of her had been too obvious to miss. It was as if he hadn't wanted his friend to know she was even there.

She had a scrambled egg sandwich waiting for Justin when he came back out, looking devastatingly handsome in a navy suit and bloodred tie and seeming as distracted as she felt. When he asked where her breakfast was, she told the first outright lie she'd ever uttered in her life and said she'd already eaten. The truth was that the knot in her stomach didn't allow room for food.

She already felt edgy staying with him, and out of place. But until he'd practically pushed his friend out the door so he wouldn't have to explain her, she hadn't felt unwelcome.

* * *

"Okay, Justin. Who's Pollyanna?"

At the sound of Rob's voice, Justin closed his eyes and stifled a groan. He'd made it until noon without running into the guy. He'd thought for sure that he was home free.

Cornered, a fist of disquiet balled itself in his gut. That was the only reaction he would allow. His motions were unhurried, his manner relaxed as he collected his change from the ex-marine operating the newsstand near his office building, plastered on a poker face and tucked the newspaper he'd just purchased under his arm. "I thought you and Beck were meeting with a potential client for lunch."

"We went to their corporate offices this morning instead. I'm just getting back. SoyCo's in the bag."

Though Justin felt himself hesitate, years of practice at the negotiating table kept his expression impressively bland. "SoyCo?"

"It's an agricultural corporation Wyler has been courting. They want to expand and they need someone more aggressive in their negotiations than the Little League firm they're using right now. You'll get the lowdown on them at the partnership dinner," he assured him, "so don't change the subject."

The disquiet cloned itself. He had no idea what sort of negotiations Rob was talking about. All that mattered to him at the moment was that with Beck, Wyler and Dunlap taking on SoyCo as a client, he could no longer help Clancy and the other farmers the old guy had introduced to him. Even though the advice he'd given them had been free, and he would mention what he'd done at the partnership dinner because he was totally aboveboard in all his dealings, he definitely had a conflict of interest. The best he could do for Clancy now was recommend that he hire himself a really good attorney.

"Come on," Rob prodded, persistent as a gnat. "Who is she?"

"Emily's...a friend."

"Emily? You've never mentioned an Emily before."

Clearly perplexed by that obvious oversight, Rob fell into step beside him, briefcase in hand. If he was just coming from his meeting, that meant he was going back to the office, too. And that, Justin realized, tamping down his annoyance, meant Rob intended to accompany him every step of the two-block walk.

"When did you meet her?"

"A month or so ago," he replied, resigned.

"Where?"

"Outside a place called Hancock. It's over by Iowa," he added to save Rob the trouble of asking.

"That would explain why she looked like she came straight off the farm." He chuckled. "What're you doing with her here?"

"I'm not doing anything with her. She has to be in town for a couple of days and needed a place to stay." It seemed best not to mention Anna. The less fuel Rob had, the better. "Like I said, she's a friend. Okay?" he asked, feeling defensive, trying not to.

"Hancock." The way Rob repeated the word had Justin bracing himself. "Isn't that where you were going fishing?"

Justin didn't say a word. He didn't have to. He could practically hear the gears grinding beneath Rob's balding pate before the man grabbed his sleeve long enough to jerk him to a stop.

"Just what were you fishing for over there?" he asked, his tone incredulous. "Is *she* the reason you kept going back?"

"Let it go, Rob."

"No way, man. Is she why you've only taken Cameron out once in the last month?"

"I didn't realize you were keeping such close tabs on my personal life."

At Justin's darkly muttered comment, Rob cut a glance at the lunch crowd swarming around them like ants at a picnic. Clear skies were a magnet for people who spent most of their day under fluorescent lights, breathing mechanically conditioned air. Half of Chicago seemed to be jammed into the plaza just then.

Ironically, they had less chance of being overheard where they were than they would in the office—which was why Justin jammed his hands in the pockets of his slacks and stayed right where he was.

"If I've been keeping tabs on you," Rob grumbled, clearly offended that his good intentions were being disparaged, "it's only because you've been acting so weird lately. You're sleeping with her, aren't you?"

"For cripes sake, Dunlap."

"Hey." His manner turned forbearing. "All I'm doing is thinking of your future. A future I've invested a lot of my own time in," he pointed out, bluntly reminding Justin that he'd been grooming him for partnership since the day he'd assigned himself to be his mentor. "I'd hate like hell to see you screw it up. What does she do? Who's her family?"

"She can't do anything for my career, if that's what you're getting at. She can barely take care of herself."

Rob lifted his hand as if to make a point, his expression incredulous. "Do you hear yourself?" he demanded, looking torn between concern and utter disbelief. "You have a shot at our senior partner's very beautiful, very accomplished and *very connected*," he stressed, "daughter. Even if you discount the social and political influence Beck would have on your career, Cameron herself could carry—''

''Cameron knows I'm not interested.''

''You told her that?''

''Not in so many words, but she got the message.''

''Well, it's obvious that you haven't,'' he growled. ''Cameron is exactly the sort of woman who could do the most good for you and your career. A man in your position needs a woman who can entertain clients and fit in with the other partners' wives. What you don't need is a novelty you're too embarrassed to mention or introduce to your friends.''

Justin felt his entire body go deadly still. He didn't doubt for a moment that Emily, with her kind heart and unaffected ways, would be shark bait for certain of the partners' wives. He'd overheard their cattiness and snobbery on occasion himself. But that wasn't what left him momentarily speechless.

It had never occurred to him to be embarrassed by her. And it hadn't occurred to him until that moment why she'd been so silent after Rob had gone. When he'd all but backed Rob out of his condo that morning, his only thought had been to spare her the man's inspection and prevent him from butting in the way he was now.

''There is nothing about her that embarrasses me, Rob.'' His tone was as flat as Lake Michigan, the look in his eyes as glacial as its undercurrents. He wasn't at all prepared to define how he felt about Emily. To himself, or to anyone else. But he wasn't about to leave Rob to his defective conclusions. ''And she's not a 'novelty,''' he clarified, with that same ominous calm. ''She's a friend who needs help right now, and I don't turn my back on a friend.''

Discomfort sucked a little of the starch from the shorter man's contentious stance. Rob took a step back, putting a little distance between himself and Justin's unfamiliar cold stare. He hadn't gotten where he was by backing down, though, and he didn't now.

"You need to work on getting your priorities straightened out here, buddy. And while you're at it," Rob added, insisting on getting in the last word before he walked away, "you might want to remember who your real friends are."

## Chapter Eleven

Emily stood at the pay phone in the deserted waiting room, the receiver pressed to her ear as she rubbed at the ache at the back of her head. When Justin had dropped her off that morning, he'd told her he had a dinner meeting that should be over by nine-thirty at the latest. He'd also told her she was to call him on his cell phone if she needed him before then.

The message she was leaving on his answering machine was for him not to come at all.

She wasn't sure of the exact moment she'd become a coward, but sometime over the course of the agonizingly long and confusing day, she'd become about as courageous as her chickens. By leaving the message at his condo, she didn't have to talk to him herself. The only problem was that by using the machine, she didn't get to say everything she probably should have.

She'd never left a message on an answering machine

before. But the message she'd heard on Justin's telephone was the same one she'd heard when the machine had gone off that morning. Hearing it again, she followed his instructions and left the day, the time and a brief message after the beep.

The brief part threw her a little, though. Because he'd said to keep it short, she told him only that she would stay at the hospital tonight, so he wouldn't need to pick her up.

She hung up, certain he would be relieved by her decision. She knew she was. She would far rather be alone and feeling lonely than be in a place where she wasn't wanted. And there was no doubt in her mind as she moved to the night-darkened window at the end of the little room that he didn't want her there. When he'd closed the door on his friend that morning, she'd experienced the same sick sensation she'd felt when she'd first been shunned and her entire family had turned their backs to her. Justin hadn't refused to communicate with her or take anything from her hand, but between his distant manner and what had happened with his friend, there was no getting past the fact that he was merely tolerating her presence.

What she couldn't understand was why he'd insisted she stay with him in the first place.

She had no idea how long she stood at the window watching the cars come and go from the parking structure below. She had no idea how long she paced between that window and the bulletin board at the end of the long hall that held announcements for staff positions and a blood drive before returning to the window again. With her arms crossed over the hollow feeling in the pit of her stomach, she was just trying to quiet her thoughts. But all she could think about aside from her baby and the produce order she'd missed that morning was that she really didn't know the man called Justin Sloan at all.

There had been moments after he'd met her and Anna

at the bus when she'd caught glimpses of the friend he'd been—the man whose quiet strength had seemed as much a part of him as his generosity. That generosity was still there, too innate to be buried. But he found no pleasure in the things he did the way he had before. He was different among his own people. Reserved and remote. Easily annoyed. Always a little on edge. What she'd noticed the most was that the friend she so desperately needed was no longer there.

She had no idea what it said for her state of mind that she still ached for him to hold her.

The green plastic cushion of the waiting room sofa creaked as she wearily settled into the far corner. Visiting hours were long over. Except for the snow-haired janitor she'd exchanged pleasantries with before he'd started running a floor polisher, she was alone in the spare and uninviting place. The older wing where the nursery was held few of the amenities of the newer sections where diagnostic tests were run. The only diversion here was the view from the window and the traffic from the two elevators halfway down the hall, though this time of night they, too, were quiet. Someone had even cleared away all the magazines that had been on the end table yesterday.

Knowing she wouldn't be able to concentrate to read anyway, she tucked her feet beneath her skirt and rested the side of her head against the back of the sofa. The nurse had promised to wake her when it was time for Anna to be fed. With any luck, she could sleep for a couple of hours before then.

The pitch of the polisher grew fainter, melding with the ping of an elevator as the little man worked his way farther down the hall. If she concentrated on that lulling sound, maybe she wouldn't think of the monitors that blinked and beeped above her baby's plastic bassinet, or of the money she had lost that day because she hadn't been there to pack her produce—money she could ill afford to lose in light of what she'd had to spend on bus tickets, much less the medical bills she was incurring.

She was thinking she'd have no choice but to accept the financial aid the woman in admitting had told her about when she became aware of footsteps moving toward her. Lifting her head to see who was there, her heart slid to her throat.

There was an easy grace about Justin's measured strides, a command that earned a deferential nod from the janitor and kept the older man's eyes on his back after he'd passed. He'd loosened his tie and he carried his navy-blue jacket slung over one shoulder, his casual manner totally at odds with the restraint in his chiseled features when he stopped two feet away.

"How's Anna?" he asked before she could say a word.

"Good. She's asleep," she added, automatically glancing down the wide hall with its distant doors leading to the nursery wing. She hesitated, tucking her legs more tightly beneath her. "Didn't you get my message?"

"Yes, I did. About twenty minutes ago." The overhead lights caught a hint of silver above his ears as he tossed his jacket over the opposite end of the sofa. Giving her a look she couldn't read at all, he tugged at the knees of his slacks and sat down a cushion away. "I called home to check messages on the way over here."

With his hands clasped between his knees, he glanced to where she remained curled in the corner. For a moment, he said nothing. He just studied her the way a scientist might scrutinize a particularly puzzling specimen under a microscope.

"You didn't say why you didn't want me to pick you up tonight."

"There wasn't time. Your instructions said to be brief."

His brow lowered a scant second before something that

very nearly passed for a smile flashed through his eyes. "I see," he murmured, watching her absently pick at the fabric covering her ankle. "Well, there's no need to be brief now. So why don't you tell me what's the matter."

"I never said there was anything wrong. I just said I want to stay here."

"You didn't have to say anything was wrong. I could hear it in your voice."

"If I sounded different, it was because I was nervous," she defended, stilling the motions of her fingers so she wouldn't look that way now. "It felt strange talking to a machine."

For a moment, she thought he might accept her excuses. She hoped he would, anyway. It was one thing to feel humiliated. It was another entirely to have to talk about it.

The steady way he studied her made it clear he had no intention of letting the matter go.

"I don't know if you realize it or not," he said, still quietly watching her, "but you're not convincing me. I know there's a problem. I can see it by looking at you. The only question is, did you want to stay to be near your daughter...or because you want to avoid me?"

Justin saw her glance jerk to his, only to falter the moment she met his eyes. He couldn't believe how tired she looked, how bone weary. Or how lost. She was sitting there, curled up into herself like an abandoned child. Yet, she was trying her damnedest to pretend she hadn't been wounded by what he'd done.

He didn't know what he admired more about her, her guts or her strength. But even steel had a breaking point. Seeing how her arms had snaked around her middle, he couldn't help but wonder how much more she could take before she found hers.

"I was afraid of that," he muttered, when her only response was silence.

"Emily, listen. I'm sorry about what happened with Rob. I didn't realize until this afternoon how things might have looked to you when he showed up."

"I'd really rather not talk about this."

"Well, we're going to," he informed her, refusing to let her close him out. "I was trying to keep him from you, but I'm afraid it looked like it was the other way around." He reached over, slipping his finger under her chin to tip her face toward him. "That's what's going on here, isn't it?"

Justin didn't expect an answer. The gentle woman looking at him in confusion and hurt had spent a lifetime denying her own ego. That was why he knew it was something more than pride keeping her silent. It was self-protection. The last thing she wanted right then was for him to know just how vulnerable she was to him.

He appreciated the feeling far more than she would ever know.

"Isn't it?" he insisted, deliberately dropping his hand.

She ducked her head, went back to picking at the thread.

"Isn't he a friend?" she asked, still wary.

"I suppose. Of course," he added, surprised at his equivocation. "He just tends to ask a lot of questions that aren't any of his business. It wouldn't have been fair to subject you to him unprepared."

Incomprehension flickered through her eyes. "What kind of questions?"

He could hear Rob now, interrogating her much as he had him.

*So, where are you from? What do you do? Who's your family. Great dress.* That one, tongue-in-cheek. *Who designed it?*

Normal-sounding questions to anyone else. Innocent sociable conversation that, with Rob, wouldn't have been innocent at all. It had only taken him seconds to size up Emily as a beautiful woman with a screaming lack of polish and sophistication. Though Justin knew the man was too civilized to deliberately embarrass her, it would have been impossible for him to hide his own sense of social superiority. Had he discovered her background, he'd undoubtedly have regarded her as the novelty he'd already labeled her. As sharp and insightful as Emily was, she'd have picked up the slights in a heartbeat.

The thought that Rob wouldn't even have noticed, much less cared, was hardly a revelation. It was what it said about Justin himself for dismissing the trait for so long that nudged hard at his conscience.

"Forget it. It's not important now," he told her, jamming down uneasiness with himself and annoyance with Rob. The smudges of fatigue beneath her eyes told him how worn-out she was. She'd always looked a little tired to him before. Knowing how poorly she'd slept last night, he suspected she was now pushing exhaustion. "It's late and you're tired. Come with me so you can get some rest."

He planted his hands on his knees, preparing to rise. Emily made no attempt at all to move. She didn't doubt what he'd said about what had happened that morning. And there was no denying how his intention to spare her his friend's nosiness eased the awful ache in her chest. But the same tension she'd sensed in him before was still there. She could feel it snaking around her, balling itself in the pit of her stomach.

She simply couldn't handle being around him when part of her hated the way he tied her in knots and another part wanted to be held in his arms.

"Thank you, Justin. But really, I'm fine where I am. I want to feed Anna," she added, seeing the set look to his jaw that told him he was about to get insistent. "The nurse said she'd come to get me when she wakes up."

"When will that be?"

"Three hours. Maybe four." She really didn't know for

sure. Anna had been going a little longer between feedings eating from a bottle, something that both encouraged and disconcerted her. The nurses were giving her formula now, too. But before her mind could start wandering any further in that direction, she saw Justin glance at his watch and release a long, low breath.

A moment later, he reached for his tie. The knot was already loose and the top button of his shirt undone. Pulling the tie off completely, he released the second button with a flick of his fingers and dropped the long length of red silk on his jacket.

Without a word, he unbuttoned his shirt cuff and started to roll it up.

"What are you doing?" she asked, cautiously.

"Getting comfortable."

"Why?"

*Because I've already made your situation harder than it needs to be,* he thought. *Because, right now, I know I should be running as far and as fast as I can, but I can't stand the thought of leaving you alone. I'm all you have here.*

His last thought felt like rationalization, an evasive technique he had down in spades where she was concerned. But the knowledge was also oddly humbling. Last night, when he'd found her at his window, he'd never seen anyone who looked so badly in need of a pair of arms. She looked very much like that now, too. Lost and alone and trying very hard not to let it matter.

It was one thing to protect himself. It was another entirely to do it at her expense.

"Because it'll be easier to sleep," he finally replied. He tucked a couple of rolls into his cuff, then did the same with the other. "If you won't come to my place, you'll just have to share your sofa with me."

His eyes locked on hers, the storm-gray depths revealing

nothing but determination—and the quiet concern of the man who once brought her a kitchen window.

She was desperately afraid to trust what she saw. "You don't have to do this."

"Yeah. I do."

"Justin." Her voice fell. "Please."

Her plea held the same conflicted emotions she'd heard in his voice when he'd turned her toward her room last night. It was so unfair of him to do this to her when she was so tired, when she was so concerned about so many other things she could do nothing about.

His tone was mild. It was only his expression that turned guarded. "Do you really want me to go, Emily? If you do," he conceded, carefully searching her face, "I will."

"No." She barely whispered the word. "Yes," she immediately amended, grasping for the sense of perspective she'd somehow lost the day she'd met him. She had no experience with a man like him. No way of knowing what it was he wanted from her, if he wanted anything at all. All she knew was what she felt, and she couldn't help feeling that he was only going to hurt her again, whether he intended to or not.

She couldn't help feeling, either, that she might be lost without him.

"I don't know what I want right now, Justin. All I can think about is that I want Anna to be well. And I want to be home so I can take care of my chores. And I don't want to be worrying about money or my chickens or the seedlings in the greenhouse or what I'll do if they can't help my baby. And if I could have anything," she added, as long as she was at it, "I'd want us to be the way we were before you kissed me because that's when everything changed. But I can't have that and now when I'm with you...even when I'm not with you..."

She shook her head, cutting herself off before needs she

wanted to deny made her admit something she wasn't prepared to accept herself.

"I know," he murmured, when she concluded her less-than-enlightened reply by tightening her hold on herself. He reached toward her, curling his fingers around her crossed arms. "I feel the same way about you."

The thought that he could be as confused about her as she was about him was incomprehensible. So was what he was doing. Last night, when she'd felt his hands settle on her shoulders, her heart had leapt at the thought of feeling his arms around her. Now, unwilling to believe she'd ever feel that sense of safety again, she braced herself to stay right where she was. She didn't want him pulling her to her feet. She didn't want him leading her to the elevator, insisting she needed to go to his place to rest as if only he knew what she needed.

"Come here," he coaxed, ignoring the way she stiffened. "I'm just going to hold you. Okay?"

The gentleness in his voice nearly undid her as he gathered her close, carefully, as if she were something terribly fragile. Never in her life had she been treated that way. Never had she felt so vulnerable to another human being. And never had she wanted anything as badly as the simple comfort he offered her now.

She didn't trust herself to speak just then. The best she could do as she dared to let her body slowly relax against his was nod.

"Good." He whispered the word against her temple, his breath moist and warm. Moving her with him, he angled himself in the corner, stretching one long leg across the cushions, and drew her against the solid length of his body so she could rest her head on his chest.

"Is this all right?"

His voice rumbled low and deep in his chest. She heard it beneath her ear. She could hear the strong steady beat of his heart, too, as reassuring to her as a mother's heartbeat was to a child. She had no idea what it was about this man that made her feel so safe when she was in his arms, but that sense of security was there. And, for now, she wouldn't question it. It was too precious, too fleeting.

Her only response was to nod against the crisp fabric of his shirt. The small movement brushed her hair against his chin. Justin slowly smoothed the shining strands, letting his hand drift down to free her heavy braid from between her and the sofa back and eased the length over her side.

He didn't let himself think about untwining those long flaxen strands. He didn't let himself linger on the curve of her hip before he drew his hand back to curve his arm around her and clasp her fingers to his chest. He'd never offered comfort before. But that was all he intended to do. It was, amazingly, all he wanted to do. And as he slowly ran his fingers over hers and asked her to tell him what the doctor had said about Anna that day, he found it far easier than he would have ever imagined.

The problem wasn't genetic. The doctors ruled out that possibility even before all the test results were in.

Emily had told Justin that last night, but there had been no relief in her voice because the doctor had yet to say what the problem was. All she'd been told was that they'd know more when some other test results came back—and that she wasn't to worry.

Justin had thought at the time that whoever told her that obviously didn't have a child himself. But when he stepped through the double doors leading to the nursery at five o'clock that afternoon with the carrier Emily had asked him to bring from his condo, he fully expected to see that worry gone.

Anna was going home. Emily had called him a couple

of hours ago and told him the doctor had said she would be fine.

Seeing her talking with a nurse outside the nursery, he walked up behind her and smiled at the little blond head resting on her shoulder.

"I'm so glad everything turned out so well, Mrs. Miller. She's just the most precious little thing." The nurse, copper-haired, forty-something and wearing a scrub top dotted with yellow smiley faces, beamed at the baby Emily held. "I put some more nutritional information for you in here," she continued, holding out a large white plastic bag. "You take care of yourself by eating properly and getting more rest. And keep Anna on the formula. You just watch. She's going to start growing like a little weed.

"Excuse me a moment," she said, looking over Emily's shoulder. "May I help you, sir?"

"I just came for Mrs. Miller and Anna," he replied, setting the carrier on the waist-high counter beside them. "Don't let me interrupt."

The woman was professional enough to mask most of her curiosity. But as she ran a glance over his dark suit, silk tie and hand-tailored shirt, she was clearly wondering at his connection with the former Amish woman in the slightly wrinkled lavender jumper.

All Justin considered just then was Emily. It occurred to him, vaguely, that she would look stunning in something long, sleek and black. She could wear anything and look incredible. His next thought was that the strain that should have been gone was still there.

"Anna has been discharged, so we can go," she said to him.

"Let's put her in her carrier here," the nurse suggested. "Then, I'll accompany you to the door."

The pleasant-looking woman flipped back the straps inside the thick mauve padding as Emily moved forward to tuck her baby into the carrier herself. The blond little girl blew bubbles while her mom told the nurse how grateful she was to the staff for taking such good care of her child. There was no doubt that Emily's appreciation was heartfelt. But her smile was forced, her eyes devoid of the relief Justin had fully expected to see.

She hadn't once met his eyes, either. The closest she'd come was his chin.

The nurse picked up the large white plastic bag to carry while Justin reached for Anna. The baby was now busily sucking on three fingers. Seeing her grin around them when he skimmed his finger over her chin, he couldn't help but smile back. It could have just been the smile, and he couldn't swear to it, but he thought her little cheeks actually looked fuller than when he'd seen her two days ago.

He would have mentioned that had the nurse not commanded Emily's attention just then.

"I hope you aren't planning to go back to your home right away, Mrs. Miller."

"That depends on whether or not I can catch the bus," Emily replied as they headed for the elevator. "The last one leaves in an hour."

Sympathy tempered professional disapproval. "Give yourself a couple of days, dear. Soak in a tub. Put your feet up. If you know anyone who can watch Anna for you," she added with a significant glance in Justin's direction, "let him take care of her while you sleep through a couple of feedings. That's another advantage to having her take a bottle."

It sounded to Justin as if the woman were trying to be encouraging. Totally sidetracked by the alarming thought of watching Anna alone, it didn't occur to him to wonder why Emily suddenly seemed even more dispirited.

Conversation came to a halt in the crowded elevator. But the nurse picked it up as they headed through the busy lobby. "Whatever you do, see that you take better care of yourself. If you don't take care of you, you can't take care of her. Good luck," she concluded, and handed Emily the bag she'd carried down for her when they'd reached the patient loading area where he'd left his car.

Justin didn't hear what Emily said in reply. His attention was on the baby who was following the flash of the gold pen in his pocket while he strapped her carrier into the back seat.

The thought that anything could have been wrong with someone so incredibly innocent had simply refused to gel. Or maybe, he reluctantly pondered, he just hadn't let himself fully consider the possibility because he hadn't wanted to admit how worried he'd been himself.

Not sure he was all that comfortable with the admission now, he somewhat awkwardly smoothed Anna's corn silk hair. Smiling to himself at the way she tipped her head back as if to see what he was doing, he then turned his attention to loading the heavy bag into the car and opening the front passenger door for Emily.

The nurse was walking away.

"Forget it," he said when he saw Emily turn to him and draw a breath. "We can't make the bus."

"We could if you hurried."

"You can't hurry in five o'clock traffic, Emily."

Her brow lowered thoughtfully as she climbed in and buckled up.

"Is there another bus company I could try?" she asked the minute he was behind the wheel. "I have to get home, Justin. I have chickens to feed and I have to water. I can't afford—"

"Call Clancy."

"Clancy can barely keep up with his own work this time of year. I can't ask him to do mine."

"I'm not suggesting you ask him to do all of it. Just ask

him to feed the chickens again and turn on the irrigation.'' He handed her his cell phone. ''You're stuck in Chicago for another night, so you might as well call Clancy now. But first, tell me what the doctors figured out about Anna. You said she was all right. You didn't say what had been wrong.''

He *had* been worried, dammit. And like it or not, he cared very much about the little girl who still scared him silly because, despite what Emily had said, she *did* look fragile enough to break.

So did her mom.

''She just needs to take a special formula so she gets more vitamins and she'll be fine.''

''That's it?''

''That's it,'' she echoed, her voice oddly devoid of emotion. ''They ruled out genetic problems, diseases and physical abnormalities. She's even gained two ounces in the past two days. That's twice what she was putting on before.''

There was no smile as she contemplated the black instrument he'd handed her. No spark. None of the optimism he'd once considered naiveté.

It had to be fatigue, he thought. He couldn't imagine any other reason why she wasn't bouncing off the walls with relief. Considering how little rest she got, something the nurses had apparently noted themselves, he wasn't at all surprised by how tired she looked. What he didn't understand was her dejection and how withdrawn she became as he headed into the heavy traffic. Even when the tension between them had been thick enough to slice, she'd never been as distant with him as she was now.

He didn't prod her again about making the call to Clancy until she'd settled the baby on the middle of her bed. Anna had fallen asleep during the drive and was now lying on her back with a fist by one cheek, one arm straight out and making little sucking motions with her mouth.

Standing in the doorway of his study with the telephone in hand, he watched Emily skim one soft little cheek before reluctantly moving away. There was such affection in the way she touched her baby. Such caring. But there was no mistaking the shadows in her pale features when she turned and saw him hold out the telephone.

He wanted to know why those shadows were there. He wanted to know what she wasn't telling him about Anna. Not wanting her attention divided, he first wanted to get her concerns with her chores out of the way.

"If you don't want to call him, I'll do it," he said, only to feel his conscience poke hard. He couldn't help Clancy anymore. Sometime soon, he needed to call the man himself. "You'll feel better when you can stop worrying about your farm."

Looking more numb than resigned, she took the phone and dug the Clancys' number out of her purse. Moments later, she'd moved to the dining room and was speaking with Mrs. Clancy. The woman must have wanted to know how the baby was doing because he heard Emily say that Anna was doing fine before expressing her own concern about the woman's hip. He had no idea what all Mrs. Clancy said in the minute Emily remained mute. His only concern was with the rigid set of Emily's shoulders as she eventually asked her favors, thanked the woman and punched the button to end the call.

"She said Mr. Clancy can take care of the chickens for certain, but he won't be able to set the irrigation. He has to drive to Davenport to pick up some bailer parts in the morning, so he wouldn't be around to turn it off."

"I take it he can't do it now?"

"He's in the field. He won't be in before dark."

Her hand was trembling when she set the phone on the

table. Aware of him watching her, she promptly hugged her arms around herself.

"Justin," she began, looking as reluctant as she sounded. "Is there any way you can take me home tonight?"

"Didn't I hear the nurse tell you to get some rest?"

"It's not her plants that need watering."

She had a point. It would also be infinitely easier on him if he did take her home this evening. He had the day from hell scheduled for tomorrow. Between meetings that began at 8:00 a.m. and the partnership dinner that wouldn't end until heaven knew when, he'd be lucky to find time to breathe. If they left in the next hour or so, he could be back by midnight.

"I'll take you home," he said, relief fighting reluctance over letting her go. "But not until you tell me what's going on with Anna. And don't tell me nothing," he added, in case she was considering it. "What exactly did the doctor call her problem?"

The chaotic swirls of purple and blue in the painting beyond Justin's imposing form had once reminded Emily of the violence of a storm. At that moment, the image reminded her more of turmoil going on inside herself.

She couldn't believe how guilty she felt. And how ashamed. She felt bewildered, too, and utterly horrified by how she'd jeopardized her little girl's health.

"Emily?"

"They called it failure to thrive," she said, her voice a little too unsteady as she slowly turned away. There were times when the unblinking way he watched her made her feel as if he could look straight through to her soul. If he could do that, he'd see how very close she was to losing the tenuous hold she had on herself. "One doctor just called it 'malnourished,'" she added, sparing herself nothing. "They said she is about a month behind in her development. She should weigh more than she does. Be able to do things like lift her head up when she's on her stomach and sleep longer at a time.''

"But I heard the nurse say she'd be fine.''

"She will. Now.'' And for that, she would be forever grateful. "They said that when the cause is found this soon and the diet corrected, babies usually catch up in no time.''

Confusion colored his tone. "So why aren't you relieved?''

"I am.'' More than he could possibly know. "But it's my fault...my fault,'' she repeated when her voice cracked, "that she wasn't getting what she needed.'' She hugged herself more tightly, trying to quell the shaking sensation in her stomach. "They told me I was dehydrating myself and burning too many calories so she wasn't getting enough nutrients to develop properly. I'd lost the weight I'd gained carrying her too quickly, too. Losing it too fast put things in my milk that weren't good for her.''

"They *said* it was your fault?''

"No. No,'' she repeated, not sure why he sounded so dangerous just then. "But it was. She didn't have anyone else. She relied on me, Justin. If I'd had any idea I was hurting her, I'd have changed what I was doing. But I didn't know. I really didn't,'' she insisted helplessly. "I don't know what I could have changed, or how, but I would have.'' The burning in her throat seared the strength from her voice. "I swear I would.''

Her oath was barely audible, choked off as much by the stranglehold she had on herself as the weight of responsibility pressing down on her.

Taking her by the shoulders, Justin turned her to face him.

With her head down he could see nothing but the first plaits of the long braid hanging down her back. He didn't need to see her face to know what he'd find there. He could hear her devastation and the weariness that was making it all so much worse.

"I know you would," he told her, gathering her in his arms. He didn't question what he was doing. He simply did it. Like last night, it just felt like something she needed. "And I can't think of anything you could have changed, either. I know one thing you need to get out of your head right now, though. You're not to blame. You knew something was wrong and you took her to the doctor. Right?"

With his hand cupped to the back of her head, he coaxed her forward. But she wouldn't allow herself to take the comfort he offered. The most she would do was let her forehead rest on his chest. The rest of her body felt as stiff as a plank.

"Maybe if I hadn't been trying to save up for a car and electricity and all those other things," she ventured, her voice strained. "Maybe if I hadn't been so selfish—"

"You're not selfish."

"Maybe if I hadn't taken on cleaning the Clancys' house—"

"That's what you traded for getting your rides into town."

"I was being greedy. I wanted too much—"

"Emily, hush."

She wasn't even being rational. The things she was saving for would ultimately save her half the time and effort she was expending now. And walking to Hancock would hardly conserve her energy.

"You're not being greedy." She'd just been doing what she had to do to survive. Considering what that entailed, it was a miracle she hadn't gotten sick herself. He ran his hand down her back, felt her breath shudder out. "You've just been given some really lousy choices."

"That doesn't make it any better."

"No," he agreed, slipping his hand over the softness of her hair. "I don't imagine it does."

"I can't even nurse her anymore."

He knew from the desolate note in her voice that somehow that was really important. Being a man, he was sure he couldn't understand what it meant to her, but he'd grown aware of the special bond it seemed to create between mother and child.

He eased her closer. "You know what will make all of this better?"

She rocked her forehead against his chest.

"Sleep," he pronounced.

He stroked her hair again, then gently tugged her head back by her braid so he could see her eyes. The tears shimmering in those liquid blue depths caught him like a physical blow.

She wouldn't have had a full night's sleep since Anna was born. For the tears to have worked past the hold she maintained on herself, that lack had obviously caught up with her.

"I really think that's what you need right now." He brushed his fingers to her temple, saw the fatigue taunting emotions she so obviously wanted to guard. "Eight hours of uninterrupted sleep."

"I'll add it to my wish list."

"No," he murmured, cupping her face. "You'll just do it. Tell me what to do with the bottles." He was going with his gut, the same way he had last night. The same way he had since he'd met her. "I've seen you burp Anna and change her enough to work the rest of it out somehow."

He expected doubt. Or disbelief. Or hesitation. Realizing what he'd just said, he was feeling all three himself. What he did not expect was for the tears she so determinedly held back to suddenly start streaming down her cheeks.

She didn't make a sound. She didn't even move. She just

stood with her face framed by his hands, her eyes on his and those crystalline drops tracking her face.

"Hey," he murmured, something tight catching in his chest. "I'm trying to make it better, not worse."

Her eyes closed, more tears leaking from beneath the curves of her dark, spiky lashes. "You're not making it worse."

"It doesn't look like that to me." Catching a tear at the point of her chin with his thumb, he slowly brushed the moisture toward the corner of her mouth. "I just want you to let it all go for now. Okay? Just lean on me for a while."

His thumb slipped over her cheek in a vain attempt to wipe the moisture away. Her skin felt like wet satin and her mouth trembled with the shuddering breath she drew, but she still made no sound.

"Stop," he whispered, skimming the fragile lines of her face, the slight part of her lush mouth.

Drawn by her naked vulnerability, he lowered his head, brushing his lips over hers. "Honey, don't cry. Please," he begged, carrying his kiss to the corners of her eyes, her temples. He swallowed the salt of her tears, hating how helpless he felt to make them go away. "I don't know what you want me to do."

He was doing it. She just couldn't tell him that. Her throat burned and her chest hurt, and she was trying desperately to hold back the sob constricting her breathing. She couldn't believe what he was offering to do with Anna. Her baby intimidated the daylights out of him, but he was willing to take care of her. For her.

That thought alone touched her more deeply than anything he'd ever done. But to be able to lean on him, even for a little while, was something she wanted so badly, she ached. Not to have to be the only one responsible for everything for one night, for one hour, would be a gift beyond imagining.

She slipped her hands around his waist, the need to take what he offered fighting its way past the will that had kept her together all these past months. The past couple of years. His mouth was on hers again, his kiss warm and full and achingly tender. He wanted to comfort her, to ease the awful feelings haunting her. And he was. And when he moved closer, gradually molding her to the solid length of him, she found she needed to get as close to him as he would allow.

The sob caught as she kissed him back. She leaned into him, her fists bunching the back of his shirt and her tears making his lips feel slick as she pressed closer. His breath suddenly went thin. She felt the brush of it against her damp cheek moments before he flexed his fingers on her hips and slowly slipped his tongue into her mouth.

The burning in her throat slid to the pit of her stomach. Within a heartbeat, he trailed that warmth up her side when his hand slipped to her waist, then moved along her ribs, around her back, down her spine. He eased his hands lower as she clung to him, his big hands pressing her to the hardness suddenly straining against the front of his slacks and drawing a moan from somewhere deep inside her.

Or maybe the sound came from him. She wasn't sure. All that felt certain was the solid strength of his body in the moments before he lifted his head and his gray eyes locked on hers.

Bridled tension snaked from his every pore. Yet, his touch was unimaginably gentle when he smoothed the dampness of his kisses from her mouth.

"You're going to bed." The smoky tones of his voice sounded a little ragged around the edges, but his decisiveness was unmistakable. Bracing his arm across her back, he caught her behind her knees and swung her up in his arms. "You can have mine. I'll stay out here and listen for Anna."

Despite the calm determination carved in his face, she could feel his heart racing when her hand flattened against his chest. The chaotic beat echoed her own. He was acting as if his only thought was to get rid of her in a hurry and the only way to ensure that she wouldn't stand there arguing with him about his plans for her was to move her himself.

She didn't get a chance to tell him the ride wasn't necessary. He'd already passed the room where her little girl still slept peacefully in the middle of the Hide-A-Bed, and was angling her sideways to carry her into his room.

He walked past a lacquered chest and stopped at the side of the huge bed. Keeping one hand at her waist after her feet hit the floor, he reached over and whipped back the deep blue comforter.

"I want you to sleep," he informed her. "I'll go get the stuff they gave you at the hospital so you can show me what to do with it. But when I get back, I want to see you in bed. I'll get you a T-shirt to sleep in so I don't wake the baby getting your things from the other room."

Justin brushed his lips to hers—as much to take one more taste as to keep her from arguing with him. But she lifted her head when he lowered his, meeting him halfway. If she hadn't done that, he would have pulled back and set to doing what he'd intended to do. At least, he wanted to think that was what he'd have done. She was vulnerable right now. More so than she'd ever been. There had even been a hint of desperation in her when she'd kissed him back and the last thing he wanted was to take advantage of her

It had felt as if she'd wanted to crawl inside his shirt.

The thought had him swallowing a groan as his hands snaked out to pull her back to him.

She came willingly. Trusting as a child, she let him loop her arms around his neck so he could feel all of her against him. Even as he drank in the sweet, drugging taste of her he immediately knew he should have left well enough alone. It had been hard enough to pull away with her clinging to his waist. With her arms stretched up so her breasts brushed his chest and her stomach pressed to his, pulling away from her now would take every ounce of restraint he possessed.

His hands were curved high on her ribs and moving higher when he gritted his teeth against the heavy ache in his loins and made himself stop. "If I don't go right now," he growled, his breathing ragged even to his own ears, "I'm going to wind up in that bed with you."

Her own breath trembled out as she lifted her head, her luminous eyes searching his. That same tremor was in her hands when they slipped from behind his neck to rest against his chest. "I know."

He didn't move. Neither did she. For a moment, Justin wasn't even sure his heart beat. He was already hard with need. Seeing that same need reflected in her lovely guileless face sharpened desire to the point of pain.

His features contorted with it as he reached out to skim his fingers along her jaw. He'd told her before what would happen if he kept seeing her. He'd had no idea at the time how much stronger that desire could get.

His heart jerked hard as he cautiously carried his touch over her hair and drew her long braid over her shoulder. He had the feeling she knew what he was going to do even before he eased off the rubber band holding the end secure. Her eyes held his, her glance faltering for only a moment, but she said nothing as he began to draw his fingers through the waist-length plaiting.

The only sound in the room was their breathing as he released the silken strands inches at a time, working his way toward her nape. When he reached the back of her neck, he gently nudged her forward and she lowered her head, allowing him to slip his fingers over her skull and free the heavy mass of the last twists restraining it.

The waving tresses fell over one shoulder in a thick tumble of pale silk. Drawing his fingers through the magnificent length, he spread it over her slender shoulders like a shimmering veil.

Emily swallowed hard. She was still fully clothed, yet she felt totally exposed. He seemed to realize that as he pushed his fingers through the hair at her temples and drew her face toward his. "You are the most incredibly beautiful woman, Emily." He breathed the words against her lips, moistening them with his breath. "And you are driving me out of my mind."

He was making her crazy, too. She just couldn't tell him that. His mouth came down on hers, a little hard, a little hungry, and she was suddenly drowning in a sea of sensation.

This wasn't about comfort anymore. It wasn't even about the security she felt in his arms. The feelings he drew from her now were like nothing she'd ever experienced, nothing she'd imagined could exist. He made her feel alive in ways she'd never dreamed possible and she wanted him and the escape he offered more than her next breath.

He turned her toward the bed as he skimmed the straps of her jumper over her shoulders and let the fabric puddle at her feet. He never broke his debilitating kiss while he patiently unbuttoned the dozen little buttons on the front of her T-shirt and unhooked the back clasp of her serviceable and painfully practical nursing bra. It was only when he tugged his shirt from his slacks and asked her to unbutton it that he moved from her mouth. Even then, he never stopped touching her. Within moments, he'd stripped away her shoes and her white cotton underwear. Then he was back, drinking from her, making her crazy for the taste of him as he shrugged out of his shirt, and reached for her again.

She felt the change in him before she saw it. His touch suddenly became cautious, almost hesitant as he skimmed his hands from her hips to her ribs. When he drew his hands up to her breasts, his touch became more tender still. Almost carefully, he shaped the sides of her fullness, lifting their weight, testing their softness.

She felt the pull of milk letting down even before he gently cupped her and lifted his head to study what he held. A host of conflicted feelings shot through the heat he'd created. But before the awful anxieties she'd been dealing with in his living room could tug her back, she saw the look on his face and found that it was all she could do to breathe.

She'd never known that the look in a man's eyes could swell a woman's heart even as it turned her weak with longing. Something that looked almost like reverence moved through the carved angles of his face as he drew his thumb over the liquid pearled at the tip of her turgid nipple.

As if he understood how hard it was for her to know she could no longer nurse her child, he lowered his head, gently caught the opalescent drop with his tongue, then touched a kiss to each breast.

When he raised his eyes to hers, the tears were back. She couldn't seem to stop them. He didn't seem disconcerted at all by them this time. He simply rose over her, kissing them away as he pressed her back onto the bed and discarded the rest of his clothes. It was almost as if he wanted her to think only of the yearnings he created inside her as his mouth and his hands played utter havoc with every nerve she possessed.

She returned his caresses, mimicking the motions that had her breathless. He encouraged her every step of the way, guiding her in a sensual game of follow the leader. Having learned so much from him, she didn't hesitate to follow him where he led her now.

She whispered his name, marveling at how free he made her feel.

He whispered hers back, all but gritting his teeth when her small soft hands ventured down his taut stomach. He couldn't believe how beautifully she responded to him, how completely she gave herself. How desperately he needed to be inside her.

Raw desire had him in its talons, but some small fraction of sanity made him reach for one of the foil packets in his nightstand drawer and roll a condom over himself before he eased his weight over her. Something like hesitation, then gratitude flickered through her flushed features when she realized what he'd done. He didn't feel grateful for the protection at all. But he didn't let himself wonder why he resented using the barrier with her. He focused only on smoothing the heavy tangle of hair from her face and watching her eyes go dark as he eased himself into her body.

Her exquisite warmth enfolded him, stealing his breath in the moments before he urged her to move with him. Sensation escalated, expanded. But something more built with each powerful thrust. Something he'd never felt before. For a moment, he had no idea where he ended and the lovely woman in his arms began. It was as if they had somehow become one body, one heartbeat. Then she was shattering in his arms and he was conscious of nothing until his own breathing eventually quieted.

All he felt then, was peace.

## Chapter Twelve

Justin had never intended for things to go as far as they had last night.

He'd never realized, either, how being with Emily could make him forget nearly everything but the sense of calm he sometimes felt with her.

The evening had seemed almost surreal, much like the weekends he'd spent on her little farm. Cocooned in his condo, the world had narrowed to just the two of them and little Anna. And while he really had wanted Emily to sleep, between him and her daughter and the need for dinner, it had been nearly midnight before she'd actually fallen asleep in his arms.

They'd been awake again at two with the baby. And while he had actually held and fed Anna earlier, an experience she suffered quite graciously, Emily, thankfully, had awakened, too. She'd been right there on the sofa with him, looking as uncertain about the whole bottle thing as he felt about the feeding thing in general.

Between the two of them, they'd gotten four whole ounces into her.

He couldn't believe how good it had made him feel to see Emily smiling because of that. Or how much he wanted her again, after making love with her only hours before. It had been nearly four o'clock before they'd fallen asleep. Yet, he'd awakened craving the feel of her.

There was just no time to consider how complicated the situation with her was getting.

As he pulled a tie from the circular rack in his closet and whipped the length of imported teal silk around his neck, his biggest concern was that he was late.

"I have a breakfast meeting in half an hour, an appointment at ten-thirty and my afternoon is booked solid." He grimaced, remembering. "And I have a partnership dinner tonight." Looping the tie into a neat knot in front of his dresser mirror, he glanced at Emily's reflection. She sat in the middle of his bed, wearing his T-shirt and feeding Anna her bottle. "I'll call you as soon as I get to the office and we'll work out something."

Holding bottle and baby with one hand, she gently pried a handful of her tangled hair from Anna's questing fingers. "You have too much to do today to worry about me, Justin. I'll call a cab to take us to the terminal." Thoughts of the work waiting for her, the chores she'd been worrying about even yesterday seemed to bow her slender shoulders. "There's a bus at three."

"Yeah. A milk run that won't get you there until after seven o'clock," he muttered, not at all impressed with her quick mastery of city transportation. "I don't want you worrying all day about your plants drying up. I'll be back for you by noon," he decided, grabbing his suit coat from a hanger. He could have her to her farm before the bus even left the Chicago station. He'd just have to figure out later how to handle the rest of his day.

Tucked and combed, his hair still damp from the fastest shower he'd ever taken, he turned from the dresser. The calm he'd felt with her had faded the instant he realized he'd overslept and bolted from his bed. What he felt now was a knot in his stomach the size of a Florida orange.

The realities of his world were pulling hard.

Bending when he reached the side of the bed, he pushed his fingers through her hair and caught the back of her neck. Hesitating only long enough to acknowledge the uncertainty in her eyes, he brushed a kiss over her lips. "Be ready. Okay?"

Emily assured him that she would, then watched him absently touch Anna's little cheek before heading out the door. He seemed to suck the oxygen from the room as he left, his long strides eating up the distance to the entry so quickly that the front door closed before she realized just how fast he'd made his escape.

She didn't doubt for a moment that he had somewhere he was supposed to be just then. And he'd mentioned the partnership dinner to her before. Yet, as she sat among the tangled sheets, turning her attention back to the little girl batting at her hair while she enthusiastically sucked her bottle, Emily couldn't help the awful uncertainty filling her.

Or the hope.

She loved him. She was his. Body and soul. And after last night she prayed desperately that he might somehow come to feel the same commitment she already felt in her heart. The fact that he insisted on taking her home himself instead of letting her take the bus was definitely a good sign. And she was incredibly relieved by the thought of getting home to her plants that much sooner. But when he'd bent to kiss her, she'd seen the same struggle she'd sensed in him when he'd said goodbye to her a couple of weeks ago.

She knew he was struggling with things he didn't feel comfortable sharing with her. She just had no idea why they made him look so torn.

She'd promised him she would be ready by noon. With next to nothing to do in his condo but take care of herself and Anna, she had time to spare. Because she couldn't figure out how to use Justin's washer, she washed out her T-shirt and jumper in the sink and dried them in his dryer, since that had been pretty straightforward, and was showered, braided and dressed by nine-thirty. By eleven thirty, when she heard Justin's key in the lock, she'd made the bed, bathed and fed Anna and was sitting on the sofa reading aloud to her from the microwave cookbook.

Anna had fallen asleep during the part about rotating foods to ensure even heating.

Looking over her shoulder when the door opened, she saw Justin walk in and glance at the baby carrier and the denim bag in the entry. He'd barely closed the door when the tension radiating from his big body hit her like one of the sonic shock waves she'd read about in the Hancock Library's encyclopedia.

"We can leave as soon as I change clothes."

"We're ready," she assured him, easing Anna to the cushions so she could put the book away. "I know you can be back in time for your dinner, but what about your appointments this afternoon?"

"I've taken care of everything."

His response sounded a little vague to her. But since he seemed wound as tightly as her kitchen clock when he cut toward his room, she let it go.

She'd put the book back in its drawer and carried Anna's carrier to the sofa to put her in it, when a demanding knock sounded on the door.

The three heavy beats repeated themselves seconds later.

"Justin, open the door. I know you're there."

The muffled voice sounded as impatient as the raps on the solid wood. She recognized that voice. Apparently, Justin did, too. The look on his face when he walked out of his room in a pair of unbuttoned khakis and carrying a pale-yellow polo shirt was nothing short of lethal.

He dragged the shirt over his head, pulling it down hard over the muscles rippling in his back when he passed her and jerked open the door.

Rob, impeccably attired in a vested pin-striped suit, looked decidedly annoyed. That was exactly the way he sounded, too. "Are you crazy?"

Justin's voice dropped to a growl. "I don't have time to talk to you now."

"Yes, you do," the stockier man insisted, catching the door when Justin started to close it. Looking as if the vein in his temple was about to throb out of his head, he pushed Justin's arm aside and walked right past him. "No one misses a partnership dinner. No one. Especially their first. I couldn't believe it when Beck told me you..."

"Oh, hell," he muttered, seeing Emily standing with Anna in the middle of the living room. "Is this what's—?"

"Emily," Justin said, his tone amazingly calm considering the quelling glare he aimed at Rob before he gave the door a shove to close it. "Will you excuse us? Take Anna into my room. Please," he added, to keep the request from sounding like an order.

Her blue eyes looked huge as she blinked back at him.

But all she did was give the uninvited guest in the entry an uncertain glance before doing as he asked.

Rob had the good sense to keep his mouth shut until the bedroom door softly clicked shut. But in the intervening seconds, it became apparent to Justin that Beck had called Rob shortly after he'd left the senior partner's office.

Justin had been halfway through the morning when he'd admitted to himself that there was no way he could take Emily home and leave her there without help. She had three days' worth of work to catch up on and she was already exhausted from months of interrupted nights—the last one, thanks in part to him.

He'd had his secretary reschedule everything on his calendar. But he'd gone to Beck himself. He hadn't hedged or come up with excuses. He'd simply told his senior partner he wouldn't be able to attend the dinner that evening because he had a friend who had a problem and he needed to help her. The timing was unfortunate, but it couldn't be helped.

Beck hadn't been pleased. But Justin hadn't been able to tell if it was because he was breaking tradition, or because the man had come to realize over the past couple of weeks that Justin truly wasn't interested in his daughter.

When he'd left his office, he'd had the feeling it was a little of both.

Rob seemed more than willing to confirm the conclusion. "It's like you've got a death wish," he hissed. "You lost your edge with the Carter brothers' case, you threw away a shot at Cameron and now you're thumbing your nose at the partnership."

"I'm not thumbing my nose at anybody," Justin snapped. "And I haven't lost my edge." He preferred to think he'd refined it. But the point would be lost on the man glaring at him across the carpet as Rob paced his way to the window and back. "Like I told Beck, the timing sucks, but there's nothing I can do about that. I'll be at the next one."

"You're damn right, you will. You'll be at this one, too. Whatever you think you need to do can wait."

"So I can do what you want instead?" Justin demanded, his voice dangerous and low. "Nothing will be discussed at that dinner that I can't be told about tomorrow. She has plants drying up and there's no one— "

"Plants? You're letting her mess you up because of some plants?"

"They're her crops, dammit."

The door wasn't thick enough to block the increasingly angry argument coming from the living room. Even standing on the far side of Justin's bed, Emily could hear nearly every word.

She could hear Rob, anyway. In some ways Justin's overbearing partner reminded her of the bishop of her old community. Rob had that same air of righteous indignation about him; as if only the foolhardy would dare test the absolutes of his doctrine. He wasn't bothering to temper his tone or his reactions at all. And though she could hear little of Justin's low rasp, it was becoming clear in a hurry that she'd been causing problems for him pretty much since the moment they'd met.

She just didn't realize why until she heard Rob's blunt demand.

"What do you mean you need to take care of her?"

"Just what I said," she heard Justin snap back. "She has a baby who's been sick, more work than any three people can handle and no family around. She hasn't got anybody else."

"So what are you going to do the next time? And the next? Are you going to keep running to Hancock every time she needs a hole dug or whatever it is she's got you doing over there? If you're looking for someone to rescue, Sloan, I suggest you consider saving yourself. Your billable time is down. You're pissing off your partners, and you're letting a woman who can't do a damn thing for you interfere big time with your career. If you value that career at all, you'll do whatever you have to do to get her back where she belongs and be at that dinner tonight.''

Emily had heard the expression about silence being deafening. She'd just never realized how very loud it could be until the quarrel in the living room suddenly stopped.

She didn't know who opened the front door; if Rob had and stalked out, or if Justin had walked over and flung it back himself, silently inviting the man to leave. But she heard it slam hard enough to make her heart jump.

She must have clenched Anna a little too tightly. The baby jumped, too. Screwing up her little face, she let out a whimper to let her know she didn't appreciate being disturbed and settled back to sleep against her shoulder.

There had been a time when numbness had protected her. Hearing Justin's heavy footsteps on the tile walkway, she prayed for its return now.

He stopped outside the door, hesitating a moment before turning the knob and pushing the door open.

He'd tucked in his shirt. Odd, she thought, that she would notice something so ordinary when her little world was being so mercilessly battered again. She'd fallen in love with the undeniably attractive and very guarded man watching her carefully from the doorway. And all the time he'd been working his way into her heart, he'd merely been feeling sorry for her.

The thought that he could well have been feeling pity while making love to her only added humiliation to the hurt she was trying desperately not to feel. She would deal with the pain later. When she was alone. It was probably prideful of her not to want him to know that she'd never felt as hollow as she did at that moment. But, frankly, she didn't care.

She swallowed. Hard. "May I ask you something?"

Justin walked past the foot of the neatly made bed, approaching her with the same caution he might a frightened doe. He didn't know exactly what she'd heard, but it was apparent she'd heard enough. She looked far more shaken than she sounded.

Wanting to touch her, afraid she'd pull back, he settled for picking a piece of lint from the back of Anna's pink romper. "Of course you can."

She stepped back anyway.

"You told your friend you need to take care of me," she said quietly. "How had you planned to do that?"

There was an edge to her question that didn't sound like Emily at all. A sort of defensiveness that hadn't even existed when he'd first met her. Back then, she'd hardly known what self-protection was.

The thought that she'd acquired the need for it because of him did nothing but add a dose of guilt to the confusion of loyalties and anger knotting his gut. The anger eating at him was directed at Rob at the moment, but there was a bitterness to it that didn't feel that specific. He wasn't even sure why some of that anger was there. He didn't even know exactly what all he was feeling just then. Except pressured. That, he had no trouble identifying at all. Pressure from Beck and Rob. Pressure from within himself. And, now, with one simple question, pressure from the woman who had every right to know what his intentions were where she was concerned.

"I don't know." He could be nothing less than honest

with her. "I don't know how I thought I'd take care of you. I haven't figured that out yet."

Emily rubbed her hand over Anna's back, wanting to ease whatever anxiety her child might feel from her mom. Her baby book said infants picked up on that sort of thing. But she hadn't read anything anywhere to guide her now. She had no idea what a woman with more experience would do when a man said he had no idea what she meant to him. She just knew she wasn't anyone's obligation.

"You don't need to figure out what to do about me, Justin. I don't need to be taken care of." She tipped her chin up, trying very hard to pretend she wasn't dying inside. "I may not be getting on the way a lot of people do, and I know I'm making mistakes. But I'm learning."

"I didn't mean to imply that you couldn't handle your life."

"And I don't mean to imply that I'm ungrateful for all you've done for me," she returned, echoing his phrasing. "I know it's your nature to take over and fix things, but I'm not your problem to solve."

He wasn't sure why her softly spoken words stung the way they did. He should have been relieved that she expected nothing from him. It was certainly what he would have felt with anyone else. At least, that was what he was thinking in the seconds before she started past him and her other remark jammed his eyebrows together. "I don't take over," he denied flatly. "What are you talking about?"

She stopped in the doorway, looking every bit as uncomprehending as he did when she turned around. He honestly looked as if he had no idea what she meant. "Straightening out problems is what you do, Justin. You were doing it when you helped me and my neighbors after the storm. You've been doing it ever since. With me. And with the Clancys. And with the other farmers."

She shook her head, quietly amazed that he had no idea what it was he did nearly every day of his life. "Everything you did for me and Anna," she said, realization dawning. "It now makes perfect sense. You saw me as needy and you wanted to help. Fixing problems is even what you do for a living."

Justin had never considered what he did in that particular light before. And he couldn't effectively argue her conclusions. Either of them. He had seen her as in need of his help. But he was in no frame of mind to consider why he'd wanted to be there for her. "What's wrong with what I do for a living?"

"I'm not accusing you of doing anything wrong. I'm just telling you what I see. And while I'm at it," she added, because something about the pain inside her demanded that it be said, "I think you're cheating yourself. You're a noble man, Justin. But you're trapped in a world that's draining the soul right out of you. I don't understand why you want to do something that never brings you any real satisfaction, or why you want more of something you fight more than you welcome, but the decision is obviously one you made long ago."

Justin said nothing. He just stood at the foot of the big bed where he'd held her, made love with her. His eyes revealed nothing, but the way the muscle in his jaw jumped spoke of the turmoil he'd been dealing with far longer than he would probably ever admit.

Determined not to look as empty as she felt, she cupped her hand to the back of Anna's head and turned for the carrier she'd left on the sofa. She could hear Justin behind her, following more slowly.

Settling the sleeping baby into the carrier, she strapped her in, then picked up the phone from the end table.

"Do you have a telephone book?"

"It's right there," he said, nodding to the drawer below the phone's base. "What do you need?"

"A cab." She was going to splurge on herself. She had no business doing it, but she simply didn't want to deal with figuring out how else to get to the terminal. "There's no reason for you to take me home," she told him, her voice hushed because Anna was right there. "I've been taking care of myself for a long time and now that I have the formula for Anna, I know how to take care of her, too. Go to your dinner tonight, Justin. Make amends with your people."

"It's not necessary for you to take the bus."

"Yes, it is," she assured him, flipping open the yellow pages.

"I can still take you and be back in time for the dinner. How will you get to the farm? Clancy will probably be in the fields until dark."

"I'll ask Mary to give me a ride. She lives right there in town."

"Emily—"

"I don't want you to take me," she finally said, wondering if he had any idea how hard it was just being in the room with him right now. She'd been so foolish to let him open her up to all the feelings he had shown her, to let herself start wanting and dreaming. Weaving dreams around Justin was as foolish as setting seed just before the snows came.

She found the listings for taxis and called the first one with a big ad.

Listening to her order the cab after she asked him for the building's address, Justin walked over to his window and looked down at the view he seldom saw during the day. He didn't really see it now, either.

Emily had already closed him out.

He tried to think logically. Analytically. It was how he functioned best. It didn't matter that he hated what she was doing. It didn't matter that he felt like a snake for hurting her. And he knew he had. He didn't care how strong she was acting; he'd seen the pain in her eyes when he'd walked into his bedroom. What was happening was the only sensible course for them to take. She had her life. He had his. Going their separate ways was what he'd known they should do weeks ago, anyway. What he'd tried to do.

She'd also just kept him from sabotaging his career. If anything, he should be feeling grateful to her for that.

"I'm going to wait for the cab downstairs," he heard her say and turned to see her heading for the door with the carrier. "It'll be here in ten minutes."

He thought about pointing out that she'd have a three-hour wait in the terminal.

He kept his mouth shut and handed her the denim overnight bag so she could loop it over her shoulder with her purse, then held out the white plastic bag with the formula and bottles the nurse had given her.

Taking it, she opened the door with her free hand.

"Goodbye, Justin," she said, and was on her way down the hall before he could do much more than lift his hand.

Anna had been smiling at him.

Emily hadn't even given him a chance to brush her soft little cheek goodbye.

The thyme had been bundled and boxed and Emily had just washed her hands at the pump when the drone of a vehicle drifted up from the road beyond her house. Since the produce man wasn't due for another hour at least, she didn't pay any particular attention to the sound as she walked back to where Anna was lying on the baby quilt under the apple tree. Her little girl was on her tummy, supporting herself on her forearms while she cooed at a red block in the quilt with *Rebecca* embroidered on it. She was drooling on the bright blue block embroidered with *Amos*.

Yesterday, she'd rolled over. She'd startled the daylights out of herself when she'd done it, then delighted in repeating the feat.

Picking up the burp cloth, Emily crouched down to wipe the drool from Anna's mouth. She'd just reached for her when Anna flipped over and got that startled look in her eyes before breaking into a grin.

"Pretty proud of yourself there, aren't you?" Emily smiled, touching the cloth to the wet little mouth before brushing the end across her baby's rounded little cheek. Pure pleasure rushed through her. Anna had only been on formula for two weeks and already the difference was extraordinary.

The drone of the car had changed pitch. But it was the crunch of gravel in her drive that had her turning around and slowly rising to her feet.

The pleasure she'd just felt vanished like wood smoke in a windstorm. She'd always believed that a person couldn't miss what she'd truly never had. She now knew that just glimpsing a possibility was enough to kindle a longing so fierce it might never go away.

The black BMW rolled to a stop at the side of her house. She couldn't begin to imagine why Justin was there. She just knew she fervently wished he'd kept on going as she crossed her arms over her denim jumper and saw him get out of his car.

The memory of having watched him like this before was as clear as the September sky. Him, standing with his hand on his door, a mountain of masculinity in a polo shirt and khakis, and her, waiting with her heart beating a little too fast in the shade of the apple tree.

She hadn't expected him that long-ago day, either. But she remembered what she'd felt; the excitement, the anticipation. The anxiety she felt as he closed his door now and slowly walked toward her was far less welcome. For a few short moments, she actually hadn't been conscious of how naive she'd been to fall in love with a sophisticated man who could never want a simple woman like her. She thought it terribly unfair that he should rob her of what little peace she'd found that day.

She watched him cross the lawn, trying to ignore the leashed power of his unhurried strides, the athletic grace of his big body. His dark hair was perfectly cut, as always. The angular lines of his face were carved with restraint. She hadn't regarded black as being a particularly appealing color, having grown up with so much of it. But when he stopped in front of her, she noticed that his black shirt turned his eyes the color of polished pewter.

She didn't think she'd ever seen him look so handsome. Or so hesitant.

"Hi," he murmured, those quicksilver eyes carefully searching her face.

Feeling far too exposed, all she could think to say was, "Why are you here?"

"I thought I'd stop by and see how you're doing. The two of you," he added, looking over to where Anna was excitedly waving the edge of her burp cloth. He let his glance linger. "She looks good."

"She is. She's growing very well now."

"I'm glad to hear that. Actually," he confessed, "Mrs. Clancy told me she was putting on weight. I'd called to talk to her husband," he explained, pushing his hands into his pockets. "She said you seemed to be doing all right, too."

He almost made it sound as if he'd asked about them

specifically. But she didn't care to know what he discussed
with her neighbors. She hadn't said a word to Mrs. Clancy
about him and, last week, when Mrs. Clancy had started to
tell her that Justin had some sort of problem giving Sam
and the other farmers advice, she'd promptly remembered
a chore she had to tend and ended the conversation before
it had even started.

The warm morning breeze rattled the leaves on the tree
as he glanced toward the greenhouse, then toward the
porch.

"Is everything here holding up?"

"Please, don't do this." Looking at him as if he were
the proverbial bad penny, she tipped up her chin. "I don't
know if you're here to see Clancy or if you drove all the
way out because you were…I don't know," she said, gesturing with one hand, "…at loose ends or something. But
you don't need to invent excuses to keep checking on us.
I don't need to be rescued."

Justin watched her arm snake back around her middle,
the self-protectiveness he'd taught her firmly in place. She
just hadn't quite mastered the finer points of the technique.
The steel of her backbone was definitely there, but so was
her betraying vulnerability. He saw it in her eyes before
her glance faltered and she turned away.

He knew he'd hurt her. But he was hurting, too.

"That's not what this is about," he said, catching her by
the shoulder. "I know you'll be all right, Emily. And I'm
not here to rescue you. Maybe I need you to save me."

She grounded him. He felt better when he was with her.
He *was* better when he was with her. But she didn't seem
ready to hear that. Not the way she'd stiffened at his touch.

He could hardly blame her for throwing up a wall. She'd
turned to him when she'd needed someone most, and that

had meant far more to him than he'd realized—until he'd made it impossible for her to count on him at all.

"I need you to hear me out, Emily. Please. I thought about everything you said before you left and took a good look around myself. I have everything I've worked for. But I don't really have anything that matters." He lifted his hand, touched it to the smooth hair at her crown before drawing it down her braid. "Not without you."

Emily felt the weight of his hand drift away before she turned to face him. His expression was guarded, uneasy. Like her own. At that moment she wasn't sure which felt stronger; the hope blooming in her chest, or the fear that she was about to hear something that would kill it once more.

"You were right," he told her, looking as if he wanted to reach for her again but not at all sure that his touch would be welcome.

"About what?"

"About everything. About what it is that I do. The way I fight the very thing I thought I wanted." He lived in a world that measured a person's worth by what he earned, what he possessed, the recognition and the power he'd achieved. He'd let the pressure to win, to stay on top, to prove himself worthy of his parents' and his peers' collective approval take him over, consume him. "About how my world is bleeding me dry."

The muscle in his jaw jerked. "I hadn't even known I could appreciate something like painting a porch."

The admission held a wealth of realization. He'd had no idea how to appreciate simple things. A sunset. A smile. But she'd shown him those pleasures, along with a kind of satisfaction he'd never found anywhere else.

"I'm leaving the firm," he said, his tone utterly matter-of-fact.

Her glance shifted over his face, concern melding with caution. "That partnership meant everything to you."

"I never should have accepted it in the first place. You said I was the one who'd decided on my career," he reminded her. "And I did. I'd just never considered why I chose it." He now understood the restlessness that had plagued him the past few months. It had begun as soon as he realized he was about to reach his goal. A goal that he now realized had actually felt more like a trap. "I know now that I did it because it was expected of me. By my family. My friends. It was how I could continue to belong in the same environment I'd grown up in. There are parts of what I do that I truly enjoy. It's the direction that isn't right. It's like you after you'd left your old community and you'd discovered a new place you needed to belong. You said yourself you'd changed too much to go back even if they'd let you."

Emily couldn't help the empathy she felt for him just then. She knew exactly what he meant. But she couldn't believe that he could simply walk away from everything that had been so much a part of his life. Even as different as her life was now from what she'd known before, there were still parts of it that would always be with her.

"What are you going to do?"

Encouraged by the quick concern in her eyes, he let himself trail his fingers along the delicate line of her jaw. The need to touch her was simply too great to ignore. "I've already done part of it. I've been staying at the Hancock Inn for the past couple of days while I looked for real estate."

"You're buying some property here?"

"Yeah," he murmured, carrying his touch to the fullness of her bottom lip. "But I'll get to that in a minute. There's something I need to talk to you about first."

He moved closer, taking in the translucence of her skin, the softness of it as he cupped her face in his hands. Rob had called him a fool. But then, Rob had said a lot of things before Justin had told him he had no desire to become the sort of man Rob was—something that had, for once, left the man speechless. He'd told him, too, that he had his own ideas about his future and they didn't include being towed along in the wake of someone else's ambitions for him. He'd also mentioned, in passing, that he'd be representing a small group of farmers against the firm's newest client.

Rob had called him a fool, he repeated to himself. But this woman had called him *noble.*

The word had stunned him because it wasn't a trait he'd ever imagined himself to possess. If he possessed anything remotely resembling it, it was only because she'd brought it out in him.

"I'm in love for the first time in my life, Emily. And I wanted to do this right, but I'm really at a loss here. I started looking for places because I thought I should have everything lined up. But then I thought we should probably make the decisions together. If you'll have me, I mean."

Emily swallowed, her heart beating heavily as his glance dropped to her mouth. "I'm not sure I understand what you're saying."

It seemed perfectly clear to him. "I'm saying I love you. And I'm asking you to marry me. Will you? You and Anna?"

He wanted her little girl. "Justin...I love you, too." Desperately. "But you're an educated man." A worldly man. She shook her head, afraid to believe what she was hearing. "I've tried to learn as much as I can, and I've learned so much from you, but there's so much I don't know."

The look in his eyes turned fierce. "You've taught me far more than I could ever teach you. And there's a lot I don't know, either. We'll just have to figure out what we don't know together. Okay?''

He drew his thumb over her cheek, felt her breath shudder out. ''As for where we'll live,'' he continued, needing her to know he truly had thought his decisions through, ''I've become pretty drawn to Hancock. There's a vacant building at the end of Main Street that has plenty of room for a law office upstairs, and Clancy and the other people I've talked to said they wouldn't mind having a sympathetic lawyer handy. There's also an opening on the town council I wouldn't mind filling.

''My only problem is that the building has this space downstairs that would be perfect for a specialty shop. The sort of place that sells organic vegetables and gourmet kitchen supplies. I'd want a tenant for it, but only if she hired a couple of other people to work in it with her.''

With her heart beating in her throat, Emily's voice was little more than a whisper. ''I can't believe you remembered that.''

''I remember everything about you.'' He pulled her closer, the brush of his body stirring the memories that darkened his eyes. ''I remember all the other things on your wish list, too. So, I'll make you a deal. If you'll consent to a home with electricity, central heating and telephones, I'll get you a car and teach you how to drive.''

''No chain saw?''

''It's in the trunk.''

''No,'' she whispered, daring to smile.

''Yes,'' he whispered back, brushing a kiss over her lips. ''So, what do you say?''

She didn't know where the tears came from. They were just suddenly there, filling her eyes even though she knew she was smiling. ''Yes.'' The word was a little choked so she thought she'd try again. But she didn't need to bother.

The gleam in Justin's eyes turned feral and before she could breathe, his mouth covered hers.

There was possession in his kiss. And longing. And need. She felt love there, too. More than she'd ever dreamed possible. Locking her fingers around his neck, she kissed him back, giving as good as she got.

When Justin lifted his head long moments later, he tugged her down to sit beside the little girl yawning on the colorful quilt.

With his arm around Emily's shoulders, he touched the baby's cheek. The little girl had stolen his heart, too. Unexpectedly. Completely. Smiling when Anna smiled back, he drew a deep breath and looked into her mother's clear blue eyes.

"You know, Emily. I have a wish list now, too. You and Anna were at the top of it," he said, dipping his head toward hers once more. "But if you're willing, someday I wouldn't mind adding another baby's name to this quilt. Three's a nice number in a family, but I'd really like to make it four."

\*　\*　\*　\*　\*

*Look for 36 HOURS:*
*THE CHRISTMAS THAT CHANGED EVERYTHING,*
*a special holiday volume, featuring*
*Christine Flynn, Mary Lynn Baxter and*
*Marilyn Pappano, on sale November 2000.*

You have just read a

# Silhouette
### Special Edition
##### book.

Silhouette Special Edition always features incredible authors like Nora Roberts, Sherryl Woods, Christine Rimmer, Lindsay McKenna, Joan Elliott Pickart—and many more!

For compelling romances packed with emotion always choose Silhouette Special Edition.

*Silhouette®*
*Where love comes alive™*

Now that you have enjoyed a
# special edition
why not try some more?

## On sale July 2000:

### The Pint-Sized Secret
### Sherryl Woods

Jeb Delacourt was supposed to find out who was selling the family firm's secrets—not fall for the prime suspect! Did Brianna O'Ryan have something precious to hide?

### Man of Passion
### Lindsay McKenna

Loner Rafe Antonio reluctantly agreed to protect beautiful Ari Worthington while she ventured through the Brazilian jungle. Could Rafe keep his own heart safe from the woman he'd sworn to keep from harm?

### Married to a Stranger
### Allison Leigh

Jaded tycoon Tristan Clay knew that a marriage of convenience was the only way to help Hope Leoni. But Hope was already in love with her groom—and now Tristan had to admit his heart wasn't as resistant as he'd thought!

### Each month there are six new
### Silhouette Special Edition books to choose from.

Silhouette®
*Where love comes alive*™

# COMING NEXT MONTH

### #1333 THE PINT-SIZED SECRET—Sherryl Woods
*And Baby Makes Three: The Delacourts of Texas*
Her daughter was all that mattered to Brianna O'Ryan. So when
unnervingly sexy Jeb Delacourt got too close, she tried to deny their
attraction. But maybe it was finally time to risk everything....

### #1334 MAN OF PASSION—Lindsay McKenna
*Morgan's Mercenaries: Maverick Hearts, 50th Book*
Loner Rafe Antonio reluctantly agreed to protect beautiful
Ari Worthington while she ventured through the Brazilian jungle.
Then Ari began to stir Rafe's long-buried passion. Could Rafe keep
his own heart safe from the woman he'd sworn to keep from harm?

### #1335 WHOSE BABY IS THIS?—Patricia Thayer
First Dr. Matt Landers had his identity stolen, then irresistible
Tara McNeal accused him of being her baby niece's daddy. But
when Tara and Matt banded together to find the child's real father,
they found that love could be a stronger bond than blood....

### #1336 MARRIED TO A STRANGER—Allison Leigh
*Men of the Double-C Ranch*
Jaded tycoon Tristan Clay knew that a marriage of convenience
was the only way to save demure Hope Leoni's reputation. But Hope
was already in love with her groom—and now had to convince
Tristan to surrender his heart!

### #1337 DOCTOR AND THE DEBUTANTE—Pat Warren
When Dr. Sean Reagan rescued Laura Marshall, his snowbound
houseguest began to melt his iced-over heart. Now that the patient
turned healer, could Laura soothe Sean's soul happily ever after?

### #1338 MATERNAL INSTINCTS—Beth Henderson
When colleague Sam Hackett was ordered on a business trip,
Lauren Nugent volunteered to baby-sit the single dad's daughter. But
Lauren got more than she bargained for when she fell for her tiny
charge—and the handsome father!

CMN0600